Praise For *That Was Tomorrow*

"For anyone wanting a realistic portrayal of yester-day's sleepy South, a more informed connection to modern Fairhope, or a working re-enactment of Marietta Johnson's Organic Education philosophy, *That Was Tomorrow* is a clear choice. Author Mary Lois Timbes escorts us into the cliffs and gullies, the dirt and the shine, the people and the place, and the village on the bay that was a utopia for the taking. Jump in. Mobile Bay hasn't felt this good in decades."

—Rex Howard Anderson, *Mobile Press Register*

"As a recent—two years and counting—permanent resi-dent of Fairhope, I found this novel by Ms. Timbes to be a very relevant and interesting read, a good way station on my own journey toward understanding this remarkable commu-nity. The range of interviews that underpin the book serves to bring to life the Fairhope founders and earlier settlers of the immediate post-World War I period...let me sum up the book thusly: it is a very good read, well-written, nicely laid out and gives just enough coverage to the somewhat raffish character of the colony in those early days to underline the point that, in a very unprogressive state, a flower grew and flourished."

—Ralph E Thayer, *Fairhope Courier*

"It's hard to believe that there was once a time in this country, between the Last Great War and the inevitable onset of the next one, when there existed utopian communities across America, testing shared principles of civic idealism, personal actualization and the common good. And it's harder to believe that one of the more interesting was located in the Red State of Alabama, in the coastal community of Fairhope. In *That Was Tomorrow* Mary Lois Timbes brings the improbable to life, complete with believable, flesh and blood characters all living out their hopes and dreams in a concretely described, lush Southern setting. Take a trip to Fairhope. You will not only discover a progressive community of the past, but also what is finest in the American character."

—Jonathan Odell, author *The Healing*

"With intelligence and clarity, Mary Lois Timbes smoothly incorporates fiction and the history of a very real place. *That Was Tomorrow* offers an enlightening peek into the past of an unusual town with far-reaching ideals. This is a book to be read at leisure, and savored, as there is much to digest."

—Judith Richards, author *Too Blue To Fly*

"Historical fiction is a much abused genre. Too often fascinating people and events are treated like museum pieces - fragile, silent, and dead. *That Was Tomorrow* avoids these pitfalls, giving us a vivid portrait of a time and place in history filled with colors, scents, sounds, and a strong sense of the future. Along with heroine Amelia, we explore the turn-of-the-century Utopian experiment known as Fairhope, getting to know the colony's eccentric citizens, their habits, their politics, their fears, and their dreams. It is a coffee-fueled, romance-filled, full-sensory trip back to a dynamic time in a very unique place - and is well worth the visit."

—Michele Feltman Strider, author *Homecoming*

That Was Tomorrow

A Novel

Mary Lois Timbes

Sibley Oak Press

Other books by Mary Lois Timbes
Meet Me at The Butterfly Tree
The Fair Hope of Heaven

ISBN: 978-0-9857733-2-8

Published by Sibley Oak Press

Sibley Oak Press

The essence of the new education is to find out what is good for the child and provide the right conditions for growth. If right growth were understood and provided for, we would have a better nation in a single generation.

—*Marietta Johnson*

One

THE TRAIN RIDE to Mobile had been long and hot, with frequent stops and views of the Southern landscape. Amelia tried to define what was so different about what she was seeing out the dusty window. She had been traveling through miles and miles of farms and fields, all dry and for the most part unattended. The difference was not in the way it looked, but in a certain mood that was at the same time relaxed, formal and old-fashioned. The American South was like no place on earth.

It was not only the speech patterns of the people crowding into the car on the train, not only their gentle, placid attitudes, not only the waft of hot, humid air every time the train opened its doors to admit more passengers. Riding through the beautiful, almost-barren fields was like sailing backwards through time. This eerie feeling surrounded her, even though she was beginning an adventure, heading to a town called Fairhope, a reformist utopia in the deepest reaches of unknown territory.

Amelia was a city child, and a Northern girl to boot, accustomed to crowds and hustle. The pace and speech cadences of the people on the train were soporific, almost hypnotic. Amelia saw fields of plants with fresh cotton growing on them—little miracles, these fluffy white lumps on weedy stalks, cloudlike puffs that would be spun into thread providing fabric for the world.

In North Carolina a man of about 20, with freckles on his face and hands and hair the color of a ripe persimmon squeezed into the seat beside her. She gave him a wan smile and turned back to the window.

"You from the North?" he asked her. She looked at his eyes, the color of light blue glass, and answered, "New Jersey."

"Guess this looks mighty strange to you." He shrugged and tilted his head, indicating the world surrounding him, including the scenes out the window. He tried to read her with those blue eyes.

"Different, anyway," Amelia responded. "A different look to the farms."

She looked out at fields of red dirt, soon replaced by vacant farms and occasional rocks from the foothills of the Appalachians.

"See them there chimneys?" he asked, pointing out two brick columns standing about fifty feet apart in an empty field.

"No house," Amelia observed after a moment.

"You're right about that. You'll see a lot of them chimneys 'round here. Houses were burned down by the Yankees. We call 'em Sherman's Sentinels."

"Hmm," Amelia nodded. She found it odd to hear the Civil War spoken of in this immediate way, as if it just happened. She observed the distant look in his eyes as he looked over the dying fields outside the window. Sure enough, the track veered close to another brick chimney without a house. "There's another one yonder."

The war, which ended over 60 years before, was still vivid to this curly-haired fellow who could only have heard of it through family tales.

"My granddaddy was in the Home Guard. They burned the bridge to town when the Yankees come close. He lost two brothers in that war."

His tone was wistful, conveying more than a feeling of personal loss. It sounded to Amelia like regret, regret that the Union had won and the South must eventually accept being part of the United States again. Amelia really didn't want to discuss the Civil War, but she heard the fellow out since the subject seemed to weigh heavily on his mind. He wanted to fill in the gaps in her knowledge of the conflict.

Amelia just listened. She sensed the hard reality of losing a great and devastating war would be a long time gaining acceptance in some areas of the South, even this many years later. Talk of the conflict made her uncomfortable, as if she were traveling to a foreign country she might not like.

She forced herself to think happier thoughts. The memory of her meeting with Marietta Johnson, her reason for traveling so far from home, the excitement of planning a future on her own—all were really a part of her life now, and the promise of a bright future was part of her daydreams. She willed herself back into the vestibule of the Women's Club of Philadelphia, where she had waited with others who wanted an audience with Mrs. Johnson.

"Amelia King?" her name was called to enter the door. It was drawing close to 4 o'clock and she knew she would have to rush to get her questions asked and to see if she could arrange a real job interview.

"How do you do, Miss King?" Mrs. Johnson's voice was as genuine and embracing when not behind a lectern as it was imposing and melodious when making a talk.

"How do you do, Mrs. Johnson," she countered. "It's such an honor to have a few moments with you."

Mrs. Johnson acknowledged the compliment with a brief flash in her brown eyes, but brushed it away to talk of more important things.

"What can I do for you? I hope you're going to say you're a schoolteacher," Mrs. Johnson said.

This was thrilling. Amelia had wanted so to impress Mrs. Johnson, who took no time at all in saying just the right thing.

"I am! You can't know how happy I am that you guessed it," she said. "Yes, I am a schoolteacher, and I am so inspired by what you have to say about education."

"What is it that appeals to you?"

"Well, for one thing, you said that all education should be designed to meet the needs of the child, rather than forcing the child into some mold conceived by adults…" Amelia stopped a moment to think. She didn't need to tell Mrs. Johnson what she had herself just said, but only to let her know how completely she agreed.

"I completely agree with that," she went on. "Children love learning, and adults must, um, must," she halted, reaching for the right words. She was acutely aware how limited her time was. She had to be sure to say something that would cause Mrs. Johnson to grant her a job interview. The words began to come to her.

"Adults must provide a place, a school, centered on the child, and based upon his needs—the needs of the growing organism that every child is."

"That's good, that's right," Mrs. Johnson said. "I think I said that." She was smiling warmly at Amelia. Mrs. Johnson had the kind of brown eyes that glistened and seemed to reveal her whole heart. "I think you would like our school in Fairhope."

This had sounded almost like an invitation. Amelia stopped thinking about what to say next and just went on talking.

"I think I would, too. I have so many ideas—but only two years experience, and that was in a city school. I'd like to talk with you about a teaching job in Fairhope."

"Well, I certainly think that could, and should, be arranged," Mrs. Johnson said, in a sentence that would change Amelia's life forever. Sometimes, Amelia realized, big things happen so quickly you hardly notice the world shaking beneath your feet.

"I must get on a train in just two hours, but would like for you to see Fairhope for yourself. If you can come there, we shall have a long talk before we decide if it would be a good place for you."

"I can make a trip to Fairhope," Amelia had said. "What is your schedule?"

"As a matter of fact, I leave for Chicago next," Mrs. Johnson said. "I have a number of speaking engagements. I'll be back in Fairhope for the summer at the end of May. We may have a position open in the fall."

Amelia's teaching job at the Ferndale School on the outskirts of Philadelphia would come to an end in the middle of June, but she could arrange to travel to the South after that, and maybe come up with a job in the exciting laboratory school for the next term. She wrote her name and address on a piece of paper—actually a page torn from her appointment book—and gave it to Mrs. Johnson.

"Write me to arrange our meeting in Fairhope," Mrs. Johnson said, taking the page of paper, folding it neatly into quarters, and putting it into her large handbag. "The address is simply Marietta Johnson, Fairhope, Alabama."

"No street number?"

"It will get to me, without a doubt. I look forward to talking with you further."

How easy their first meeting had been! From the beginning she felt it was preordained that she would get the job in Fairhope and move there for as many years as it might take to master the principles of Mrs. Johnson's theory of Organic Education.

On the train, half a year later, Amelia looked in her overnight bag for the letter that brought her this far. The red-headed man had dozed off in his seat next to her. Finding the letter she was looking for, she swelled with joy and read it again.

Dear Miss King,

After our brief talk after my little speech to the Educational Society of Philadelphia, I was most happy to learn that you are interested in teaching at my school in the fall. I look forward to discussing the possibility with you.

I gather that a trip to Fairhope is not out of the question for you, and I feel that is the best place for us meet again and talk further. I shall be free on Monday, July 11 to meet with you. My niece and secretary Esther Pierce will make arrangements for you to stay at the Gables Hotel, a very comfortable hostelry in Fairhope. I think that will be a good place for you to get acquainted with our town.

I shall ask Captain and Mrs. Cross, who manage the Gables, to make a reservation for you. I wish you a pleasant journey.

The letter was signed in a clear, schoolteacher's hand, *Marietta Johnson*.

Southern Alabama seemed an odd location for Marietta Johnson, with her Minnesota accent and her reputation as an education reformer. Nevertheless the settlement of Fairhope, in southern Alabama, was the place she had chosen to start her experimental school. Amelia was traveling to Fairhope to have her official job interview with Mrs. Johnson. This was the kind of school she dreamed of working in.

Amelia attached herself to the new ideas in education because of her own childhood, overindulged in some ways and deprived in others. Her upbringing in the crowded immigrant town of Hoboken, separated from New York City by the wide and serviceable Hudson River, had been privileged and protected. Her parents were part of what was known locally as the "upper crust," the Germans who had settled in Hoboken in the 1870s, before waves of Irish and Italians came to fill the town at the turn of the century. The wealthy families now resided in prestige houses on Castle Point Terrace and Hudson Street, some with views of the growing Manhattan skyline.

Until the age of six Amelia had not been exposed to the normal rough-and-tumble activities of other children. Her education had been placed in the hands of her nanny, Miss Pritchart, in order to prepare her for the kind of life her mother thought proper. Miss Pritchart was an old fashioned despot, certain that children should be seen and not heard, and seen only in their cleanest finery. A spinster in her fifties, Miss Pritchart tied her white hair into a severe bun on the back of her head and except for the occasional lace collar wore no ornament or color. Since her early twenties she had been charged, as a teacher and governess, with exposing children to a strict academic regimen and seeing that they were obedient and well-mannered.

Miss Pritchart's brisk, no-nonsense style appealed to Gertrude King, Amelia's mother. From the day she was hired, Miss Pritchart struck the right chord of assurance and sense of purpose. There was a look of self-satisfaction about her face, with thin lips that almost appeared to be smiling, but not quite. Amelia mistrusted her from the beginning.

"I see you have experience with young children," Amelia overheard her mother say to the nanny when she was interviewing her for the job. "What do you find is the most important part of their upbringing?"

"The fear of God—and respect for their parents, Mum," Miss Pritchart answered automatically. Fear of Miss Pritchart was more like it, Amelia thought now. Even remembering the old lady made her shudder.

※

In her portfolio Amelia carried a magazine with an article Mrs. Johnson had written, "Principles of the New Education," which she had already read half a dozen times, and the latest edition of *The Fairhope Courier*, a newspaper published in Fairhope every Thursday. Mrs. Johnson's approach to education emphasized that education should be based upon the nature and needs of children and not, as was usually the case, upon arbitrary standards set by adults. Adults were inclined to set benchmarks a child should reach by each grade level.

Her system honored each child's own pace and did not test the child to see if he was reaching certain goals. She did not allow tests or grades. Mrs. Johnson felt that hand work in ceramics and wood, folk dancing and music, and frequent breaks for study and play out of doors were essential to the normal development of every child. Apparently reading was not emphasized in her school, but teachers in the early grades—Amelia's area—were advised to read folk tales, fairy tales, and stories of ancient mythology to their students. Amelia was enchanted with this idea, so different from the way she had been taught.

She was drowsy as the train moved southward, thinking of what she might encounter in the next few days. The young redheaded man had gotten off the train at a crossroads stop just outside Atlanta. He was her first Southerner, and she would not forget him.

She leafed through *The Courier,* a folksy publication which extolled the pleasures of living in Fairhope. The newsletter praised everything—Fairhope's gardens, its ubiquitous study groups, forums and meetings to govern and manage problems that arose in the town and promote its mission of spreading the economic philosophy of the single tax throughout the world. Fairhope was a center of this economic philosophy.

She hardly noticed when the red-haired fellow had stood up, taken his tattered, homemade-looking suitcase from the rack overhead, nodded goodbye to her and departed the train, replaced on the last leg of the trip by an older lady with white lace cuffs appearing on the sleeves beneath her navy blue traveling suit.

The lady spoke in a voice so soft Amelia could hardly hear her, and with an accent so thick she could hardly be understood.

"Ah see yo readin' *The Fairhope Courier,*" the lady said, shy as a bird.

Amelia nodded and managed a smile.

"It's a lovely lo-cay-shun," her seat companion said. "But Ah can't say as Ah quite agree with awl the things about the taw-un."

Now she was curious. "What do you mean?"

"It's a sawt of a poe-lit-icle essperiment, you know?"

"I guess so," Amelia said.

"The way Ah unduh-stand, the community owns the land and rents it out."

"Single Tax," Amelia said. She knew that Fairhope was a utopian colony founded to prove Henry George's theory as outlined in his best selling book *Progress and Poverty* at the end of the last century. She didn't understand it thoroughly and was quite sure the lady would not be good at explaining. The idea was that the yearly payment on land was to provide revenue to run the town's utilities and be the only tax the citizens would pay. However, Federal income tax, instituted for just a few years now, was probably making the single tax theory obsolete, Amelia thought.

Although she was well aware her companion probably didn't find it so, Amelia thought it was interesting to consider a colony established to try new theories. Probably that was why Marietta Johnson found it such a congenial place for her radical school. Amelia could not help but ponder what she might find ahead of her. Surely not traditional Southerners like her new red-haired acquaintance or this little woman beside her now. Fairhope was a community founded on ideas and ideals—not of restoring anything, but of reforming almost everything. It looked forward into the 20th century, not back at past wars and dreams of recaptured glory.

Since first learning of the school and of Fairhope, Amelia wanted to like both. As she listened to the train clicking over the rails, she had a feeling of meeting her destiny.

Nothing prepared her, however, for the sweltering blast of humid air that hit her on deboarding the train in Mobile. She had known in her mind that it was going to be hot, but until one has experienced the combination of high temperature and high humidity in South Alabama in summer, one simply does not know what to expect. A redcap moved slowly in her direction, dripping sweat in his once-spruce uniform, with a hand truck to move her luggage.

Two

WHAT SHE SAW on her first look at Fairhope was a rudimentary, primitive community, situated on a bluff. At the base was Mobile Bay, a gently rolling body of water that gave a sense of serenity to the town. Tall, lean pines flanked the bluff, pointing like arrows to the sky.

Being on the eastern side of the bay afforded views of sunsets every evening. The closer one was to the water, the more seductive was the soothing sound of the gentle waves lapping the shore. The waters of the bay were brackish, not unlike the Hudson with which Amelia was so familiar, but wider so that the other side wasn't visible as it was in Hoboken. From the western bank of the Hudson, Hoboken's location, the buildings of New York City hovered over the water, almost close enough to touch. In Hoboken she had to turn to the other direction to see the sun set into the cliffs that provided a border between her town and Jersey City. It was strange to Amelia to be where the sun set into the water side of town—but she thought, how beautiful the sunset views would be as the sun dropped like a glowing rubber ball into the bay every evening!

A little railway took riders up the steep hill from the dock, a municipal pier which served the boats to Mobile and back, stopping in other villages along the way. Fairhope's unpaved streets were crawling with chickens, goats and some hogs. There was a butcher shop, a bakery where fresh bread could be obtained, and a creamery for local milk and even the summer treat of ice cream; produce was available intermittently from the backs of trucks and from the food markets in town, but most people also maintained their own plots for vegetables and fruits. The community was populated with former city dwellers, from Iowa and other Midwestern locations, who prided themselves on the notion that they were now farmers. They loved working in their gardens in spite of the fact that the sandy soil would hardly support real crops.

The first settlers had assumed this warm, damp climate would provide a Garden of Eden for them. By now they had learned that the soil of Fairhope was alkaline and not ideal for agriculture of any kind. But they endured in a spirit of cooperation and optimism, and many had accepted conventional wisdom that citrus, particularly the new Japanese satsuma orange, might be the salvation of Fairhope's economy. The growing season was a long one, and they experimented to extend it even longer if they could by growing and preparing vegetables and fruit unknown to them before their move to the South. They tried loquats and mulberries and planted chinaberry and tung oil trees as well as vegetables long known in the South. There was a bounty of okra, which was quite tasty when you got used to it, and there were varieties of peas, beans and nuts which they had come to enjoy over time.

On that initial visit, Amelia stayed at the Gables, the rambling two-story wooden building, where Mrs. Johnson had arranged lodging for her. The Gables was less fashionable and less expensive than The Colonial Inn, which sat a few blocks west on the bluff overlooking the bay. The

Gables was right in town and just a few blocks from the school. It was comfortable and old-fashioned—a pleasant place to stay.

The Gables was run by Captain and Mrs. Jack Cross. Mrs. Cross was a busy, funny lady—and her husband a raconteur with an English accent, who held forth with his pipe and a cup of tea on the front porch every morning and afternoon, as cronies and neighbors stopped by to discuss the fate of the world with him. They often talked about the politics of the village, about the future of the single tax system, and about books they were reading and authors they admired. Captain Cross was known in town as a "walking encyclopedia." His knowledge of a wide range of subjects made him extremely popular and made the hotel a natural meeting place.

"I see no reason it wouldn't work," Amelia heard a man saying as she had a cup of coffee at the table in the dining room. A white tablecloth covered the mahogany table, and there was a vase of fresh blue hydrangeas in the center. Amelia sat in one of the stiff dining chairs and relaxed while she breathed the aroma of the dark brew and sipped. She felt as if the conversation on the porch was a performance, perhaps for her. The voice was that of one of Captain Cross' morning visitors on the porch.

"Just saying, old man, that I don't see it happening as yet," came the captain's clipped English accent in response.

"To my mind, it won't be long before our demonstration exerts its appeal to all the neighboring villages. They'll all have the single tax system when they understand it."

"I hope you're right," answered the captain. "But all I hear is objections from people in Daphne and out in the county—to say nothing of the total rejection of it in Mobile."

"What is it they object to, do you think?"

"What they say to me is that they want to *own* the land, not to *pay rent* on it to a central community fund. What do you say to that?"

"I say that mankind cannot *own* land at all. That is a mythology. The land was here when we arrived on the planet and it will be here when we leave. We are but stewards during our time."

"The word 'tax' seems to be anathema to Americans," Captain Cross was saying.

"I prefer the word 'rent' myself," the visitor said. "The colony is landlord, the citizens are tenants on the land, paying only a yearly rent. And that's the only tax—"

"Ah, but that's difficult to defend now that the government has imposed a tax on income," the captain countered.

"Rent, then. *Rent* on the land, for its use, for 99 years. It's just a bully idea!"

"I agree with that, but I don't see converts outside of this community," the captain said.

Amelia would soon learn this discussion was typical on Fairhope mornings, here and all over town. The town elders often stopped at The Gables to air their thoughts on the latest issues they were dealing with—even E.B. Gaston, the editor of *The Courier* and virtually the founding father of Fairhope often came on his morning walk to exchange pleasantries with the Crosses. This simple hotel was the hub of the community, Amelia thought, but as she got to know her way around, other such hubs were revealed to her. There were three or four cafés in the village of about 1,500, and about 15 hotels with dining rooms, and coffee urns all over town were hot with fresh brew all day long. The Colonial Inn, elegant in its plain Craftsman style, was on the bluff with views of the bay. It was the site of intellectual meetings both organized and impromptu.

"Wherever there's people in Fairhope," Mrs. Cross said to her, "There's coffee. Or maybe that should be, wherever there's coffee, there's people." She made tea for her husband and his friends, but always hot coffee as well. The Crosses, both devoted to the cause of single tax, had moved to Fairhope with the idea of running a farm, but, like many idealists who had never farmed before, they changed their minds after a year or two. Then they took over the management of the Gables Hotel, where Mrs. Cross cooked and supervised the workers in the kitchen. She laid an old-fashioned boarding house type of table, which was popular with locals as well as transients.

Amelia found both the Crosses fascinating people. She noted the visitors from town were a certain breed—earnest, wordy, and wise, with one central agenda, which was how best to put Fairhope on the map and change the world through single tax philosophy.

These citizens hadn't yet realized that the wave of the immediate future of Fairhope was actually Amelia and those like her who were moving to town to participate in Mrs. Johnson's school. Seven years before, the famed educational philosopher John Dewey had come to Fairhope to review the school for a book he was writing. His visit had set the village on its ear with excitement. The children, informed that the only day Dr. Dewey had available to observe the school was Christmas Eve, voted to keep the school open its regular hours that day so that he might get a fair picture of it in operation. Mrs. Johnson took some of them outside, as was her custom so often, to teach a class. Dewey's daughter photographed the scene which became the frontispiece of his book.

After Dewey's book *Schools of Tomorrow* was published, the town rapidly changed. Mrs. Johnson's philosophy of a utopia, not only in Fairhope's political system, but also as a paradise for children in her school, brought coverage in the *New York Times* and other newspapers, and subsequently brought hundreds of families to the town to live. Amelia was among those who were coming to Fairhope in order to observe progressive education in action, and she knew there were many like her.

Amelia's first impression of Fairhope was that she was in the middle of one large citrus grove with a few chickens and goats running about. The satsuma orange had been developed to be frost resistant for the occasional freezes and hardy enough to withstand Fairhope's high summer temperatures as well. It was a delicious and popular fruit, easy to peel and section, just as tasty but less juicy than an orange. Soon after its introduction in Fairhope, the satsuma was being planted all over town, in large yards and small—anywhere that there might possibly be room for a small tree. Satsuma trees had the advantage of not growing to too great a height, having the appearance of a large, bushy shrub. In the spring, she would learn, their blossoms exuded a heady, sweet fragrance; but now, in early June, the bushes were heavy with the golden-orange fruit. Every square foot of land that would support a tree had a plant on it. Children, who explored freely through the town, often pulled satsumas off the trees, which were so laden that the owners were not likely to notice one or two fruits missing. It was a common sight to see a youngster peeling and eating a satsuma, spitting the seeds anywhere he liked.

There were oaks—some of them large, draped with Spanish moss that resembled nothing so much as grey ragged scarves hanging from their huge limbs. They added a grace to the heavy trees, as if a fashion designer had decided to drape a dowager with a complement of chiffon handkerchiefs.

The founders had bought the original tract of land for their utopia in the late 1800's, at which time it had been lumbered out until the land was bare and parched. Early settlers had established a park on old Indian mound property just above the bay hill, where they planted dogwood and azaleas, and named it Knoll Park, arranging through Colony mandates that Fairhope would maintain this and the whole beachfront as public parkland in perpetuity. They had a clear idea of what Utopia should look like, and they adhered to this principle of beauty as well as economic purpose in planning all aspects of the town.

Compacted dirt paths provided sidewalks for the unpaved streets. The main street, Fairhope Avenue, boasted a millinery shop, a general store, a harness and carriage shop, and several cafés. Amelia walked through town, seeing few pedestrians like herself, but those she passed smiled and greeted her. Children played freely on the paths and roads, and some were climbing in the trees, hanging upside down like monkeys. The train track ran down the center of Fairhope Avenue for the railway car that brought people up and down the hill to and from the steamer to Mobile.

Houses nestled in tree-lined lanes, unassuming bungalows next to wooden two-story homes with steep roofs, such as one would find in a northern climate, designed to shed heavy winter snows. The locals called the bigger new houses "Fairhope's castles," but as Amelia walked, she couldn't avoid comparing the landscape to that which was more familiar to her. Next to the ornate Victorian architecture of Hoboken, Fairhope's homes were very plain indeed.

🌺

The long anticipated job interview with Marietta Johnson took place the morning after Amelia arrived in mid-June. Amelia was unused to such weather this early in the summer season; in the Northeast, temperatures in June and July generally ranged in the high 70's and low 80's. However, there was seldom humidity like this. Her lacy white shirtwaist was not so comfortable as usual when she walked up the slope of Fairhope Avenue to the 10-acre campus of the School of Organic Education.

She was to meet Mrs. Johnson in her office in the dormitory building called the School Home, which was half a block south of the corner where the new community auditorium was under construction. As she neared the building, Amelia noted that most of the construction workers on the large, barnlike structure were teenagers, male and female, with a few men alongside.

A sawhorse was set up at the side of the building, under the shade of a blooming magnolia. A teen-aged boy and girl were busy sawing two-by-fours and stacking them on the ground in front of the building.

"You got your measurements, Ella?" the boy asked. "Looks a little long to me."

"I got 'em and got 'em right," the girl said, smiling proudly at a stack of evenly-trimmed boards.

"We'll see," he said, pulling out a tape measure and stretching it across the top board. "Looks about right—four and a half exactly," he said. "This measuring is a fine way to learn math!" He grabbed her boards, stacked them with an equal number from his side, and strolled into the building with them.

This was how she realized building the edifice was largely a project of the school, and that this was what Mrs. Johnson meant by hands-on learning under the supervision of qualified adults. This was the kind of natural learning environment she had only read about. It was what Mrs. Johnson called *organic education* at work.

She had no time to dawdle, but how she yearned to, just to be a part of the experiment!

"George Ray! We gotcha some more two-buh-fours!" He called as he entered the room.

A tall, lanky boy of about 15, with dark hair and brown eyes, took charge in a way that indicated he was head assistant to the gentle man on the ladder. He must have been George Ray. His own assistant was a boy who looked to be his age but was slighter in stature and had darkish blonde hair, falling in his face just a bit. Three girls were working together to build what looked to be the frame of a window. Ten or fifteen youngsters populated the hall with workers, each obviously enjoying the work and feeling a part of something very important. Hammers hit nails, making a great cacophonous orchestra of sound competing against the saws cutting wood. The smell of lumber and sawdust filled the air, and young voices called out for answers to their questions to the grownups in charge about how to do their jobs.

Amelia stood at the site longer than she thought, but had done so without realizing it. She had not noticed the time. The important thing was to get an audience with Mrs.

Johnson, to have a real job interview, so she might work in this environment, in this extraordinary town. She knew the time for her appointment was upon her, and, having seen the spectacle of Organic School students in action, she now knew her life would change forever if she had to opportunity to work here. She viewed the large dormitory building with a light heart and a head full of ideas.

She stepped onto the porch, and Marietta Johnson herself opened the screen door to greet her. Small in stature, Mrs. Johnson nonetheless had the imposing look of a matriarch. Her kind brown eyes didn't miss anything, and, although aging, she radiated the energy of a much younger woman. She was quick to smile when she recognized Amelia.

"Oh, dear!" Amelia said, "I'm a little late—I just had to see what was going on over there," gesturing toward the construction site. "It's wonderful!"

"Yes it is," Mrs. Johnson said. "That will be an auditorium for the school and a center for community events and activities. I'm having it named for Lydia Comings, the best friend my school and I ever had. She and her husband also happen to have built The Gables."

There was so much to say about Lydia Comings that Marietta Johnson sometimes had to stop herself. This was one of those times. She and Lydia had dreamed the school together, and it grew to reflect a shared vision of education for the future. Lydia and her husband had staked the school by coming up with $25 a month for the Johnsons to live on while Marietta worked out her theories and practiced on local children.

"And the students are helping to build this new community center?" Amelia asked.

"Of course." Mrs. Johnson showed some surprise at the question. "They'll be using it all the time, for celebrations, sports, plays, assemblies—it will be an essential part of the school and of Fairhope. As for the building of it, that's the kind of thing they must learn to do in life. It is what our school does best—in fact, in a way it's the only kind of thing we do! Come inside, Amelia, I'm looking forward to talking with you."

Amelia dutifully followed the older woman, with her heart in her mouth. They walked into a cool, dark room, furnished with comfortable mission-style pieces. A Morris chair, a number of dark tables—two large ones obviously for dining—and a fireplace with several hand-made chairs facing it made the room comfortable and welcoming. There was a door at one end to Mrs. Johnson's office, which barely had room for her heavy Mission desk and a small table with a typewriter on it and chair for the lady who Amelia rightly assumed was her secretary.

"Esther, this is Amelia King," Mrs. Johnson said. "I met her in Philadelphia. Amelia, this is my niece and irreplaceable secretary, Esther Frederick."

"Yes, how do you do," said Esther, "Welcome to Fairhope. I hope we see more of you soon." She then discreetly took some papers from her desk and left the room.

Mrs. Johnson closed the door.

"I've received your letter and your *curriculum vita*," Mrs. Johnson said. "Mount Holyoke! That's a fine college. How do you like teaching?"

"I love teaching," Amelia heard herself saying, although it wasn't entirely true. She knew Mrs. Johnson would want a more specific answer than that. "What I love is sharing what I know with children, watching them absorb it, watching them use it. But the educational system as a whole doesn't allow much leeway for creativity in a teacher."

Mrs. Johnson's brown eyes suddenly had a light in them, the same light she had seen when she met with her in Philadelphia.

"What do you think you could bring to this school?"

"I have to admit that I think mostly about what this school could bring to me," Amelia said. "I think it is an exciting direction for education everywhere—but first I want to learn your theory. I want to be almost as good a teacher as you."

"That's a worthwhile goal, dear, and very flattering," Mrs. Johnson said. "The world needs more schools like this, and more teachers that understand the thinking behind it—I don't call it a theory, by the way—but what do you think you could bring to this school?"

Amelia felt caught. She had to come up with a good answer.

"I am a pretty good teacher. I like the idea of teaching *life* rather than subjects. I like the idea of respecting the child and allowing him to follow where his curiosity leads—"

"And do you love all children?"

Amelia had to think a moment. There had been children she found difficult, children who tried her soul, but there had been moments of clarity even with them. It was easy to love some children, not easy to love others, but *all* children?

"Yes," she said, after thinking it over.

Mrs. Johnson was smiling.

"I guess you noticed I hesitated. I had some problem children in my class—"

"Tell me about them."

23

Here Amelia began a monologue she hadn't expected to deliver. In her second year of teaching she had encountered a situation concerning Andrew Martin, a child with a pronounced stammer that inhibited his learning and his social development. She related the story.

Amelia had had to enlist the help of all the children in her class to ignore the stammer. After Andrew had gone out at recess she huddled down with the rest of his classmates.

"I know you think the way Andrew speaks is funny," she began, and with that the whole group giggled—some quite self-consciously.

"He can't help this by himself. It is up to us to help him by looking past his stammer and learning to know Andrew the boy."

Chastised, the class nodded and shuffled out onto the playground. In coming days she saw a marked improvement in their behavior, except for one boy who continued to make Andrew's stammer a butt of jokes. After a day of this she asked him to stay after school.

"Edward, you know why I've asked you to stay in."

"I guess so," he responded, his eyes on the floor.

"Andrew is beginning to make progress," she said. Edward didn't look up.

"I can't help it. I think it's funny when he does that," Edward said, and then darted a glance at his teacher.

"He is trying to learn. The only way he can learn is if he's not laughed at. Making fun of him only makes his condition worse."

Amelia had noted that when not under pressure Andrew was bright enough. He was insecure, but had a generous nature and very seldom stammered except when called upon in front of the class. Edward seemed to need the attention of the class and considered himself a harmless class clown who could gain acceptance by using another as a brunt of his jokes.

She told Mrs. Johnson about her solution.

"Edward, the bully, was intractable. Andrew, with the support of the rest of his class, was making progress. I went to the administration and got Edward transferred to the other class and had him met with me after school one day a week, where we explored jokes and humor. We read Twain, some of Will Rogers, even funny papers. He brought in jokes he'd heard and we discussed them. I saw he had a gift for comedy—and his teacher in the other homeroom class noticed a definite improvement in his attention in academic classes.

"I worked with Andrew after school on other days, and never called on him in class. I saw that Edward needed the positive attention every bit as desperately as Andrew did. I had both of them reading Horatio Alger and stories from *Boys' Life* about boys who triumphed over adversity. I brought both their mothers in and let them know how I was handling the situation and how well their sons were doing. Not that I had to tell them!"

Mrs. Johnson was alert to everything the young teacher told her. There was the look of a smile in her eyes.

"By the end of the school session I asked the boys to meet with me. Together. There was a great deal of tension in the air—some of it my own," Amelia said.

"Finally, Andrew asked Edward, 'Do you still think I'm f-f-funny?' just like that. Edward answered, " 'No, I know you couldn't help it. I just used to like to show off.'"

"You'll find miracle stories like that are commonplace here," Mrs. Johnson said. "You handled it well, and I would say your instincts will probably serve you well as a teacher here or anywhere you choose to work. You are aware that if you take the job here there is no other class to which you can transfer your problem child."

"Mrs. Johnson, I want to work here."

"I'm pleased. We are going to need a good teacher for our students in First Life. If you can be here the last two weeks of September, our school begins October 3."

"You can count on it," Amelia said, and extended her hand. She was aware the school was small and money was tight. Mrs. Johnson told her the salary she could expect, which was certainly meager, with no allowance for holidays or vacations.

She had not expected much. In fact, she probably would have taken the job for nothing and considered it an extended education. Luckily she did not need the salary. She was the only child of Dr. and Mrs. Frederick King of Hoboken, New Jersey, and the granddaughter of the late Conrad King, one of the leading merchants of the city. He left Amelia a comfortable trust fund and she would never have to worry about not having enough money. This fact came vividly back to her when she learned the pittance Mrs. Johnson's school paid.

She marveled at Mrs. Johnson's ease with people. At their first brief conversation in Philadelphia she had all but offered Amelia a job, inviting her to Fairhope. Unlike the stern and tyrannical schoolteachers and head mistresses Amelia had known before, Marietta Johnson exuded strength and warmth in equal measure.

She could sense the school demonstrated the character of its founder, expanding the possibilities of everybody who came in contact with it, student and teacher. For her, the opportunity to work here would be better than any graduate school program.

Three

WHEN AMELIA EMERGED from Mrs. Johnson's office in the School Home, she didn't know if she'd been an hour or all day. Her stomach told her it was getting close to lunchtime and she heard sounds and voices coming from what must be the kitchen—the room to the rear of the building, just off the big reception room that was also set up for dining—that made it sound as if meal preparations had begun.

It was summer vacation now, so the small staff prepared meals only for Mrs. Johnson, her family, and the few faculty members who were still around before they took their summer break. Amelia didn't know who the people were who were beginning to gather. Mrs. Johnson's mother, a sister and a brother, along with her son Clifford Ernest—home from college for the summer—and Esther, the secretary-niece Amelia met earlier, all lived in this dormitory along with a few faculty members and some 15 or 20 students during the school year. Fairhope in general and the school in particular were generous with their hospitality.

Mrs. Johnson had not let Amelia out of the job interview without exacting a promise from her to study some reading matter. She gave her two books on education: *The Education of the Child* by Nathan Oppenheim, and *Education and the Larger Life* by C. Hanford Henderson, both of whom were mentors to the lady herself and shared her radical ideas about the education of children. Amelia was excited at the prospect of reading both books. She had one more day in Fairhope and was looking forward to using the time well. She could start the books here and still would have plenty of time for reading on the train home.

She could not resist stopping by the new Comings auditorium on her way back to The Gables. The building was almost complete, she could see. She couldn't hear as much activity as she had before, so she walked inside and looked around at the spacious room with high ceilings, exposed rafters, and light coming in from the windows at all sides. At one end of the room was a stage, built some four feet above the large main floor. What uses the students would make of this marvel of a building—a floor big enough for parties, banquets, folk dancing—a pet class of Mrs. Johnson's—and a stage at the other end for theatricals and concerts!

Most of the workers had gone home for lunch, which to the students meant they went home to hot meals cooked by their mothers, but the man she had seen on the ladder earlier was eating out of a black metal lunchbox and talking with a few of the young people. He looked up at her with soft blue eyes and said, rather shyly she thought, "Howdy, Ma'am."

Amelia had not ever heard the vernacular actually used like this and hearing it, suppressed a laugh.

"My name is Will Hodges," he said, smiling back. "This is Ella and this is my little brother Wallace." The dark-haired tall boy, whom she had seen on the ladder before, was introduced to her—George Ray Collins. He and his smaller assistant, Wallace Hodges, were hammering something onto the floor of the stage, and were not available for formal introductions but they nodded at her from their work. She noted a silent man with straight, almost white blonde hair and dark circles around his icy blue eyes. His cupid's bow mouth turned up at the corners. He hung in the background of the busy room, observing more than he was working.

"That there's Curry Cumbie," Will Hodges said of the man in the background.

From his corner, Cumbie glanced up and nodded. His look was like a dark cloud; he appeared to be a man of much internal conflict and unresolved anger. Maybe it was just the shadow, Amelia thought. He looked as if he needed some sunlight and fresh air.

"Glad to meet you," Amelia responded, only beginning to realize that Will Hodges' 'howdy' had been something of an affectation of Southern country charm. Will was clearly not a hick. His accent didn't even sound Southern.

"Are you going to be a teacher here?" Will asked.

"I just came from my interview with Mrs. Johnson," Amelia said. "And she's offered me a job teaching first and second grades. I'm very excited to be here."

"Better learn not to use the word 'grade,' then," Will said with a sardonic grin that moved only one side of his mouth. "Miz Johnson doesn't like that word. You'll be teaching First Life." He paused a moment, letting her take that in. Then he broke into a full smile and said, "Welcome!"

"First *Life*—oh yes, of course. Mrs. Johnson did explain that to me. I must not even say the word 'grade'!" One of the tenets of the school was that students were grouped by age; another was that there was no such thing as a "grade." Letter grades were not given for any course—therefore the aversion to the word even being spoken. Amelia had loved teaching the first grade in Ferndale, but she could see the efficacy of combining grades, particularly in a school with a small enrollment. The Organic School had an average of about 150 students, counting both kindergarten and high school.

"Well, I'll be teaching six- and seven-year-olds," she said.

She knew it was time to get back to the Gables while lunch was still being served, so she started out of the open, big room. "My name is Amelia King, and I'll be seeing you in the fall," she said as she reached the door. "I love what you're doing here!"

Her remark was intended to include more than the spare simplicity of the construction of the building. By "what you're doing here" she meant the ease and immediacy of everything in Fairhope that she had observed so far—the comfort and commitment to the community and the school. The school itself appeared to be the home for the whole village.

As she walked down Fairhope Avenue, past the big intersection of the town's main streets, she realized she had spoken to three different people this day and all three had said the word "Welcome." That surely could not have been a coincidence!

To her left was a pharmacy and across the street was a big store with the name H. Crawford General Store emblazoned across its front. An old man with a long white beard, neatly dressed but without shoes, was walking up the steps onto Crawford's porch.

Next to the general store was a quaint structure that proclaimed "Millinery" from its sign. Two boys were shooting marbles by the side of the unpaved street, and two young women, one in men's attire, held hands as they walked into the millinery shop. A man in very dirty clothes, looking as if he'd slept outdoors and was not yet quite awake, sat on the porch of the general store. A regal-looking woman rode astride a white horse down the center of Fairhope Avenue and turned left on Church Street, in front of The Gables. On this sunny day, everything seemed out of the ordinary, heightened for Amelia by the knowledge that she would soon be at home amid the magic.

She was late for lunch, although Mrs. Cross had set aside a plate for her as she had stopped serving the public.

"I thought you'd like my chicken pie and vegetables," Mrs. Cross said as she set her place. "It's a favorite of all my usual diners."

Amelia was more than pleased to be presented with a plate of steaming food. The chicken pie was full of meat, and had its share of carrots, potatoes, peas and celery swimming in white sauce under the golden crust. The meal would have been quite complete without the side dish of cabbage cooked with ham. Always having freshly made tea on hand, Mrs. Cross managed one of the first dining rooms in Fairhope to offer iced tea with every meal. Amelia thought twice about eating so much food on a hot day, but on the third thought she applied her knife and fork and ate.

She had to ask about the woman on the white horse, the most striking of the Fairhope citizens she'd seen.

"Oh, that was Madame," said Mrs. Cross.

"Madame Mercedes Morehead, opera singer and veterinarian," Captain Cross added. The juxtaposition of occupations was unusual, but the captain didn't bat an eye at it.

"She cuts a striking figure," Amelia said.

"That she does," said the captain. "She's an asset to the town, with both her music and her way with animals."

"And her personality! I never met a woman quite like her," Mrs. Cross said, smiling and shaking her head. "She's so sure of herself. It's like talking with a man, yet she is feminine at the same time."

Amelia told the Crosses of her interview with Mrs. Johnson, and that she had accepted the offer to teach First Life the next year. She was so excited, she told them, to be included in the experiments that were both Fairhope itself and its unique school.

"So, are you now a single taxer?" Captain Cross asked.

"I would say so, yes," Amelia answered. "I'm really not sure how it works, but I would think a year or two in Fairhope would clear that up."

"It'll take more than a year or two," Mrs. Cross practically bellowed. "There's people here been discussing the finer points for fifty years and they still don't understand it!"

"They weren't discussing it here for fifty years, dear," Captain Cross said. "The town wasn't founded until 1895."

"Oh, they were discussing single tax long before they got to Fairhope," his wife said.

They all laughed, and Amelia thought of the men who came by The Gables to discuss economics and philosophy with the captain every day. They were old-time contrarians who had moved to Fairhope to prove a point, but each of the individuals apparently had a different point in mind.

"Is there as much difference of opinion about Organic Education?" Amelia asked, innocently expecting the Crosses to assure her that everybody in town approved that particular philosophy.

"Much more!" Mrs. Cross was emphatic.

"Oh, Idella, I wouldn't say much more—maybe not even more. But as much, surely." The Captain patted his wife's hand.

"Jack, don't deceive the girl," she said.

Amelia was stunned into silence, wanting an explanation from one of them.

"Well, nobody argues with Marietta," Mrs. Cross said. "She's very persuasive, very artful. And she is on a mission."

"No doubt about that," said Captain Cross.

"Her methods work because she is an extraordinary schoolmistress," Mrs. Cross said. "She has a way with children, and she is committed to change the world, just as E.B. Gaston is with his commitment to single tax."

"And what is the single tax theory, exactly?"

"Basically that the colony owns the land and leases it to the citizenry, using that leasehold money to finance community services. It is a scheme to circumvent the rapacious exploitation of land by real estate developers." Captain Cross said. "It puts the colony in charge of developing the land to its best use for the community."

It sounded logical enough to Amelia, but then she hadn't had time in her young life to consider the kind of objections this would raise among people who had spent their lives with the dream of owning property. It was a constant subject for debate all over town.

"In many ways, I think Marietta's radical school has a better chance of succeeding," Mrs. Cross put in. "And even she says her school is a 'demonstration' of what a perfect school should be. It's progressive because it's still a work in progress. She's still working the wrinkles out."

Amelia did not know if Mrs. Cross was playing devil's advocate or speaking her own thoughts, but she was formulating a response to in her mind when the front door was opened with a bang.

"Saw that there was some activity in here!" said a booming voice. She recognized this big, effusive man. She had seen him on the boat ride from Mobile. He wore a jacket and cap then, indicating he was the purser of the steamer Apollo. Now he was in shirtsleeves, rolled up, and his collar was unbuttoned.

"You never miss a thing," Captain Cross said to the big man with the ruddy cheeks and big smile revealing teeth slightly yellowed.

"Amelia, this is our friend Jacob Pilcher," Captain Cross did the honors. "This is Miss King, who will be teaching First Life for Mettie next fall."

Amelia had not heard the nickname *Mettie* for Mrs. Johnson before that moment, but she would hear it a great deal from now on—even from the children, who always called Mrs. Johnson "Aunt Mettie."

There was an upright piano in the front room of The Gables, one which Amelia had heard Captain Cross trying out a Chopin prelude on in the morning. Now Jacob made his way to it and performed a showy glissando across the keys. Then he leafed through the sheet music on top of the piano and began playing a medley of ballads: "My Wild Irish Rose," "A Bird in a Gilded Cage," and "None But the Lonely Heart." He sang them all too, with Capt. and Mrs. Cross joining in. Since her early childhood in her home with the Chapman family, her cousins in Philadephia, Amelia had always loved the custom of group singing around the piano. The piano in that parlor had seldom been silent.

"I have my work to do in the kitchen," Mrs. Cross said, but just then E.B. Gaston himself was coming up the steps to the porch.

"I hear music," Mr. Gaston said.

"Do come in, Ernest," Mrs. Cross, who was at the door, said, summoning him into the room. "I don't think you've met the newest citizen of Fairhope, Miss Amelia King."

Mr. Gaston was tall and saturnine, with a lean, wrinkled face. "How do you do," he said to Amelia. "Don't tell me— I'll wager you're a schoolteacher!"

"Does it show?" Amelia asked.

"No, I wouldn't say so," Mr. Gaston recovered quickly. "It's just that all the pretty girls who move here seem to be schoolteachers."

Jacob had not stopped playing the piano, but now he had subdued the music into a quiet mode as background to the conversation.

"I was on my way to the kitchen," Mrs. Cross said. "But you must join our song fest, as long as you're here. Would you like coffee or tea? How about you, Jacob?"

Both the guests asked for coffee, but Amelia and Captain Cross requested tea.

"I'll be right back," Mrs. Cross said and went into the kitchen.

"What were you playing?" Mr. Gaston had turned to the piano and leaned on it. The son of an Iowa minister, he loved to sing the old hymns as well as entertain at ice cream socials, picnics, and other such gatherings.

By now Jacob was into the verse of "Alice Blue Gown," singing it too, and E.B. joined right in. This was a treat for Amelia, who actually owned a dress of what was called Alice Blue, after Alice Roosevelt—who favored the shade, it was said, because it matched her eyes. Amelia, like so many American girls her age, loved the color, and that particular dress.

Mrs. Cross had discreetly placed a tray with the coffee, tea, cream and sugar on the table beside the sofa and left for the kitchen again.

"Here's the coffee!" Amelia announced, taking her teacup and hoping the singing would go on for a while. Group singing went straight to her heart.

The men took their coffee and E.B. asked her, "How do you like our town?" He fairly beamed when he spoke of it, he was so proud of Fairhope.

"Very promising," said Amelia, and all the men laughed.

"Promising, my girl?" Jacob boomed. "You picked the perfect word!"

"And Fairhope shall deliver on its promise!" Mr. Gaston said.

"I'll drink to that," Captain Cross added. "Tea, of course."

There was more laughter and then Jacob said, "We'll sing one more song, in honor of that promise."

"Oh—I know what that's going to be," said Captain Cross.

"I'll wager you do! E.B.'s favorite song!" said Jacob from the piano.

"Everybody's favorite song," E.B. ventured.

With that, Jacob drained his coffee cup, returned it to its saucer and put the saucer on the table. Then he wheeled around on the piano stool to face the piano. With a flourish, he began to play.

It was the first time Amelia was to hear the song that Jacob had written, the unofficial anthem of the town—an old-fashioned waltz called "Fairhope." All three men sang at full volume, E.B. adding the harmony, and Mrs. Cross came in from the kitchen and joined them.

"There's a verdant shore, by the waters blue, where we dearly love to stay/There's a village fair and we long to be there, on the banks of Mobile Bay!"

They came to the rousing chorus. By the last line of the chorus all in the room had tears in their eyes, including Amelia.

"Fairhope, Fairhope, Down on Mobile Bay/Fairhope, Fairhope, that's where we love to stay.

"Down where the roses are blooming, down the waters blue, Fairhope, Fair-hope"—there was a long pause between syllables "fair" and "hope" and then the song's great payoff line—"I love you."

The song went on and on, five full verses, and the singers sang each verse, even the one about the single tax, with full conviction and ardor.

Enveloped in the warmth of their song and surrounded by pairs of tear-filled eyes, Amelia was transported back to the Philadelphia parlor, with her aunt Althea at the piano and her Uncle Ned and three cousins joining in song. She recalled the lonely child she had been, taken in and transformed by the simplicity of love.

It was begun as a temporary arrangement, but Amelia thrived and found herself begging to stay with the Chapman family every year until she attended college. She went to Hoboken only for summer vacations and at Christmas.

This evening in Fairhope reminded her of the childhood days with her aunt, uncle and cousins. This was surely a place she would feel safe and realize the possibilities of her deepest self. With the traumas of her own childhood behind her, she might be able to make life more positive for children by allowing them to grow and learn on their own terms, to be their best selves.

In joining the final chorus of the "Fairhope" song, Amelia felt all of them were right in loving this particular place, this community full of energy and ideas, this dream they were all dreaming and all working to make come true. Some innate shred of optimism overpowered the sense of impending doom she had carried as long as she could remember.

Four

ERNESTINE CUMBIE HAD a nice hot meal ready for Curry. She was expecting him any minute. She was not as disturbed about being back in Fairhope as she had expected to be, even though it did bring up a lot of memories that she and Curry had both been trying to forget. He had all of a sudden decided it was time to return and get used to it again, he said. His brother Curtis had told him that things were pretty much the same at the school and all.

Curtis and his wife Lou Ellen lived in a house on the edge of town, where they managed to grow enough vegetables and keep enough chickens to feed themselves and even sell some to people in Fairhope from time to time. Curtis had an old truck and when there were collards, turnips and okra to package for sale he and Lou Ellen would box them up and ride into Fairhope where they could sell them by the side of the road. The Cumbies had lived in Baldwin County since before there was a town called Fairhope, and the family farm was only few miles out in the country. Their daddy and momma had worked it before the boys were born. As the oldest child, Curtis took it over when the folks got old and sick, and he inherited the place when they died.

Ernestine was putting on weight all the time, and she knew it. At first it bothered her, but she couldn't help eating more, and it didn't seem to make no never mind to Curry, who had changed too, but only to become a bitter man. Not that he had ever been a sweet one, but he had the Cumbie face with lips that turned up at the corners slightly, like a smile even when he was mad or sorrowful. His family all had that mouth. On their sister Vesta's face, the Cumbie look was very pretty, and their own daughter Alice Ann had inherited the Cumbie face along with the disposition of a rattlesnake.

Ernestine still grieved the little girl Alice Ann, even though the Lord had taken her five years before. She had tried so hard to make the girl obey, but Curry spoiled her. She was just like her daddy anyway—willful and stubborn. She wouldn't listen to any grownups. Curry didn't mind it; he thought it showed she had spirit. But he didn't have to deal with her all day long. He was as like as not to blame Ernestine if Alice Ann acted up. Nobody could really please Curry; he was in his own mind too much of the time.

Cornbread was in the oven, and a mess of greens was in a pot on top of the stove, cooked with ham hocks the way Curry liked them. It made a good solid dinner and then he could go about his business. Ernestine tried her best not to worry about her man, but she knew his ways and never knew when he might explode in anger or even in tears.

They were staying with Curtis and Lou Ellen until they could find a place of their own, which might be never. Ernestine was good at cooking and thought she could find a job cooking for someone, but Curry insisted she hold off until he made up his mind what she should do. He didn't like the idea of his woman working for money, but there was no question they could use the income, especially so they could get a house of some kind.

There were always a few cottages available in Fairhope, pretty cheap, too, since you didn't have to buy the land. You could add to your own house, and all you had to do was pay a yearly rent to the single tax colony for the land. Curry and Ernestine liked the idea more than Curtis and Lou Ellen did, but then they owned the farm and didn't have to think about it. It was always better to own your own land and house, but the single tax idea had its merits when you didn't have much money.

She and Curry took the single tax and the Organic School with a grain of salt, except that now and forevermore they would have no truck with the school. She would grant that many of the people there were good-hearted, and she knew what had happened to Alice Ann was an accident, but Curry wouldn't hear anything about it except that the school should be closed once and for all.

All the same Ernestine knew to get some kind of work at the school was her best chance for a decent shake—maybe cooking in the dormitory, or cleaning up part-time, maybe both—while Curry took odd jobs and worked at electrical and such. She was surprised when Curry said he thought it was a pretty good idea. At least he had said she could try when the time was right.

She was pulling the skillet of cornbread out of the oven when he came in and let the screen door slam as usual.

"Home again," he said, without any emotion that she could read. He looked serious and smelled of stale beer and white lightning from the night before. He went straight through the kitchen to the outhouse and then came right back and started washing his hands along with the dirty dishes in the sink.

"Curtis around?" he asked.

"He and Lou Ellen went to town," Ernestine said.

"Smells like you got some dinner," Curry said.

"Cornbread and greens."

"Any tea?"

She was glad he was asking for tea instead of beer at this hour. Sometimes he liked iced tea with his dinner, although plenty of times he just skipped both and went straight to beer. She tried to see that there was always food available. Curtis and Lou Ellen liked to have some food too, but she didn't know when they'd be home.

She had made the tea in the morning and put plenty of sugar in it. She and Lou Ellen kept a pitcher of it in the kitchen all the time, hoping the more there was of other stuff to drink, the less Curry and Curtis would drink the beer and home brew that made them get to fighting. The ice box seldom had ice in it, but the tea, at room temperature, was still called iced tea because it wasn't hot. The men wouldn't think of drinking hot tea. Strong coffee was their breakfast drink.

She cut a chunk of cornbread and put it in a big flat soup bowl, took the bowl to the stove where she ladled greens and pot liquor onto it, adding a ham hock for Curry.

Curtis and Lou Ellen had a cow, so there was always butter for cornbread, potatoes, or corn on the cob when they wanted it. There was a churn the old folks had always used and every week or so the womenfolk would skim the buttermilk and churn some butter. She put another chunk of cornbread next to the butter on the table.

Chores like churning butter and making sweet tea meant a lot to Ernestine, and every once in a while she could tell herself that she and Curry were happy—at least as happy as they could be.

She wanted to ask if he'd found work, or what work he'd been doing, but she had long since learned that it was none of her business, and that asking about his day would likely set him off. He was less edgy than usual this day, but all the same it was up to him to tell her if he so desired.

"Workin' with Hodges today," he said. It was unusual for him to volunteer information, and he wouldn't have said anything if he wasn't having a really good day. He knew she liked Will Hodges and felt comfortable that he'd let Curry help with some of his paying jobs. Will often worked for nothing, but when he got a job that paid he would bring other people on sometimes.

"That's good," she said.

"Yeah, he's got a few jobs workin' for new people in town." He took a big chew of ham hock before he spoke again, with food in his mouth. "Has a house he thinks we should look at."

Curry talking about getting a house could only mean that he was thinking about letting Ernestine take a job of some kind, although she wasn't sure she should bring that up. He saw the look on her face when she heard about a house, and so he even said something more.

"Course we can't think about it now, things being how they are."

"Well, we could think about it. I could go look for work cleanin' houses, or cookin'," Ernestine said.

"Yeah, you could." Curry was shoveling food in his mouth and Ernestine couldn't always understand what he said. It was hard to believe he was thinking about them buying a house and her getting a job, but that seemed to be what he was saying.

"Got any more of this cornbread?"

She knew he had seen her take the skillet of cornbread out of the oven. This was his way of complimenting her cooking.

"You know we do," she said.

He sidled over to the stove, served himself another plate of greens and cut a chunk of cornbread and crumbled it into the plate, soaking up the pot liquor.

"I bin thinkin' about what we was talkin' about," Curry said to her. "It don't mean we're gonna buy us a house or nothin', but if we're gonna start thinking about that, we're both gonna have to have jobs."

"You know I don't mind havin' a job, Curry."

"I know you don't. I don't like my wife workin', but sometimes it's a necessity, for a short spell anyway. I think you ought to go ask at the school."

This was a real surprise. The terrible accident had happened to them years before at the school, so serious they never even talked of it now. Their only child, Alice Ann, had passed away and Curry had always held Mrs. Johnson personally responsible. Whenever bad things happened in Curry's life, he blamed some other person. Ernestine never thought Curry would come around about the school, feeling the way he did, but today he plowed right on.

"They have some nice people," he said. "Hodges says there might be work over at the School Home, where the boarders live. You might have a chance to give Mrs. Johnson a piece of your mind."

Ernestine had nothing but respect for Mrs. Johnson, but Curry despised her with all his heart. She knew that what he was saying was that with her working there *he* might have a chance to give her a piece of *his* mind.

"A piece of my mind or yours?" she said.

Curry laughed.

"You know what I mean," he said. "You know just what I mean."

"Pretty much," she said. She did not always know what he meant, but it felt good that he always thought she did. He had his ways of talking around a thing, and it was best not to question him to explain. Ernestine had learned that the hard way.

"Me and Curtis may go huntin' later," Curry said. Hunting this time of year meant shooting birds and squirrels, sometimes a wild turkey. Sometimes they brought home food, but mostly it was an excuse to use their guns while they were drinking.

"We could use some turkey for the weekend," Ernestine said, thinking it was not likely they would bag anything like that. The turkey was the excuse, but she and Lou Ellen would be lucky if they got anything more than a squirrel or two for stew.

"Some big 'uns around," Curry said. He started sucking on a ham hock and Ernestine went to the sink to wash up. Out the window she could see the hardscrabble land the Cumbies had tried to farm for generations—sand mostly, but over the years they had built up a few spots where vegetables would grow. The cow gave milk and the chickens layed, but it was not much of a place and there was no hope of it ever being hers and Curry's anyway. A house in Fairhope might do for starting over and maybe helping Curry into a better life. She liked the people in Fairhope, although she did not really socialize. She liked the feeling in Fairhope, that people there would help you through hard times—and she had never known anything but hard times. It was not easy to hope for life to be better when you were tied to a man like Curry, who was suspicious of people and never looked on the bright side even when things were good.

"What you thinking about?"

Curry hated it when she had private thoughts, but then he usually got mad when she told him her thoughts anyway.

"Oh, I don't know," she sighed.

"Yes you do."

"Well, it crossed my mind that it might be nice to have a house in Fairhope," she said.

"Yeah. That crossed mine too."

All it would take was for her to get the word to the school that she was looking for a job, she was sure. They might not have anything, there was that; but maybe she could get a job in the kitchen at one of the restaurants or guest houses. They were all busy these days, with the enrollment at the school growing and so many people visiting Fairhope just to look it over. She would start at the school, since Curry had mentioned it.

The very next day she went into town with Curtis and Lou Ellen on the truck, and stopped by the dormitory to talk with Mrs. Cora Myhers about possibly working there. Mrs. Myhers said she'd have to think it over and would arrange an appointment for her to speak with Mrs. Johnson. All very professional and intimidating, but Ernestine knew Mrs. Johnson and was not to be deterred. If she didn't get this job there were other places she could work in Fairhope.

Five

FROM THE DAYS when her school was first getting started, Marietta Johnson knew the little ones of Fairhope
regarded her as someone out of the ordinary, a grownup
who understood what they were interested in and had ever
so much to share with them. When in one of her classes
they would sit where they were comfortable, on the floor in
a circle, in rapt attention to her every word. There were no
desks screwed to the floor, she saw to that. The children were
eager to answer the questions she posed and they flocked
to her with questions of their own, showed her the projects
they were working on, and just liked to follow her around
when she walked through town. Townspeople seldom saw
her without at least two children, chattering, in her wake.
Just knowing that they counted on her, that her work with
teachers would benefit them, signified to her that she must
go on.

Marietta delighted in the way her teachers used the
natural surroundings in Fairhope for lessons. There was a
harmony with nature in Fairhope, inspiring her in a deep
spiritual way. She considered it to be God's own harmony.
The town was threaded with deep gullies, which made for
unique playgrounds for young and old. One bordered the
south, cutting off the main street, and on the other side of
that the Negroes lived. There were gullies all through the

town, some made passable by bridges, some simply there to be explored, from sand floor to the top of the clay walls on either side. With the thrill of the danger of scaling their heights and the possibility of exploring the length of the ravines, the gullies were fun for children, and even the adults would venture into them to explore at times.

It was an easy step for Marietta to incorporate the gullies into the children's school life. Much of their day was spent outside, and some of it was spent in learning Greek mythology and old folk tales. With their teachers they would take walks all over town, acting out the myths as they did, climbing into the trees, climbing up and down the gully walls. They sometimes did their sums on the clay walls of a particular gully, and whenever a child was playing a character of power, off he would go to the highest point to which he could climb to assert his dominion over the others. They took bows and arrows with them to practice archery, which was sometimes used in their theatrical events. They loved playing Robin Hood and King John, and planned presentations to show the grownups. The teachers cleverly guided these projects and took their classes throughout the town, teaching details of the local flora and fauna along the way.

One day she saw four-year-old Chauncey Wilson with his older sister and another child at the post office. Chaucey was a particular favorite boy, bright and a rather serious fellow. His sister Emily had him firmly by the hand. The little girl with them appeared to be Emily's age, which would be six, or just a bit younger. She had long blonde hair and icy blue eyes and was nervous for a child her age. Her lips were full, cupid's-bow style, and naturally turned up just a bit at the corners. It was the first time Marietta had ever seen Alice Ann Cumbie.

"Good morning, Chauncey," Mrs. Johnson said, addressing the young man as the full-fledged person he was. No irony colored her tone of voice. And he took it that way as well.

"Hi, Aunt Mettie!" Chauncey said.

"Good morning, Emily," she went on. "Who's your new friend?" Emily told her Alice Ann's name, and Chauncey looked to be very proud that everybody had gotten all the etiquette right. Alice Ann, however, dropped her eyes and appeared uncomfortable.

"I'm sure you'll like me when you get to know me better," Marietta said, instinctively wanting to put the child at ease.

"It's Marietta Johnson, Alice Ann!" Chauncey chimed in, and he, Emily, and Mrs. Johnson all laughed together. Alice Ann wasn't laughing, but she managed something like a smile with her already-smiling lips. She wore her self-consciousness like a badge. Alice Ann was a child with troubles that a child should not have—perhaps an unhappy or unwholesome home life, Mrs. Johnson noted. She hoped she would see her Alice Ann at her school and the school would help provide the child with conditions for normal growth and self-respect. Thinking it a definite possibility, she formulated how she would advise the teachers of her observations and suggest that attention be paid to care and handling of this child.

She went to the postmistress, Mrs. Totten, to get the mail for the school, which came in a nice big bundle. As she walked toward home, the three children were just behind her.

The town of Fairhope was now full of adventurous children and young teachers who had come to town for one reason—to learn Mrs. Johnson's methods. It was a paradise of nature and learning, intertwined into what she truly hoped

would be a school to demonstrate the future of education—her school, the vanguard of Organic Education. Her
dream, as she often said in her speeches, for every child, was
that he develop a sound, accomplished body, a sympathetic,
intelligent mind, and a sweet and sincere spirit. What was
education for if not that?

Into this pristine paradise for children, there had to
come some tribulations and tragedies. Mrs. Johnson had
learned to accept this as a fact of life on this planet. She
tried to teach this to the older children but in her heart she
understood there is really no way anyone is ever prepared
for tragedy. No one is exempt from its occurrence.

One such tragic event was to befall her school on a fine
spring morning in 1916, when Mrs. Johnson was away on a
fund-raising trip to California. The Second and Third Life
Groups were together on a hike to Stack's Gully, a deep
ravine with high bluffs for climbing, not far from the campus. The two groups together—comprising what would be
third, fourth, fifth and sixth grades in a traditional school,
numbered about 25 children.

It was a bigger group than usual, but their two teachers each had an assistant, a student-teacher, and they had
been on these gully trips many times before. Their objective
was clear. They would walk to the gully where the teachers
would work with them in four groups, each studying a different facet of what they found. One group was to collect
clay from the walls, one would study cloud formations, and
the other two groups would investigate various aspects of
the plant life. The children were excited, as they always were
readying for these trips—noisy and chaotic and eager to
leave. Mabel Edgar was in charge. She was an older teacher,
one Mrs. Johnson had recruited from Minnesota—a no-

nonsense, hearty woman, and the perfect leader for such an outing.

On the way to the gully the children broke into smaller groups, comparing their plans for what they expected to gather. There was a din of child-noise—high pitched squeals amid the conversations. The teachers did not admonish for quiet, but would occasionally say, "Calm down, class. This is fun for all of us," and the voices would fall silent for a few moments. Then the noise would ramp up once again. Two girls chattered on the periphery of the group—Alice Ann Cumbie and her best friend, Emily Wilson, the girl Mrs. Johnson had seen with her at the post office and told the teachers about. Alice Ann was more fidgety than usual, Miss Edgar noted. Marietta had told her about this child, warning her that she seemed to bear the weight of an un-happy home and would need special attention. Alice Ann's idea of play was to punch her friend in the arm until she yelled "Ouch!" A few minutes of this and the Wilson girl would leave her side, but then Alice Ann sought her out again. Sometimes Alice Ann would punch her hard and then run and hide behind a tree.

Miss Edgar was just beginning to know Alice Ann, and could tell drawing her out and helping her to have normal social interactions was not going to be easy.

Alice Ann and Emily were not in the group that was assigned to collect clay, but Alice Ann insisted that that was what she wanted to do, and squirmed her way into the group of boys with clay buckets. More than content to get away from her, Emily went straight to the group of girls her age collecting leaves from the bushes.

"The idea is to learn the name of the bush," the student teacher of Second Life said, "And then take just one leaf.

We are here to help you identify, and we'll all take the leaves back to the campus where we can write down the name of the plants we've learned."

The clay collection appealed to Alice Ann because it involved climbing high on the bluff, a favorite activity of Fairhope children. The children had small buckets in which to put the clay they'd dug, which they would take with them to the campus to soak, sift clean of sand, and ultimately use in making pottery. Alice Ann pushed into the group working with clay.

Climbing on a bluff was a hazardous activity. The sides of the bluff were covered with sand, some grass, and some brush. The older students knew this well and were digging carefully into the sand for clay. Sand would slip and occasionally children slid, but they had long ago learned how to handle themselves in the gullies of their home town. Exploring gullies and climbing were activities enjoyed by young and old in Fairhope.

One of the boys had dug quite a hole, almost a cave, high up toward the top of the cliff, by the time Miss Edgar spotted him and brought him back down to the sand at the base of the gully.

"That's enough up there, Kenneth," she said, and he brought his pail to show her, quite full of good red clay.

As she examined it there was a cry from above. It was the voice of Alice Ann Cumbie. She had climbed high, dug herself even more deeply into Kenneth's cave and suddenly a landslide had started above her filling the hole with sand and causing a cave-in across the side of the gully. All at once all the children, sliding down the cliff, were running and screaming.

"Quiet, quiet!" Miss Edgar and the three other teachers tried to assess the situation and to quell the screams at the same time. None of the teachers understood what was happening, but a few of the children had seen Alice Ann disappear as the cave-in began. One by one the children came to realize that one of their number was missing, but the teachers did not know until it was too late.

Emily Wilson dropped the handful of leaves she was holding. "It's Alice Ann!" she cried.

"It's all right, it's all right," Miss Edgar said. "Did anyone see where she went?"

No one had. It had happened quickly and she had not been seen climbing into the cave which engulfed her as the land slid all around her, sweeping other children down the hill to safety on the gully bed. Many were covered in sand and dirt, and they all were profoundly frightened in a way they had never been in their lives. The all-embracing gullies of Fairhope were suddenly fraught with danger and death.

"Alice Ann!" a child called. Soon they all were calling her name, hoping for a response so they could locate her and bring her to safety. No response came.

Mabel Edgar knew how to handle this. She dispatched the Second Life teacher to town to find able-bodied men—Mr. Dooley the constable, if possible—as soon as she could. In the meantime she and the other teachers had their hands full quieting the children and digging. After a few minutes she perceived the gravity of the situation and took the two assistant teachers aside and admonished them to gather all the children except for three of the sixth grade boys she chose for their size and ability to keep their heads. Most of the children would be walked back to the campus, and she and her chosen three would start digging in the spot where Kenneth's cave had been dug until Miss Temple, the Second Life teacher, had time to return with the men.

"If you can keep your head when all about you—" She began.

"Are losing theirs and blaming it on you!" came the three boys' voices in unison, as clearly as a church responsive reading.

"If you can trust yourself when all men doubt you, and make allowance for their doubting too..." Miss Edgar instinctively had picked a poem the boys knew, one that applied at least obliquely to the situation and might provide a distraction from their profound task of finding the lost girl.

"If you can wait and not be tired by waiting..."

Miss Edgar spoke above the voices of the boys, chanting rhythmically as they followed her instructions. Kipling was a favorite, and his masculine vigor helped distract as well as inspire the boys.

She and the boys were now near the spot where the cave had been dug so deeply.

"I'm afraid Alice Ann must have gotten very deep in the cave," Miss Edgar said. "Before the landslide started. Miss Temple will be here soon, with Mr. Dooley and some other big strong men, and we'll have this all straightened out."

"If you can dream, and not make dreams your master,

"If you can think, and not make thoughts your aim..."

As they recited they went ahead with the work of digging, with their hands and using the pails they had brought for clay, going far deeper into the cliffside than anyone had any idea they would have to. Apparently Alice Ann had found a real cave, and been caught in a cave-in. The hot Alabama sun and the physical exertion caused them all to break out in sweat, including the usually fastidious Miss

Edgar. She endeavored to keep her sense of panic from showing as they dug deeper and found no sign and heard no sound from the missing child. The poem came to an end, and the boys went on with their work, more somberly now. They sensed what they would find, and the seriousness of the task weighed on them.

Within the hour, Miss Temple came back with Will Hodges and George Ray Collins.

"Mr. Dooley wasn't home, but I told his wife we needed him," she said. Will and George Ray had shovels and they helped with the digging.

By the time Dooley arrived they had found the body of the little girl, suffocated and still. She had so quickly gotten into the cave, the landslide overtook them all before any of the adults had missed her, and by the time they did it was too late to save her. They were astonished and heartbroken to learn what had actually happened.

Miss Temple quickly took the boys with her back to the school and Miss Edgar and the two men took the remains of Alice Ann back into town to the undertaker's office at the rear of Crawford's store. It was up to Miss Edgar and Mr. Dooley to face the parents with the dreadful news.

Curry and Ernestine Cumbie were simple country people who had moved to Fairhope to live with relatives. He did odd jobs around town, helped with electrical and repair work, and was known to become boisterous when John Barleycorn was in him. Ernestine took work cleaning houses, and occasionally showed up with bruises on her face and upper body, but nobody knew the kind of scars she covered where it didn't show. They always were down on their luck, and this would be a blow they might not be able to take. Mabel Edgar wished for the wisdom of her friend

Marietta when she faced them, but she didn't know if she had it in her.

The Cumbies were living in a one-room house they had managed to buy on Single Tax land, an economy they appreciated. Because they paid only for the house and the Colony owned the land, they were entitled to free tuition at the Organic School, which they thought was a wonderful idea for their only child.

When they saw Miss Edgar approaching with Dooley, the town's only policeman, and they saw the looks on their faces, they knew it was trouble. They assumed Curry had committed some infraction that they didn't know of, and they prepared for the worst.

"Mr. Cumbie, Mrs. Cumbie, we have terrible news—" Miss Edgar started.

The looks on the faces of the couple was something Mabel Edgar knew she would never forget. They started with guilt, which melted into a kind of defensiveness, which, before the word was out, had turned to anguish. They realized they were to hear monumentally bad news, news that changes lives.

"I don't want to hear this!" Curry Cumbie said emphatically. "Get off my property!"

Ernestine was already beginning to cry. It was as if she was anticipating, in addition to the unbelievably bad news, a beating within an inch of her life.

Miss Edgar tried to summon the courage to comfort this couple.

"You have to hear it, Curry," said Dooley. "Just take it easy now."

"Easy?" Curry's face was blotchy and inflamed with rage.

"Now, son, you have to get quiet and listen," Dooley said, the voice of reason.

"Alice Ann has been killed in a terrible accident," Miss Edgar said, realizing it simply had to be said.

Ernestine shrieked, and Curry's face went scarlet. He put his arms around his wife and the two of them dissolved in sobs as the reality of the words gradually became real to them.

The next hour was almost unbearable. Dooley and Edgar took the couple inside their house, sat down with them on the makeshift chairs and threadbare sofa, and quietly gave them the details of the afternoon. Miss Edgar offered to make tea, a custom which she often found a comfort in such situations—although she knew she had never faced anything quite like this. It turned out that Ernestine did have some tea, and a saucepan handy for heating water. The water in the house was in a pitcher; it had been drawn by the pump outside.

The Cumbies had calmed down somewhat. Miss Edgar told them Alice Ann's body was at Mr. Saltz's and it would be up to them to make further arrangements. Ernestine was in a state of shock. Curry was nothing but mad. They were not church people, but Miss Edgar said she would tell the pastor about it and suggested he might visit them to talk. Curry was not the least bit interested in hearing what the pastor might say, but it was clear that Ernestine would need counsel and was willing to ask for it.

As the news spread the trauma extended to all of Fairhope, particularly the school. Mrs. Johnson was back in town in time for the funeral, and she made a trip to the shack where the Cumbies lived. She extended her condolences and tried to talk with them both, but they were stubborn in their insistence it was not an accident but the fault of the school and even of Marietta, subjecting their child to a situation in which her life was in danger. As Mrs. Johnson expected, Ernestine was more receptive to her than Curry, who was distant, almost in a trance state.

Marietta had several meetings with Mabel Edgar, who tendered her resignation and planned to return to Minnesota.

"I was responsible, Mettie," she said.

"Nonsense."

"The child wandered up to where she shouldn't have been, and I knew it."

Mrs. Johnson thought for a moment. The Cumbie child had problems—she had seen that at once—but it was her hope that constructive play with others would work its wonders on her as it did on almost all the children in her school. She could not lay the accident on Mabel, even though it was Mabel who had been in charge.

"She was a child with a lot of problems, Mabel. She had not yet learned to listen to adults—"

"Marietta, I want you to think about this."

"I am thinking about it. You know I am. I'm very distressed for the family, and I just know that with time we could have reached that child…"

"I mean, the trips to the gullies are far more dangerous than we knew."

"I have curtailed trips to the gullies," Marietta said. She still believed that trips to the gullies would be reinstated at a future date, but she knew that they would never be the same. She, the school, and even the town, had lost their innocence.

"You did all that was humanly possible," she assured Mabel, who had been so devastated by the experience that she confided she was considering giving up teaching. "There is no one among us who would have met the situation better."

"That's what you think," Mabel said, sadly. "I appreciate your support. You know I've loved working here—it was my dream to help you in our vision to create a perfect school environment. I so believed that this was the right way to teach." Mabel's voice trailed off as she thought of herself and Mettie in normal school those years ago, talking after reading Henderson's book, dreaming of having such a school to work it. Then she looked straight into her friend's bright and gleaming brown eyes. "I just don't think this is right for me. I have my doubts whether this is right at all."

"That's a strong reaction, but, Mabel, I do understand." Marietta was loath to lose one of her best stalwarts, one of the lieutenants in her battle to change the world by educating children in a different way. "You've had a challenge here. You were taking our theory to its highest level and you've been overwhelmed by events."

"How are we to continue with such projects, when things like this happen?"

"We must."

"I know you feel that way." Mabel shook her head and could not meet her friend's eyes. "I trust that you can make a go of it. I agree with you in principle. But I need to get away—I want to go back to Minnesota for a time and see if I can come to understand this."

There was nothing to discuss. Mabel was more traumatized by the event than anyone but the Cumbies. It had apparently shaken her to the core, even to the point of causing her to consider giving up her calling as a teacher. Marietta wished Mabel well, yet she could sense that her friend probably would not return to Fairhope. But it was her decision and she must be the one to make it and live by it. Mabel had used the word "want," but both the women understood this was not a matter of what either of them wanted. Mabel must leave and Marietta, on the other hand, must stay the course no matter what.

Trips to the gullies were ended altogether for several years. Marietta still favored teaching out of doors, keeping short walks and extensive exploration of the outdoors as part of organic education. In a few years gullies were added back to the curriculum, limited to groups of ten or fewer children and only when there were two teachers supervising. In anyone else, Marietta's consistency might be seen as stubbornness, but as far as she was concerned her adherence to her principles meant success. As long as she lived she must demonstrate what she believed through her school.

Over the years she had heard intermittently from Mabel. She wrote that it had taken a year before she was comfortable returning to teaching, but she did return to a traditional school, and reported that she found it possible to integrate much of what she had learned in Fairhope into the conventional classroom situation. Perhaps the good things she had learned in Fairhope would stay with her, Marietta thought, even though she had endured such a tragic accident. Her abilities as a teacher had not been compromised, but Marietta had to face that she would not likely try to be an "organic" teacher again.

Six

WHEN SHE LEARNED that Ernestine Cumbie was looking for work at the school home, Marietta Johnson couldn't help reflecting on the traumatic accident of five years before in which the Cumbie's daughter Alice Ann had lost her life.

It would not be easy to speak with Ernestine under the circumstances, but she regarded Ernestine's approaching the school as a positive move. When she had seen her last she had been so devastated that Mrs. Johnson feared she might not ever pull out of it. She braced herself for what meeting with Ernestine might bring.

Marietta had just had a pleasant interview with Amelia King, an enthusiastic young teacher she hoped would be a long term asset to the school and to Fairhope. Miss King seemed to be a sensitive young woman and likely had the makings of an excellent teacher in the organic style. If only all her tasks were as pleasant as talking to such bright young people and persuading them to join her in her mission! What was coming next was certain to be more difficult.

Marietta understood the Cumbies were a troubled family. Soon after the funeral they left the area, relocating to rural Louisiana, she was told. The tragedy had occurred four years before and now they were back in Fairhope. She didn't know whether to be happy or not, but Ernestine had let it be known that she would like a job in the school home if there was an opening. Curry had found something part time out at the lumber mill but they would need more of an income and it was possible she could do cleaning or help out in the kitchen.

That the Cumbies returned at all struck Marietta as somewhat strange. She had not heard anything about them for several years. They had been so devastated, it would appear, after the accident that Curry had become almost deranged with his grief. But the extended Cumbie family were longtime residents of Baldwin County, mostly living on farms and doing work as handymen and day laborers. Likely, Marietta thought, that being closer to their people would be the balm that Curry and Ernestine needed to begin to heal old wounds and get on with life.

She reflected on what to say to Ernestine on the subject of working at the School Home. If Ernestine were willing and able to work, and not embittered or damaged by her tragedy, she saw no reason not to take her into the fold, where she might begin to heal the wounds the trauma of losing her child had inflicted.

She heard a knock at the door, and shot a look to Esther, who sat dutifully at the typewriter, signalling her to answer it. Esther put a stack of letters on her desk for Mrs. Johnson to sign as she crossed to the door.

"Why, hello, Ernestine," Esther said, rather too sadly, Marietta felt. It was best to move on and not dwell in deep pain, as the sympathy of others, however sincere, could be as salt in the wound.

She need not have worried. Ernestine wore a smile. Not a big smile, not an inappropriate one, but a look of anticipation and something like a sense of joy to be home.

"Good afternoon, Ernestine," Mrs. Johnson said, extending a hand. "It is good seeing you looking well."

Actually Ernestine, prone to being overweight, looked even heavier than she had the last time Mrs. Johnson saw her, and a bit unkempt. Mrs. Johnson saw a purple bruise on her shoulder, which seemed to extend across her back but was covered by her flowered housedress. The look on her face was unmistakably gentle, even happy, and she spoke at once.

"I guess they told you I'm looking for a job—" she spoke directly to Mrs. Johnson. Esther was preparing to leave them alone when she was summoned to stay.

"There's no need for you to leave, Esther. I think Mrs. Myhers has said there is room for one more worker in the School Home. It's certainly a job you can do. Talk to her about wages, Ernestine. It will probably be just three mornings a week, with some time in the kitchen, I think."

"That's just what I was hoping for," Ernestine said. "I appreciate this."

"Not at all. I'm just hoping for good things for you and Curry at this time, and hope that Fairhope will offer you the peace you need. I like to think that Fairhope is a place where things are made right for people."

"Yes, ma'am," Ernestine said. "Thank you very much."

That was all. Marietta had an odd feeling about it, but she sloughed that off as the awkwardness of the moment. She would have to see a good deal more of the Cumbies in Fairhope to feel entirely comfortable around them under the circumstances. She still felt grief for their tragedy and knew that was not anywhere near equal to what they might be feeling.

Before she walked out, Mrs. Johnson said to Ernestine. "I know it took great courage for you and Curry to come back."

"Thank you, Ma'am," Ernestine said, looking awkward for the first time as she closed the door behind her. Mrs. Johnson could tell she was still in some conflict, but she had no way of knowing the deep, nagging fear Ernestine harbored that Curry had led her to ask for this job for some reason he would not admit.

Seven

AMELIA WOULD SPEND a week in Philadelphia telling her aunt and cousins about her experiences in the extraordinary little town in the middle of nowhere and gathering up her things to pack for the move. Then she would go to Hoboken to explain her new life's plan to her parents.

She would always regard her Aunt Althea as a hero who all but rescued her from the sterile life of privilege her parents lived. She had reason to feel this way, going back to her early days.

A child of wealth, Amelia was required to behave as if her life were a beautiful picture. She had few toys to play with—one porcelain-headed doll named Patricia, which she thought to be the most beautiful of names, and a stuffed bear she had named Nicodemus. These companions helped her create a separate world to inhabit, a world which transported her out of the ordinary. She did enjoy the bear more than the delicate Patricia. He withstood rougher treatment and inspired more challenging games. The doll was always herself, stolid and mature, and not receptive to bumptious play, if any real play at all. Patricia had to be handled carefully, and with that frozen face, made Amelia think of her mother, Gertrude.

Hoboken was a rugged town. Approximately one mile wide from the cliffs of the Palisades to the Hudson, it ran a mile in length north to south, bordered at the southern end by Jersey City and Weehawken hard by on the north. The poor were everywhere, from soot-stained children referred to in Hoboken as ragamuffins to the shabby shops along the side streets and the bars in the waterfront district nicknamed The Barbary Coast by locals. On the lower streets near the river there were vaudeville theaters, dingy cafés, saloons, and brothels—all kept quite busy by a lively, noisy contingent of stevedores and sailors. The section known as "downtown" was actually on the Western border at the cliffs upon which stood Jersey City. The Western area was mostly vacant lots, for sale cheap, encouraged by the city elders to be used as small farms. Many were as close to farms as they could be, worked by the Italians who had recently come to this country seeking to make a better life for themselves. There were old houses in Hoboken—built in the early 1800's—and there were some quite elegant ones in the Kings' neighborhood. The two elements of town were separated by the invisible wall of class, education, and money.

Her mother's sister Althea, now living with her husband and children in Philadelphia, on a visit took Amelia on her lap and gave her a hug. Aunt Althea smelled of cinnamon and peppermint, and being in the soft arms of a motherly woman was a surprising joy for Amelia. She adored her cousins, who laughed and broke rules and showed her a side of life that she had not known about. Althea and Ned Chapman ran a happy household and provided Amelia with the warmth that had been missing in her own.

She had been changed by this visit. Now she felt herself to be a part of something—and she would feel closer to this family than her own for the rest of her life. Yet there was always the awareness that she was somehow outside the circle.

Her nanny, Miss Pritchart, was consistent and unyielding, and to her mind and to Gertrude's this was good for children, who were, in the way of thinking of both women, always on the verge of breaking something, whether it be a material object like an piece of heirloom crystal or an esoteric academic principle like "i" before "e" except after "c."

Amelia learned to keep her fears hidden. The surface of serenity concealed that in her heart there was a fear of almost everything.

Miss Pritchart imposed her doctrine of original sin on the child. It was her contention, and that of many early childhood educators of her day, that children would do anything to outwit the adults in charge of them, and that the devil lurked near them at all times to lead them into sins of misbehavior and ultimately seduce them into lives of debauchery. Only by constant relating to a child what was wrong and impressing upon him how deficient he was could an adult gain the proper respect of the child and get him to focus on work, the most important facet of his young life.

Until Althea and her children Lettie, Carl, and Rose visited, Amelia had been in the almost exclusive care of Miss Pritchart. She saw her parents only at breakfast and after her bath in the evening, when she was asked to recite for them the activities and lessons of the day. Amelia was becoming more withdrawn and shy, and Althea thought she was destined for a loveless life motivated by fear and conformity.

When left alone in her room Amelia closed the door and talked with Nicodemus, creating extremely passionate scenarios for her little friend. In these dramas he was in grave danger of being tortured by giants who sought to do him tremendous harm. He fell off cliffs simulated by the old highboy in the corner of her room; he was trapped in dark caves occupied by bats and frightening flying things; he was tortured by a wicked witch who threatened him with the fires of hell. All the while the stoic soft toy stared with his shoe-button eyes at Amelia, the one kind heart in his stuffed-animal life. He could take anything, knowing that she would come to his rescue and hug him until he fell asleep every night. Amelia had no one to do the same for her.

It was all to be handled, quite by surprise, when Gertrude's sister Althea came from Philadelphia for a month-long visit with her three children, when Amelia was five years old.

The cousins, Lettie, age 11, Carl, 8, and Rose, who at almost 6, was Amelia's age, were well behaved around grownups but quite noisy and playful when alone. Lettie kept watch and treated her younger siblings as if she thought she was their mother. A very lenient and mischievous mother she was—to the grownups this was most amusing. In Lettie her siblings had the model of behavior—a capacity for fun tempered by a certain innate propriety. For her part as a mother, Althea was as warm and sunny and Gertrude was dignified and unapproachable. Althea enjoyed playing with her children, and reading to them, holding them on her lap and hugging them.

One afternoon on this visit Amelia had been put down for her nap, and the room to her door was closed. She promptly climbed out of her bed and went to the shelf where Nicodemus sat, awaiting his daily game with her.

Althea happened to be in the upstairs hall on this particular afternoon and heard talk in Amelia's room, behind the closed door. She heard the child's voice, and the word, "Wicked! Wicked!" repeatedly. She walked closer to see if she could discover what Amelia might be talking about in such harsh tones.

"You will suffer for your sins!" Amelia, in the voice of the wicked witch, said to her teddy bear, who was appropriately very much afraid. "You have bad thoughts! I know it!" the witch shrieked. "Hellfire will be your eternal punishment!"

Althea could make out the words "hellfire," and "punishment," but she couldn't imagine them coming out of the mouth of the gentle, shy child. She stood at the door for several minutes, trying to make sense of what she was hearing, as the voice softened and the little girl at last became quiet. Amelia had finished her daily quota of torture for her long-suffering bear and taken him to bed with her to sleep. After the quiet had lasted for about five minutes, her aunt opened the door a crack to see Amelia angelically sleeping with her teddy bear beside her.

The incident caused Althea some concern, but she didn't think it right to mention it unless she could discover that it occurred with some frequency. So the next afternoon she waited until the children were all tucked in for their naps and she stood sentinel in the upstairs hall. Again she heard the violent shrieking of "Punish you! God will punish you!" and she knew Amelia was going through a daily ritual.

On the third day, she waited until it started, and she went to Amelia's door and rapped gently.

"Amelia, dear, it's Aunt Althea."

The talking behind the door stopped immediately.

"May I come in?"

"No! No!"

"Amelia, I just want to visit a minute," she said, and then opened the door a crack. She did not want to give the child time to cover what she had been doing.

"No! Go away now—Aunt Althea!" Amelia said, starting off firmly but ending in a whimper. Althea opened the door and came in on the child with her teddy bear.

"I think your bear is being very naughty," Althea said.

"No, no he wasn't. He's very good, really, but the witch always tries to punish him." Amelia told her, sharing a dark secret.

"And she sends him to hell?"

"No—I always save him," Amelia said.

"I see. That's really nice of you."

"Well, I'm his mother, and I protect him. Or else the bad witch will get him."

Althea took the child in her arms and assured her that Nicodemus couldn't have a better mother in the whole wide world. She sat on the bed and rocked the child in her lap and tried to think of a plan to rescue her, so smothered and yet so lost in this house of coldness and unrecognized rage. It was as if Amelia was one of her own, she so deeply felt the need to take her in.

A few months after observing Amelia in Hoboken, she and her husband hatched a plan.

Althea arranged a shopping trip to New York, staying overnight in Hoboken with Gertrude and Frederick. She had a motive that had to do with Amelia. Indeed, shopping had been nothing but an excuse to visit her sister and persuade her.

"Amelia would do well to get her education in Philadelphia rather than Hoboken," Althea said to her older sister. "The children go to an extraordinary school, a private school with extremely high academic standards. If Amelia came to live with us during the school year she could take advantage of this." She allowed Gertrude a few moments to think on this. Then she added, "I also think she enjoys having her cousins for company."

Gertrude's inability to form the kind of bond her sister and so many other mothers seemed to have with their offspring was a source for some self-reproach, but she did not dwell on thoughts that made her uncomfortable. It did not require a great deal of reflection to realize that the most loving thing she could do for Amelia would be to accept her sister's offer. The child would be with them in summers and on vacations; it might turn out to be the tonic the three of them needed, and it could well benefit Amelia most of all.

❦

On the train back to Philadelphia, Amelia looked forward to the visit with joy and anticipation of the Chapmans' delight in all she had seen. She would tell them about the chickens in the street, the new barnlike community building and Marietta Johnson, the famous lady who already felt to her like someone she had known all her life. There was no doubt in her mind that every one of the Chapman family would support her choice, and that her cousin Rose, closest to her age, would even be a bit envious, even though she was now married and expecting a child. Lettie and Aunt Althea and even Carl and Uncle Ned would have a great deal to say, and she could not wait to talk with them of Fairhope.

In Hoboken it would be a different story, more serious, as once again she would have to explain to Frederick and Gertrude that she truly wanted a career as a teacher, and an unconventional one at that. To convince her parents she was doing the right thing she would need to make Fairhope sound less extraordinary, and emphasize Mrs. Johnson's worldwide reputation as a leader in the field of education. They must not be allowed to join those, who, as Mrs. Cross told her, believed the theory of the school that children were simply allowed to do as they pleased, certain to lead the world into chaos.

She wanted them all to love Fairhope and the school at least as much as she already did. In the case of the Chapmans, this would not be difficult. In the King household, however, there was a question whether they could accept either.

She took the familiar route from Pennsylvania station in Philadelphia to the house on 14th Street. It was late afternoon when she arrived, but enough sunlight remained that the gaslights and electric bulbs inside the homes were not yet turned on. She twisted the old familiar doorbell, and sure enough, as always, the door was flung open in a cascade of laughter and squeals. Lettie was home, and Rose had come over for her arrival.

Rose hugged her warmly and took her hands.

"Amelia! You must tell us everything!"

"Wait for me—I want to hear this too!" called Aunt Althea from another part of the house. Amelia adored the informality of this home, where voices were raised when necessary, and the group expressed its will freely, often all at once. It was an atmosphere one never took notice of because it was natural to all.

Soon Aunt Althea was standing in the arch of the door that led to the hall. Her arms were open, and Amelia all but ran to her to be embraced.

"Now, tell us what you found in your peaceable kingdom," Althea said.

"Oh, Aunt Althea, how sweet of you to call it that," Amelia was overwhelmed by her memory of that childhood attachment to the old Quaker and his Peaceable Kingdom paintings, and by her aunt's ability to identify just the right image for her. She had first seen the paintings on an outing to the Philadelphia Museum of Art when they were all children.

"Well—utopia, then," Aunt Althea said.

"I did find it quite companionable," Amelia said. "And I have a position for the fall!"

"Do you like Alabama?" asked Lettie.

"I don't know yet, of course," Amelia answered. "But Fairhope is a very special place, no matter what state it's in. And Marietta Johnson! She's just what I hoped she would be."

She told them of the Crosses, the new community hall being built by students, the lady veterinarian who swooped about town on a horse, the old man with the long white beard walking through the streets barefooted, the dirt roads and satsuma orchards, the songfest around the piano.

"There were chickens in the streets!" Amelia said.

"Chickens! Did they have any automobiles?"

"Well, there were a few—there's a railway car that carries people up the hill to town, running on a track right up the main street. Oh, and that hill! Such beautiful views— the sun sets into Mobile Bay every evening!"

"Except when it's raining…" Aunt Althea said.

"I'm sure it never rains," added Lettie.

"Well, I'm told it does," Amelia said. "And anyway, the humidity is so heavy it feels like it's raining even when it isn't."

The women were laughing together, sharing Amelia's joy, but with their own reservations, knowing that relocating to the utopian community might be taking her a long way from them for an undetermined length of time. Her move was too remote for them to fathom—so different from both Philadelphia and Hoboken—that they had been wondering amongst themselves if moving there might prove too difficult an adjustment for their little Amelia.

Amelia was still based at home in Hoboken although she had been teaching for two years at Ferncliff, a private elementary school for wealthy students in northern Pennsylvania. She would go to Hoboken for a week to see her parents again before making the trip to Alabama. She assumed that her parents were going to put obstacles in her path if they could. What she was choosing for herself was not what they would want for her. She would have access to the trust fund left by her grandfather as needed, but she determined to live frugally and save the money until she might need it in the future when she used what she might learn in Fairhope.

Her way of dealing with her parents had always been to withhold as much of the information about her plans as she felt necessary. She knew what would disturb them, what they would resist, and even with the prickly relationship that had developed between them over the years, she still wanted approval from them for her life choices. They were the Kings, after all, and her own parents. There was some of both Gertrude and Frederick in her, and in her way, she loved them. She would always feel the Chapmans were truly family to her, providing her with siblings and the chaos of a loving family; however, it had been the decision of her own parents to part with her in order to provide that. She would never know how aware they might or might not be of what they had done for her, but she did not question the wisdom of their choice. Just to remember the hardness of her nanny Miss Pritchard, the limitations of Hoboken itself, and the queerness of the King home she was born into, made her appreciate her youthful escape from it.

She wrote her parents from the house on 14th Street.

> *Dear Mother and Father,*
>
> *I have just returned from a most exciting journey, to a town in Southern Alabama where an experiment in education is well under way, and promises to change the educational systems of the world for the better. I will be here in Philadelphia with Aunt Althea and the Chapman family until the end of the week, but on Saturday next, I shall take a train to Hoboken to tell you all about it, and about my place in it.*
>
> *I hope you understand my choice, and if you don't now, I hope that a few conversations and my availability to answer questions you may have will put to rest any uneasiness you might have about my decision. I so look forward to seeing you again in the Hudson Street house and seeing the inevitable changes in Hoboken as it is developing into a city and not just the vacation spot for New York that Grandpa King knew.*
>
> *I shall arrive on the 4:20 train from Philadelphia on Saturday. If you cannot meet the train I will be happy to walk home by myself and see you at about five, in time for tea.*
>
> *Your loving daughter,*
> *Amelia*

Amelia never had a normal relationship with either parent. Her grandfather, Frederick's father, had sought to correct this himself by overindulging her, showering her with all the affection he genuinely felt for her. But her father and mother, for their own separate reasons, had been distant in all their dealings. There was only one incident in which Amelia could recall a lapse in either of them.

Miss Pritchart had her rules, and all Amelia had to do was conform to them to avoid the harsh stings of her criticism and constant reference to the Bible and its assurance of eternal damnation for the wicked. Adults were so judgmental. Gertrude was much the same as Miss Pritchart, but without the frequent invocation of God. Satan, and wickedness.

Frederick, however, appeared to be removed from that high post on which the women placed themselves. He was a different breed, like Grandpa Conrad. He was a man. She loved the sound of his deep voice, the smell of shaving cream and hair tonic that surrounded him.

One afternoon Amelia, almost five, awaited him in the hall as he arrived home from the hospital in the city, where he worked.

"Good evening, Little One," he said to her uneasily, off his guard.

"Good evening, Father," she said. She regarded him silently, yearning for him to bundle her up in his arms the way Grandpa sometimes did. She thought Frederick the handsomest man in the world, with his sleek black hair and his always crisply elegant clothes. Why did he spend so much time in his study, with the door locked? Why did he not take her for walks or talk with her about the things around them, as Grandpa did?

"Would you pick me up, like Grandpa Conrad does?" It was an extremely difficult question to get out.

Frederick froze. This was not much to ask, this beautiful child wanting to be held in a parental hug. He was embarrassed nonetheless. He did not know what to say or if there was anything he could.

But for one uncharacteristically spontaneous moment his heart was with his child. He gathered her up, kissed both her cheeks, and swung her high in the air and brought her down for a full hug. It was such a pleasure to him that he felt himself blushing, and soon went into his study for a drink.

Amelia stood tranfixed as he closed the door behind him. This was her father, then, mysterious and desirable, now leaving the room, closing the door between them. She never forgot the incident.

After this there were occasions when Amelia would stand next to him, close enough to feel the warmth of him, just content to feel the masculine aura of him. If she stood this close, would it not be clear to everyone that she was his little girl?

Over the years Gertrude had continued to compensate for her insecurity by keeping her distance from people, but now she had the assurance that she was once and for all a doctor's wife. She had begun to find activities that interested her. Unlike her daughter, she was not inclined to go out into the field and do settlement work or teach reading to immigrant children, but she did join the Tuesday Study Club and the women's auxiliary at her church, and she had a few lifelong friends in Hoboken who kept her company.

It was into this atmosphere that Amelia bravely made her way that August morning in 1921. She had left her belongings, most of them, in the 14th Street house, but carried a small carpetbag to the home of her parents. Her mother met her train at the Hoboken Terminal and they walked together up Hudson Street all the way to 7th Street and up the steps of the brownstone.

"It's awfully warm to take such a walk today," Gertrude said as they came out of the terminal. "We can take a cab. You know you can get a motor-cab these days."

"Nonsense, Mother," Amelia said. "I enjoy the fresh air."

"Not all that fresh around here, I'm afraid," Gertrude responded as they passed the grimy, lower-class business establishments that lined the area around the train station. Prohibition had not had all that much effect on Hoboken, a waterfront town that provided bootleg whisky and illegal activities for a bustling crowd of longshoremen. Gertrude and Amelia both knew that it was easy to avoid River Street and its dingy speakeasies and go the next block over, past the raffish men's bar known as The Clam Broth House and walk north on Hudson Street, where they would see a few butcher shops and bakeries, and the Empire Theater. By the time one reached Third Street one was safe in the comfortable homes and hotels on the fringe of the one of the nicest neighborhoods in Hoboken.

They passed Naegli's and Meyer's Hotel, both respectable hostelries that gave Gertrude a sense of security and even grandeur. Meyer's was more architecturally interesting, with its bay windows and gingerbread trim, and it was quite a fine hotel where weddings and other significant celebrations were held. Never did Gertrude feel more estranged from Amelia than when any discussion of marriage or traditional plans came up. She did not deign to bring up the topic as the pair approached Meyer's.

"Any nice weddings at Meyers recently, Mother?" Amelia mischievously opened the topic.

"Annabelle Schlish married Thomas O'Reilly," her mother said.

"I don't remember Thomas," Amelia said.

"You wouldn't have known him," Gertrude said. "The family moved here a few years ago. I believe the couple met at church."

Met at church. Amelia did know Annabelle, and knew her not to be Catholic, but with that name the O'Reillys would be.

"Is Annabelle a Catholic now, or is this O'Reilly some kind of Irish Lutheran?"

"Certainly Annabelle is not a Catholic," Gertrude said. "But the boy is not either. He would have been at the Presbyterian church, but there isn't one in town."

"That explains the wedding at Meyers," Amelia said, and that was an end to the conversation. Her friends getting married did give her pause from time to time, but she had other things in mind, and if marriage were to come it would come in due time, not before she had completed her studies and was well on her way in her career of schoolmistress and changing the world.

"Do you not mind this warm weather?" Gertrude saw an opportunity to change the subject.

"It is summer, Mother, and I rather enjoy the relaxing feel of a warm breeze." Amelia marveled at how some words were not used by Gertrude's generation—the word, "hot," for example. It was all the rage for young people to use strong words and to be proud of knowing the latest slang.

Gertrude was lightly fanning her face with a lace handkerchief. They sat in the shade for several minutes without talking, but Amelia could not help observing how her mother had aged since she saw her last. She could not have been the age of Marietta Johnson, yet she looked settled, as if she were ready to grow old, whereas Mrs. Johnson, probably ten years older, still radiated vigor and energy.

Women her mother's age thought wearing makeup gave them a youthful appearance, but in reality, it did the opposite—too much powder, too white, rouge on the cheeks, and red lip color brought to mind the look of the embalmer's waxy brush. Amelia was certain her mother was sweltering in the old-fashioned corsets propriety dictated, while at least the advent of the new women's undergarment, the brassiere, had freed her own body.

"Are you hot, Mother?" Amelia used the forbidden word. "Let's sit on this bench in the shade for a moment."

Gertrude started a bit at Amelia's saying the word *hot*, which she had been automatically avoiding, but she did allow as how a moment's rest would feel good as they strolled home. Wrought iron benches offered rest stops on every other block on Hudson Street. At some of them, nannies parked with perambulators to chat briefly with one another while the infants slept. At the corner of 7th Street, at Hudson Square Park, they sat, and Amelia recalled the Sunday afternoons she had spent there with her grandfather so many years ago.

"My, this town is getting fuller and fuller," her mother said. "So many Italians and Irish now!"

Amelia wasn't about to get into a discussion of immigrants and social conditions with her mother, but she did say she too had noted a change in Hoboken. She had never really felt at home here, except when she was teaching and trying new things at the settlement house, helping Italian children with their English and observing their mothers and grandmothers doing needlework and other hand crafts they had brought from the Old Country. They had an artistic and artisanal heritage of an untold number of years. People like her mother would never see that these new people, learning to be citizens, were bringing with them a rich heritage of talents that might well add to American life.

They sat silently for a moment, Amelia allowing her mother a moment to collect herself and rest before they walked the few blocks left to the family home. When she felt refreshed, Gertrude suggested they walk on.

"I know you have a lot to tell your father and me," she said. "I'm interested in learning about these plans you have for a career as a schoolteacher."

Obviously her letter had had some impact, but she could not quite discern Gertrude's feelings about the situation. The choice of the words "a career" might be promising, yet in Gertrude's mouth they had great ambivalence. Amelia knew that her mother's plans for her to be a traditional wife, mother, and pillar of the community had never included any particular career outside the home, and that the word *schoolteacher* had the ring of poverty-stricken spinster to her. Even if she squandered the trust fund her grandfather King had left her Amelia never would be poverty-stricken, and even if she never did marry, the word spinster did not fit her. She had every intention of using the yearly stipend from her trust for basic living expenses and was well aware how useful it would be in her time in Fairhope.

They climbed the steep stone stoop that led to the entrance hall of the house Amelia had spent such anxious days in, another life ago. The mahogany-paneled walls spoke of wealth and position, and there was a vase of large white roses on a table.

"Your father will join us for tea," Gertrude said. "He is most eager to hear of your recent adventure in—Alabama. And to discuss your plans."

"I'll wash up and be with you in the study right away," Amelia said, knowing the parlor was too formal for such a family meeting.

❧

It didn't take long to ready herself. She went upstairs to her old room, brushed her hair and washed her hands. In the mirror she looked flushed—maybe she was more anxious about this meeting than she realized. She gave herself a few moments to lie on her bed and take deep breaths. This was an important meeting and she must acquit herself well or things might go badly after all. She knew both her parents wanted the best for her, yet it was not likely they would think she was making a good choice. She armed herself for the discussion with the knowledge that a few years' education in Fairhope was just that, whether they chose to understand or not. She was of age, and—with the legacy of Conrad King—of independent means, which they could not argue with. The plan was not to argue at all, but simply to present her case for herself and allow them the opportunity to accept it. But this would be the first time in her life Amelia would do this, and she felt the impact of her new position.

There was a surprise for Amelia when she sat in one of the leather chairs by the tea table. She recognized the young woman who brought the tray of tea—it was was Constanza Garbarini, the child whom Amelia had coached in English at the settlement house, just a few years before.

"Miss Amelia?"

"Connie! What a young lady you are!" Amelia wanted to put her arms around the girl, but knowing the position that would put her in, restrained herself.

"Thank you, Ma'am," Constanza said, promptly dropping the big smile from her mouth, yet keeping a happy look in her eyes.

"Mother, I once taught Connie English—"

Gertrude understood at once. "How nice, dear," she said simply.

"Connie, how is your mother? And Carlo?"

Constanza was reluctant to go too far. "My mother and father are doing well," she said. "My brother Carlo went into the Army—"

Awareness of the Great War suddenly filled the room.

"He came home, Ma'am. But he is still in the military."

"Well, I'm so glad he came home," Amelia said. "Please tell him and your mother I asked about them."

"They will be happy," Constanza said, and put the tea tray down. She left the room quietly, leaving much unsaid between mother and daughter.

"Your father should be right in," Gertrude said.

"Connie was always such a merry little thing," Amelia shook her head at the change. This serious, brave young woman, in service in one of the big houses of Hudson Street...she should not have been so surprised, but she had to adjust her mental picture to a new reality. Time was passing; children grow up.

It was into this familiar room, with his wife and daughter obviously engaged in some awkwardness, that Frederick King walked that afternoon, anticipating a confrontation he would have preferred never to face. He recalled many such conversations with his own father, who always found him deficient, and he recalled young Amelia going off to life with Gertrude's sister's family as a frail and unhappy child, while he suffered in a silent fog induced by combinations of drugs and alcohol. He always felt inadequate as a father, and usually so as a man, except when practicing his chosen profession. His work gave him constant reinforcement as a brilliant and sympathetic human being. But facing the two dragons, his wife and daughter, was daunting.

"Good afternoon, my dears," he said, crossing to his wife and putting an arm about her waist. She extended a cold cheek which he dutifully kissed.

Amelia smiled, relaxed at last to see this renewed father, no longer the distant, somewhat depressed man of her young childhood. She went to him and planted a kiss on his other cheek. He still inspired a thrill in her, as he had when she was a child. Today he looked much more solid than he had in years. The three of them seemed almost like another family altogether.

"I see we have tea," Dr. King said.

Gertrude poured three cups and added cream and sugar to them all, in the traditional way, smiling elegantly as she handed the cup and saucer to her daughter and husband. Everybody took a sip. Amelia was warmed by the ritual as well as by the taste of tea. She thought what a civilized custom the taking of tea was, how important to have such distractions to smooth the impending rough waters.

"Very nice," said Dr. King. After a moment he went on, "Your mother and I gathered from your letter that you had news for us. We take it that you have made a decision for your life."

"Yes," Amelia answered. Where to begin? "You both know I have always wanted to teach school—"

"And so you are, teaching school," Dr. King said.

"I have become aware of new methods," Amelia said. "I heard Marietta Johnson, an extraordinary lady, give a talk in Philadelphia about a different way of teaching—a school for tomorrow."

Both her parents moved forward in their seats on the settee as they heard what she was saying. Amelia went on to describe the theory behind organic education, how children respond when they are allowed to follow their natural curiosity under the supervision of qualified adults, rather than forced to follow a rigid schedule designed and monitored by adults to meet an arbitrary standard.

"What has this to do with you?" her father asked.

"It is what I want to do. It is the way I must teach!" Amelia said. "I have been to this woman's school and she has offered me a position teaching for the next term."

"This school—it is in Alabama, we understand," Gertrude said.

"It's in a remote location, only reachable by boat. But it is a charming town, populated by"—she had to choose her words carefully here—"by intelligent, wise people who want to live their best lives, and those who want their children to have the advantage of this kind of education."

"It has a small population." Dr. King asserted. "Under fifteen hundred. in fact."

Amelia smiled. Her father had done his research.

"Yes, but they—" She started to search for words.

"They are all wise and intelligent?"

"Truly, they are. All the people I met there share a vision for a better life."

"A utopian community," Dr. King said. He had seen such colonies in his life, particularly in connection with medical clinics and health.

"It is a single tax colony," Amelia went on. "Established to promote Henry George's economic theory. But the school is becoming the engine of the community."

"Very interesting, Amelia," Dr. King said.

She had broken the ice. They understood her plan. It wasn't clear whether they would support her, but they were not going to oppose her either.

"I remember Henry George," her father said. "I once heard him speak when he was running for governor of New York. You realize that the wise and intelligent people you speak of are politically radical and could be plotting the overthrow of the government?"

"They are Progressives, Father," Amelia responded. "You may not agree with their politics, but I assure you they plan no anarchist revolution. The community was founded by a very sweet-tempered gentleman from Des Moines. I've met him. He publishes Fairhope's weekly newspaper today. I have a few copies if you would like to read them."

"I would appreciate that. You know your Uncle Ned and I have been at odds over politics ever since we first met. I should have anticipated his influence over you."

"Father, this has nothing to do with Uncle Ned, or radical politics. I have no inclinations about politics—that is something I can decide in my own good time. I am simply explaining that for my own reasons I must move to Fairhope, the town hosting the most exciting development in education in the world. I have not met anyone there who could remotely be considered a threat to our government." Her exasperation was beginning to show; she sought to relax it.

Gertrude was quite at a loss to understand this suggestion of politics, a topic which confounded and annoyed her.

"What is it you like so much about this Miss Johnson?"

"It's *Mrs.*, Mother. She was widowed several years ago and has a son who is in college. She is inspirational—that's the only way I can describe it. She is a lecturer, a visionary, and a charming and down-to-earth person. She put me at ease at once, and agreed with me that I could do good work in her school. But the main reason I must go there is that I can learn from her!"

Her eyes were shining as she thought of the doughty little lady who had won her over personally and professionally.

"The town is rustic, the school appears to be quite primitive—but that is to the advantage of both, as far as I can see. In another location the school might not thrive so much, and without the school—even with Mr. Gaston's high ideals and proselytizing newspaper—the town would have probably languished years ago.

"Education is the hope of the world." Amelia was warming to her real subject now. She found herself unable to stop talking, hoping she did not seem compulsive.

"We all need productive work in the 20th century, Father, just as you need medicine to define and inspire you. As a physician, you contribute to the betterment of man, in small, personal ways as well as the big picture. I intend to do the same. Civilization is changing; all people are called to do what they can. And I shall do this, and proudly. It is a young century; I want to be part of the new thinking."

Frederick and Gertrude watched their daughter in rapt silence.

Gertrude could not help but think of that insecure child of her memory, how she suddenly blossomed in the company of her sister's boisterous children—now a grown woman in her own home, talking of plans and promise and even a mission for her life. Her eyes glistened as she felt emotion generated by the passion this young stranger was presenting to her. Amelia Katherine King reflected something of herself and of Frederick, to be sure, but tempered so beautifully for the future by her sister and her family—given a place in the larger world that Gertrude would never have been able to dream for her.

Frederick bristled internally at his daughter's emergence as a spokeswoman for causes she deemed "progressive," yet at the same time he could respect her commitment and the practicality of her mind. As she said, it was not coming from her Uncle Ned or from this Mrs. Johnson, or anyone else but the impressive young woman who sat with them, having afternoon tea and talking of a life of her own.

"I've never seen you like this, Amelia," said Frederick.

"Am I getting carried away?"

"Perhaps, my dear. But at times it is good to be so." He thought of his discussions with his own father, himself belligerently resisting being pressured to work into the family business, King's retail establishment in Hoboken, instead pressing his own commitment to going to college and then to medical school. Had he the same kind of determination his daughter was now exhibiting? Probably, quite so. The tea conversation had a familiar ring to it, and he knew he was witnessing a rite of passage unique to the 20th century. In this case it was a girl-child moving forth, standing on her own feet, becoming an adult, with or without the permission of her forebears.

Unlike his own father, he would bid his child godspeed.

Eight

THIS WAS IT, for now: all her things packed in a nice sized trunk and two suitcases full of clothes and a couple of items for living: A copy of John Dewey's *Schools of Tomorrow*, the two books Mrs. Johnson had given her, plus the Froebel and Rousseau. A small bag carried her hairbrush, a hand mirror and the personal grooming items she needed, plus a lightweight waist and skirt, and a change of underwear. She knew enough to expect unbearable heat in Fairhope now that it was August. She would not need the heavy woolens and long underwear to which she was so accustomed in the winter.

It was even hotter when she arrived in Mobile than it had been on her first trip, and, if possible, more humid. Her natural excitement at taking this step to a new life was tempered by the sheer discomfort of feeling she was sweating through her clothes as soon as she stepped off the train.

A cheerful young black with a red cap and a luggage cart wheeled up to the arriving train and shot a bright smile at the passengers getting off.

"I'm going to the docks," she told him, handing him a crisp dollar bill. "Going over the bay to Fairhope."

"Ovah da bay," he said, almost to himself, his smile never wavering. "Nice place to be dis tahme a year." He wheeled her luggage to a loading area where she was to wait for enough people to fill a carriage going to the boat. It was there she saw another young woman with a cart full of luggage. They smiled at each other immediately, as if they both hoped and expected to be going to the same place for the same reason.

"Are you going to Fairhope?" the young woman asked. She wore her hair bobbed, falling in brown curls over a simple headband. She was dressed more suitably for the climate than Amelia, and had large brown eyes and full lips, with, Amelia noted, no lip rouge. Her look was informal, almost masculine, and she had a way of facing strangers head-on, making friends of them without effort.

"Yes!" Amelia said, so delighted that this person would be joining her in her journey. Maybe she was one of "pretty girls" that E.B. Gaston had referred to, who came to Fairhope to be schoolteachers. "My name is Amelia King—from Philadelphia and New Jersey. I'm going to teach at Organic Education."

"Well, how do you do, Philadelphia and New Jersey! I'm Avery Buchanan, from Boston and Rhode Island. I'm going to the same place you are for the same reason. It's my second year there, and your first. Welcome!"

"Everybody says 'Welcome to Fairhope,'" Amelia said. "That's so nice."

"Fairhope is a welcoming place," Avery said. "It's a place where conflict is rife but resolution inevitable—and everybody is welcome."

"Well put!" Amelia marveled at her new acquaintance's way with words. She would find that everybody had a different definition of Fairhope, but she would never hear a better one than Avery had come up with on the spot.

Soon the platform filled with passengers, who filed into the carriage with all their luggage, being helped by a cadre of porters, all ready to take the brief ride to board the Apollo, the two-wheeled steamer that had brought her to Fairhope for the first time. This time she looked forward to seeing Mr. Pilcher, who had serenaded her so enthusiastically in the living room of The Gables that afternoon on her previous trip. And he was there, greeting her with recognition, as he did the other passengers on the spacious Apollo, a steam powered sidewheeler with the capacity to hold 500 passengers. She had taken this ride once before and felt a certain familiarity with it now.

On this trip she had to see to a great deal of luggage, but she kept the small bag with one change of clothing and her female necessities with her, along with her handbag for money and handkerchiefs. The smell of the bay brought to mind marshes, sea life (both floral and piscine), and there was a light breeze which provided some relief from the oppressive heat. She found a seat on the bench on the south side of the boat, so as to feel the breeze and see Fairhope as soon as she could.

Avery plopped beside her.

"What will you be teaching?" she asked Amelia.

"First Life," Amelia took a moment to be certain she was using the proper term. Not "first grade," which came so automatically to her to say.

"I teach Junior High," Avery said. "It's the age for me. I'm not so good with little tykes."

"And I'm not so good with those entering their teens," Amelia said. "I like to see the little ones when an idea first comes to them."

"I know what you mean," Avery said. "But you know, all teaching is about the look on their faces when an idea comes to them—and it's the same whether they're two, six, 13—or 18!"

"I guess so," Amelia was willing to concede the possibility. "But I never thought of it that way."

An older lady, quite richly dressed and well covered in make-up, came to where Amelia and Avery were sitting. She had a very heavy southern accent, and actively wanted to engage in conversation.

"Mah, isn't it wawum today," she remarked, carefully dabbing her upper lip with a lace handkerchief, so as not to smear lip paint and powder on it. "Are y'all goin' to Pawint Cle-ah?

"Fairhope," Avery answered.

"Oh I luv Fy-uh-hope!" she said. "I bet you gayulls are going to be woikin' at Thawganic School!"

"You guessed it!" Avery said.

"Oh, I just *luv* Thawganic School," the lady said. "Miz Johnson is just *wun*-da-full!"

Amelia was perplexed at this creature, but the lady did want to talk and so they kept up the conversation with her, with Avery at times playing the role of a translator, until the lady abruptly rose.

"Well, Ah'm goin' over to this sahde to have a look at the uh-thuh vyew," she said. "It was so nahce tawkin' with you gayulls. Good luck to you next ye-ah." She walked to the other side of the boat and took up with a group of people talking animatedly.

"Mind telling me what that was?" Amelia said when the lady was out of earshot.

"That was an example of the distaff side of *Homus Mobilus*," Avery said, pronouncing *mobilus* as "Mobile-us," making clear the specimen was typical of the denizens of Mobile. "Speaks a different language, but essentially harmless. At least to us non-members of the tribe."

Amelia hoped the accents of Fairhope would be more decipherable. Clearly, she had come a long way from Hoboken.

"Please tell me what to expect at the school," she said, still somewhat in shock from the encounter with the Mobile lady.

"Lots of nature study, for one thing," Avery said. "Classes outdoors, hands-on, hand crafts—things they don't teach you at normal school."

"I have a degree from Mount Holyoke," Amelia said, trying not to make it sound like bragging.

"Even worse!" Avery said, and they both laughed.

Avery told her a about what to expect for the first few days in Fairhope. One thing for certain--Mrs. Johnson would hold a welcome assembly for the new teachers and the returning teachers would conduct tours of Fairhope.

"Tours?"

"Well, let's just say those of us who know are to show those of you who-don't-know around," Avery said. "Once you get to the pier, find the school and Crawford's general store, you pretty much have had the tour."

"I know the way to the school from The Gables, where I'll be staying until I find a place," Amelia told her new friend.

"I'm looking for a house to rent myself," Avery said. "We might find a place big enough to share."

This sounded like a good idea to Amelia, who, in the short time since she'd first set eyes on Avery, had come to like the young woman very well. They could become good friends.

"I notice you already know Mr. Pilcher," Avery said.

"Yes—he came by The Gables when I was here for my job interview in June. He played the piano and we all sang. Even Mr. Gaston stopped in!"

"He manages to be in the center of everything," Avery said.

"Who—Mr. Gaston or Mr. Pilcher?"

"Both of them!" Avery said, and they laughed again.

The ride was exhilarating, but with all the excitement Amelia was feeling, it was hard to separate in her mind what caused the greatest reaction. Was it the beautiful view of both shores of the bay, observing the city of Mobile recede as the two-hour ride brought her and her new friend closer to the eastern bank, with its narrow stretch of white beach and the cliffs behind it? Or was it the solid feeling that she had made a friend with whom to share her experiences? Or, underlying it all, was she most buoyed by the uplifting feeling that she was now a part of a revolution in education? The Apollo docked first at Daphne, disgorging some ten passengers, and then at the pier in Montrose, where one family got off. From there, Fairhope's wide pier was visible as the boat drew closer.

Amelia wondered if her elation might simply be the thrill of knowing she would soon be working with and for the great Marietta Johnson, in a school "of tomorrow" and living among the nonconformists and iconoclasts in this remote town at the southern tip of Alabama, a state about which she knew almost nothing. Her mind raced with questions, but all she could think of was the warm reception she had gotten from all she had met involved in the Fairhope experiment, from E.B. Gaston, founder of the single tax colony, and Marietta Johnson, proponent of the new education, to the young woman beside her looking at the crowd gathering on the pier to greet the boat.

"It's like this every time the boat docks," Avery told her. "Fairhope looks at the arrival of the Apollo twice a day as an affirmation of its existence."

"Twice a day, every day, an affirmation of its existence?"

"Well, yes. They absorb a lot of affirmation here," Avery said.

There were at least 30 people on the pier, including some tow-headed, barefooted children. A sigh of joy went out from the crowd as the first of the passengers disembarked, rather like the sound a crowd makes when a skyrocket is launched on the Fourth of July. It made Amelia smile and glance back at Avery.

"Affirmation," they said in unison.

It was not easy, unloading the luggage both the young women had brought for the school year in Fairhope. Avery had brought less, since she had left some of her wardrobe from the year before—and had a clearer idea what clothes would be needed in the southern climate.

She nodded toward Amelia's trunk.

"I hope that's not heavy with woolens and furs," she said.

"I didn't know what to expect," Amelia said.

"Oh, don't I know it. Nobody does. It can get cold here, but nothing like Philadelphia. And it's not an area that thinks much about fashion."

"I'll manage, I'm sure," Amelia said. "I like the idea that clothes aren't everything."

"It's different," Avery said. "I'm glad you like it—but it does take some getting used to."

They were helping load their baggage into the People's Railway, a one-car motorized railway that carried heavy items and passengers up the steep hill to the heart of town. The men on the pier were cooperating, and extremely friendly, in helping load the cart.

"Southern hospitality, or eyeing the new girls?" Amelia said to Avery, under her breath.

"Hah! A little of both, I'm sure. But most of these men aren't really Southerners, as you'll see. They're expatriates from everywhere, trying to find heaven on earth."

A curious comment, Amelia noted, but she didn't hear a trace of the accent that the one the lady from Mobile exhibited so aggressively. It took her back for a moment to the red-haired fellow on her first train trip South, the young man who had told her about Sherman's Sentinels and seemed to be reliving the Civil War. Fairhope seemed a world away from that—except maybe for those like the lady from Mobile, people who regarded the eastern shore of the bay as a place to vacation.

There was a lot of chatter in the crowd, and one teen-aged youth recognized Avery.

"Miss Buchanan! Hi! May I help you with something?"

"I could use it, Joe," she answered. "I'm going to be staying at the School Home until I find a place of my own."

Joe helped both Avery and Amelia lug their bags to the cart, and then he hopped on beside them.

"You'll need help getting it out too," he said, as the little train rattled its way up the hill. It made a stop at the corner of Church Street and Fairhope Avenue, in front of The Gables.

"Here's where we part for now," Avery said. "I'll be seeing you."

"That's for certain," Amelia responded, and smiled at her new friend. Before she knew it Joe and a tall, gangly man with unruly brown hair, cowlicked at the crown of his head and and flopping foreward onto his forehead—were working together to carry her bags to the door.

"Thank you so much!" Amelia said, fishing in her handbag for a change purse.

"No, Ma'am, no charge," Joe said and exchanged a glance with his moving partner. "Happy to do it." He grinned widely, looking embarrassed to have been taken for a bellboy or perhaps a beggar. But his eyes regarded her kindly. He shrugged and shambled his way back to the railway. The man with hair almost in his eyes followed her onto the porch. She stopped and gave him a puzzled look.

"I'm staying here too," he said, and walked ahead of her into the building and took the stairs two at a time.

"Oh, my stars, Mr. Taylor!" cried Mrs. Cross to the man going up the stairs, but he was already upstairs and likely halfway down the hall. "I meant to introduce you to Miss King at dinner! Do come in, Miss Amelia!" Mr. Taylor mumbled something from the top of the stairs, but a door closed and he was out of sight.

"I've kept your room for you," Mrs. Cross said. "The same one you stayed in before." Amelia smiled at this friendly gesture. Her room.

Amelia negotiated with Mrs. Cross to keep the large trunk downstairs on the back porch, as she had packed it with things she would not need for weeks—until she was in a place of her own. The two of them managed to move it into place on the porch, and then take her suitcase and the little bag of toiletries to her room, the same one she had occupied in June. Mr. Taylor was obviously at the other end of the hall, but the hotel guests would all share a bathroom.

"Would you like some coffee or tea after your trip?" Mrs. Cross asked. It was, in fact, almost time for dinner and smells of a pot roast were coming from the kitchen.

Amelia wanted to lie down for a while, so she demurred on the offer of coffee. She made her way to the bathroom, washed her face, and came back to the wood-paneled room and saw that the window gave a view of a few trees and a house down the block. Her room was at the south side of the building, so when she looked, she could see a white frame church at the corner. This was the Disciples of Christ church, she knew, the first to be built in Fairhope, attended by most of the original contingent in town including the Gastons. E.B.'s father had been a minister, and he himself was a stalwart member. She craned her neck to see more of the church, and told herself that tomorrow she would walk down there before leaving for the school. But now, she lay down on top of the white chenille bedspread that covered the single bed, closed her eyes gently and drifted into the sleep she needed, every muscle at last relaxed after her arduous journey and a thrilling arrival. She felt no anxiety, but a great deal of happy enthusiasm. She was able to take a nap that must have lasted almost an hour and was awakened by the sound of dishes clattering together and voices downstairs.

The large, noisy alarm clock on the dresser indicated the time was 6:30. Dinner at The Gables was always at 7 P.M. It would be very welcome on this day, after the meals she had

had on the train. Mrs. Cross served heavy, old-fashioned food, and the smell of pot roast alerted her this one would be hearty. The Gables had four guest rooms, and she knew at least one of them besides hers was occupied. Mr. Taylor, who had carried her luggage in with the boy from the school, was at the other end of the hall.

As she descended the stairs Captain Cross was playing The Moonlight Sonata softly on the piano. Amelia took one of her books and went down to the front room and sat in a rocker.

"Good to see you, my girl," Captain Cross said. "Did you have a nice journey?" He continued playing. Amelia allowed as how she had had a good journey, especially the last lap of it—the ride across the bay on The Apollo, meeting the nice teacher named Avery, and the clattery trip up the hill in the rail wagon. Then she opened the book to the page on which she had left off on the train. The atmosphere at The Gables was gentle and homey, smelling of old books and pot roast and gravy, perfect for reading a book about progressive education and the development of the child. It was what she would come to feel was the paradox of Fairhope, a revolution going on in the coziest of surroundings.

In a few minutes Mr. Taylor's clumsy gait sounded on the stairs, and Amelia looked up only for a second.

He made a nasal sound, something between a growl and a greeting, and headed toward the kitchen. Amelia heard him ask Mrs. Cross if he could do anything to help. Immediately Amelia felt slightly guilty that she had not done so herself; this was obviously a town where no one was truly a guest. Mrs. Cross and a young Negro girl were dishing up the food for the table, and Mr. Taylor was pressed into service to carry the platter with the pot roast.

Just as she wondered if she should also be up and helping out, Captain Cross swiveled the piano stool and announced, "Pre-prandial concert is over. It's time for dinner," and moved to his chair at the head of the table. The meal was again old-fashioned food, with lots of vegetables and iced tea, just what Amelia had learned to expect at The Gables.

"I think Mrs. Comings will stop by after a while," Mrs. Cross said. By now Amelia knew enough about Lydia N. Newcomb Comings to be excited about this visit.

"Have you met Mrs. Comings yet, Amelia?" asked Capt. Cross.

"Amelia hasn't even met me yet," said the man with the cowlick, which tonight was suitably tamed and held in place with pomade in fashion at that time. "Maxwell Taylor," he said, and nodded at Amelia.

This very informal outburst caused general hilarity all around, and even Amelia found it somewhat amusing.

"I'm Amelia King, Mr. Taylor," she said and smiled at him.

"I'm Mr. Taylor to my students," he responded, "but around the dinner table, I'm just Max," he said.

So she learned that Max Taylor was also a teacher at Mrs. Johnson's school, which put her a bit more at ease with him, at the same time causing some discomfort about what to expect from her colleagues.

"I understand you'll be teaching at the school, too," he said. "I teach high school English and drama."

"What play are you going to do this year, Max?" Captain Cross said.

"If Comings Hall is ready for it, we're going to try *The School for Scandal*," Max said. "Have you seen our new theater, Amelia?"

"Oh, yes—I love it." Amelia beamed at the thought of a full-fledged version of *The School for Scandal*, done by Alabama teenagers, performed on the stage of the building she saw under construction.

"Do you really think the youngsters are up to Sheridan?" Captain Cross' accent had never been more English.

"Of course they are, with the right director," Max responded.

"Maybe you could sign on as a dialect coach," Mrs. Cross said to her husband. Everybody laughed at that, but to Amelia it was a valid idea.

"Ah, most of these kids don't have much of an accent," Max said, "Not Southern accents anyway. Transplants and boarding students."

"Well, they don't sound English to me," Captain Cross said.

"Naw, they don't sound English. We'll see what we can do about that," Max Taylor said, now obviously thinking about the enormity of his theatrical project.

"Why not a bit of Shakespeare again?" Mrs. Cross added.

"We'll no doubt do that in class. I'll leave the full-scale productions to Mrs. Hiestand."

"Have you ever heard of Sarah Willard Hiestand?" Mrs. Cross asked Amelia.

Amelia thought the name did sound familiar, but she didn't know exactly where she might have heard it.

"Mrs. Hiestand has been wintering here for years," Mrs. Cross told her. "She's a well- known Shakespearean scholar from Chicago, and she's started doing a Shakespeare's Birthday Festival here. Everybody in town is employed in it in some way. It will be bigger and better next spring."

It occurred to Amelia she had seen the name Sarah Willard Hiestand on scholarly articles on classical theatre she had read in college.

"It looks as if I'm going to meet some interesting people," Amelia said, and just as she did, a little white-haired lady with her hair in a bun gingerly opened the door.

"Enter 'An Interesting Person,' Stage Right!" said Max Taylor with a sweep of his hand.

"Oh, I didn't mean to interrupt the meal," said the old lady, "I just couldn't wait."

"We're just finishing up here, Lydia," Mrs. Cross said. "Would you like to join us for a piece of cobbler and a cup of coffee?"

"I'm having tea," Captain Cross said.

"I think a cup of tea would be lovely—it's late for coffee, even for me," the lady, who was introduced as Lydia Comings, said. "I assume this is Amelia King. I've heard about you from Marietta."

Lydia Comings was, aside from being the owner of The Gables and the namesake of the new community hall on the campus of the Organic School, the kind of personage Amelia had come to expect to meet in Fairhope. She was small and spry, and had been, with her husband, Mrs. Johnson's original benefactor and one of the most influential backers of the school. She was an educator and one of the people who had been in the single-tax colony from its early days.

"Hope you don't mind, Idella, but I've invited Marie to drop in tonight," she said to Mrs. Cross.

"Oh, that's lovely, Lydia. I'm so glad for both of you to meet Amelia—"

"And see me, too, of course," piped in Max, feigning feeling neglected with extreme theatricality.

"We all love seeing you, Max," said Lydia with a wickedly flirtatious old-lady smile. Then she turned to Mrs. Cross. "I'm sure she'll be along any minute."

Mrs. Cross was pouring tea and the colored girl was clearing the table. She had brought in a deep-dish peach cobbler which Amelia could sense was still warm because of the fragrance it spread throughout the room. Amelia wasn't accustomed to the big meals Mrs. Cross served, and she watched her dispense the large wedges of cobbler with some apprehension.

"I think I'll just have coffee, Mrs. Cross," she said.

"Oh? You'll love the cobbler— but then maybe you'd like it for breakfast."

"That would be wonderful, I'm sure."

Mr. Taylor accepted both pie and coffee, yet there was still enough left over to think about having a small slice with coffee in the morning.

Just then a large and serious-looking woman made her way heavily up the front stairs. "Greetings, all," she said as she flung open the screen door.

A general round of responses ensued, surrounding the large lady, and bringing a warm smile to her wrinkled face.

"Oh, my, Fairhope's coming to life these days, isn't it," she said. "I'll be so happy for an end to the summer."

Amelia was introduced to Marie Howland, obviously a great friend to the Crosses and to Mrs. Comings. As she talked, it became clear she was one of Mrs. Johnson's greatest admirers.

"Mrs. Howland is the benefactor and gatekeeper of Fairhope's library," Captain Cross said. "And a regular writer for *The Fairhope Courier.*"

Like most prospective newcomers to Fairhope, Amelia had been subscribing to the town newspaper for some time. She had seen Marie Howland's name on a regular column as well as on numerous opinion pieces on the editorial page. Mrs. Howland had lived in a number of utopian communities and preferred Fairhope above all of them. She had been so useful to Mr. Gaston in recruiting new residents that he employed her as an assistant editor of *The Courier.*

"I've read your columns," Amelia said. "I'm so pleased to meet you here—tell me, how is your garden growing?"

Mrs. Howland had written in many of her columns about the garden she kept in Fairhope, specifying which fruits and vegetables were doing well, and how the change in season affected her plantings. Spontaneous warm laughter broke out when Amelia commented on this.

"Bless your heart for asking, my dear," Mrs. Howland said. My tomatoes are all played out now—I don't do well with vegetables these days. But my zinnias are spectacular!"

Mrs. Cross was already cutting a piece of cobbler for her guest.

"Idella, you know I shouldn't. I know I shouldn't, and I guess everybody knows I shouldn't," Mrs. Howland said, in obvious response to the dessert. "My doctors say it isn't good for me—but all I worry about is how difficult all this added weight will make it for my poor pallbearers!"

She did, of course, accept the dessert. Amelia thought it sad this lady was thinking about her pallbearers, but she was clearly old and not very well. She had a jolly spirit, however. She was partaking of the cobbler with gusto. And she kept the conversation going with her knowledge of the school and Fairhope.

"Marietta's enthusiastic about the new school year," she said. "Lots of interest from the Northeast apparently. She's got her folk dance teacher lined up, a true expert on English folk dance. I expect the School Home will be full."

"I should say so," Mrs. Comings said. "Fairhope's coming to life."

Nine

"FAIRHOPE IS CHANGING, no doubt about it," said Captain Cross, holding the pipe in his mouth with his teeth. "Every fall more people move into town because of the school, and every year the town grows.

"It's not the settlement I moved to years ago," Mrs. Howland said. "But I think that's all to the better."

"Progress," someone said.

"Not 'poverty,'" Captain Cross added, alluding to *Progress and Poverty*, Henry George's book which had had such an influence on the founders in the 1890s. His little joke was not lost on the group. All contentedly sipped their coffee and lapsed into a dreamy reverie about their adopted home. They clearly held great expectations for its future. Amelia looked at Max, who gave her a one-sided smile, rolling his eyes subtly for her benefit.

She observed the group in a new way tonight, seeing them as idealists who had lived their lives following a dream of a perfect society and bundling all their separate life's dreams together in this place. Silence descended upon the group as they thought of their own first days in town, compared to its new bustling atmosphere.

"Thanks to Marietta, I would say," said Marie. "I doubt that E.B. could have gotten this far without her."

"You're right about that," Captain Cross said. "Single Tax is a strong concept, and Ernest is a worthy man. But before Marietta came upon Fairhope with her radical ideas about education, the project that was Fairhope was a bit on the wane."

"Until Dr. Dewey came and his book was published," Mrs. Comings said. "Ever so many people have come to have a look at Fairhope as a result of *Schools of Tomorrow*— and it would seem they all decided to stay."

"And Marietta's lecture tours!" said Mrs. Howland. This brought a group response, with almost everybody saying yes in one form or another. Even Amelia and Max spoke up.

"That's what got me here," Max said. I heard her in New York three years ago."

"And I heard her in Philadelphia last year," Amelia said. "But I had read so much about her before that."

"And what did you young people think?" Mrs. Howland asked.

"It's obvious," Max said. "We had to come here."

"And you, Amelia?" asked Mrs. Comings.

Amelia thought a minute.

"I had to come here," she said, realizing it herself for the first time. "I had to be in the vanguard of the new education."

"Ooh, so that's what Mrs. Johnson's little school is," Mrs. Cross said.

"I think so. I'm sure of it." Amelia said. She was emboldened to position herself in the coterie of Mrs. Johnson's followers, and felt, as the rest of them did, that this approach to education was the wave of the future. The School of Organic Education was, as Dr. Dewey had confirmed, a school of tomorrow.

All the old people in the room applauded quietly and beamed at each other and at her. "We love to hear that," said Mrs. Howland. "Now, with all that said, I must go home and let you all get some sleep. Tomorrow will be the first day of work for some of you."

"I'll walk you home, Marie," Max said. "Would you like to join us, Amelia? It's just a few blocks."

Thinking she would love a brief walk before bedtime, Amelia readily agreed. Everybody rose and said good night to Mrs. Howland, and the three walked down the steps from the porch, Max holding Mrs. Howland's elbow. They turned toward the bay on Fairhope Avenue. Amelia could not imagine that it would still be hot outside even at night, but it was. Crickets chirped loudly and the air was thick with warm summer fragrances—the smells of flowers, grass, even damp earth and the bark of trees. There was a bit of a breeze coming from the direction of the bay.

"That breeze feels nice tonight," Mrs. Howland said. "You never get used to this climate, Amelia dear, I can warn you of that."

"Well, you just wear fewer clothes," said Max.

"I suppose you want to take Amelia to the camp," Mrs. Howland said, a bit slyly.

"Never thought of it," said Max. He was a little defensive. Then he gave Mrs. Howland a sharp look and she chuckled.

"I'd be surprised at that," said Mrs. Howland.

"It's a little early to talk about this," Max said. "Her first night, after all."

"Now you must tell me what you two conspirators are talking about!" Amelia was suspicious, but was certain it was nothing unusual to have a "camp" in a little town, whatever it might be. A fishing camp? An outdoor park of some kind?

"It's a nudist camp," Mrs. Howland said matter-of-factly. Amelia blushed in spite of herself, only making it worse when she made an effort to stem it.

"Now, Marie, look—you've embarrassed her!"

"Oh, my dear, it's nothing to worry about. A little open-air exposure of the body, to cleanse the spirit. Strictly an optional attraction of Fairhope!"

The three did not talk much more now that this shot had been fired as they strolled along, turning on Summit Street to walk to Marie's home, which was, as it turned out, in the same building as the Fairhope Public Library.

"I'm sorry if I shocked you, dear," Mrs. Howland said to Amelia as she opened the gate to her picket fence. "There are probably any number of things that we in Fairhope take for granted yet others never think about. There are forums and meetings, amateur theatricals, picnics--you can pick and choose what you want to participate in. And Maxwell can assure you you're going to be awfully busy with the school all year long, and will have precious little time for open air—anything! Except maybe bathing in the bay!"

They bade the old lady goodnight and turned back toward the hotel. A few houses dotted the landscape and the dirt road. Lights flickered from the houses and a huge moon lit the streets. Not quite full, it still cast a gentle flood of light on the leaves of every tree, every stone in the street, every dew-dampened blade of grass, like a distant stage light from above. Amelia had not become accustomed to Southern moonlight and felt it contained some kind of eerie magic. She would later say that a Southern moon could make a pile of old tin cans look romantic.

"Cat got your tongue?" Max asked.

"I've got a lot to think about." She regarded her companion in the moonlight. It would take more than the Southern moon to make this gawky young man into an object for romance, but something about him was likable all the same.

"Tell me, what's your impression? It's not Philadelphia, is it?"

"Certainly not. I'm not actually from Philadelphia anyway," she said. She had no idea why she said that. Probably just to shake from her mind the image of all the villagers bathing in the bay and cavorting around a nudist colony on weekends.

"Where then?"

"My parents live in Hoboken, New Jersey. I was raised with cousins in Philadelphia and graduated from Mount Holyoke in Massachusetts."

"From Hoboken to Philly to Fairhope," Max said. "By way of Mount Holyoke. For me it was Baltimore to Pittsburgh to New York to Fairhope. What do you think of your journey so far?"

"So far I just love Fairhope," Amelia told him. "It's a very unusual little town."

"I wouldn't argue with that. It has an elderly population that perceives itself as young. And its young people perceive themselves as having the wisdom of the ages." Amelia wondered what he meant by that. Was she one of those self-important young people?

But Maxwell Taylor didn't elaborate. They walked the quiet dirt road the few blocks to The Gables in a contemplative silence.

"What are those—crickets?" Amelia asked.

"Tree frogs."

"Noisier than crickets, but I'd never have guessed frogs."

"No, they don't sound particularly froggy, do they?" Then they were at the porch of The Gables. A light was on in the living room but they didn't see the Crosses.

"I do want you to know, though, before we retire for the night—that I don't go to the camp," Maxwell said, confidentially. Amelia smiled at this and felt relieved. She had a lot to think about now. She closed the screen door and left him standing on the porch looking at the moon and listening to the tree frogs.

Max thought about this winsome girl, coming on her own to this remote place. One minute she seemed sophisticated and wise; the next, tremulous and in need of protection. That was it—Max felt had to protect her. He was smitten, although not entirely ready to admit it even to himself. He had not perceived himself as lonely until the moment she was out of his sight. From then on he sought ways to be near to her.

Her room was sticky and still, with its alarm clock ticking loudly, but Amelia knew this would not interfere with her sleeping. She was exhausted as well as exhilarated. She yearned for sleep and for dreams that would help her cope with her experiences in Fairhope so far and the new life that she would face in the morning. The ticking of the clock blended with the sounds from outdoors—crickets and tree frogs, and the occasion "hoo" of an owl somewhere in the distance.

Before she could drop off to sleep she found her mind full of images. The Chapman family would be so at home here—she could just see Althea joining with Mrs. Comings in the many forums and clubs and volunteering at the school. Lettie would make a wonderful teacher in the Organic system. She and Rose could explore the community together, and Carl would be helping the students build the new community center. None of it was likely to happen, of course. She was on her own now, a long way from home. She had to say goodbye to her family for the time being even though it was clear they would never be far from her thoughts in days to come, possibly for the rest of her life. Maybe someday they would all visit Fairhope.

As she lay on her back and closed her eyes, she felt gratitude for having found this particular place. Before she could even form words to describe this new emotion, she had an understanding that she meant more than the physical place of Fairhope, an idyllic location with its views of Mobile Bay at sunset, its sounds and smells of nature—it was a place in her own soul where she was ready to grow in new ways.

She relaxed and took deep breaths, sorting out the sea of benevolent faces—Captain Cross, his wife, Marietta Johnson, Mr. Taylor, Marie Howland—then a familiar fear overtook her. For an instant, she was back in the house in Hoboken, looking at Miss Pritchart's bland smirk, hearing the gospel of sin and guilt, being forced to memorize, yet always being made to feel she was coming up short. For the moment she was helpless and frightened once again. She sat up in bed and looked around her. No, this was not that life. This was a place to shed the fear and shame once and for all, a gentle place far from those dark halls and the sense of ill feeling behind her teacher's cold, superior face with its the thin lips. Tree frogs outside and the ticking clock soothed her back to rest, with thoughts of the beautiful experiences that lay ahead. She called those gentle faces and voices back into her mind.

She was soon asleep, dreaming of again being on the boat to Fairhope, surrounded by strangers and people she had now met. Maxwell Taylor was one of them. He came up to her and said, "Are you sure you want to be here?" and she said, "Yes, yes, of course!" but he shook his head and walked away. As he was going to the other side of the boat she called to him, "Are you sure we are going to Fairhope? Can you tell me where the school is?" but he was not answering her. Out of nowhere Mrs. Johnson came up to her. "Stay with me," said Mrs. Johnson. "I know where you are going."

꽃

She had set the alarm clock for 6:30 but was awakened earlier by the smell of bacon frying and coffee brewing, and the sound of water running in the bathroom down the hall. She had laid out her clothes the night before—a simple skirt and blouse, her plain "teacher shoes," and a gray ribbon to match her skirt, for her hair. She took all to the bathroom, which was already made steamy from having been used before her. She drew a bath and soaked for a very short time, and dried herself with the thin towel Mrs. Cross had left in her room. While in the tub she heard the striding step of Max Taylor, coming down the hall and then tromping down the stairs.

She had never known the likes of Max Taylor before. Teetering on the border between brilliance and downright strangeness, he had a way of saying the almost-right thing and looking almost right as well. But he was off the center somehow; not handsome, not ugly, yet not plain either. The thought of him as attractive just didn't materialize. He was like an old man in some ways, pompous and stolid, yet he was surely no older than she. He was more serious than the people her age she knew; yet he was playful in a way as well. There was no question he was in her life now, a part of this educational experience. Just where he might fit in perplexed her.

She brushed her hair and pulled it back, securing it with a tie at the nape of her neck and then tied the ribbon over that. She decided not to apply rouge to her lips or cheeks, thinking of Avery with her clean-washed look. Avery seemed sure of herself, like a New Woman should be. Amelia strove for that designation for herself. But this was not Philadelphia, and to look like a serious young school-teacher she would rely on her natural looks.

She went downstairs and accepted a cup of coffee from the same Negro girl who served dinner he night before.

"How do you do," she said to the young woman. "My name is Amelia King."

The girl nodded uneasily.

"What's yours?"

"Sadie," said the solemn young black.

"It's nice to meet you, Sadie," she said, determined to break down the barrier between them. Whether it was a servant-mistress barrier or a Negro-white barrier Amelia could not be certain, but either way, she resented its existence, especially in what she took to be the egalitarian setting of the single-tax colony.

"Thank you, ma'am," said Sadie, her eyes on the floor, and left for the kitchen.

"There's some of this cobbler left over from last night, Amelia," Mrs. Cross said, coming in from the kitchen. "Would you like some eggs and bacon?"

Amelia accepted a plate of scrambled eggs with a slice of cobbler on it and sat at the table. Max was just backing his chair away from the table.

"I'm going early," he announced. "They'll all be gathering already. Some of the teachers are staying at the School Home until they find places to rent." Immediately Amelia thought of Avery, who had said she was staying at the School Home.

"I'll be there in a few minutes," Amelia said, and watched Max lope to the door and across the porch. Then she gulped the rest of her coffee and quickly ate what she could of the leftover pie before dashing upstairs to get her books and bag of supplies for school.

Ten

OUTSIDE IT WAS muggy and already warm, but the air was charged with a note of apprehension—perhaps it was just Amelia's own unease about what might lay ahead. The screen door snapped behind her and she scurried down the steps to the street, her mind full of anticipated images of what to expect on this auspicious morning. She yearned to see Mrs. Johnson again, and to greet Avery, and to meet all the people she could only imagine she was going to get to know. Never had she had such a sense of the importance of what she was about to do.

"What's your hurry?" someone called as she walked past the offices of The Fairhope Courier. "This is Fairhope, you know—there is time for everything!" It was E.B. Gaston, chiding her from behind the screen door.

"Good morning, Miss King. Don't look so worried—you're going to love your job." There was a glimmer of a smile on his face and his eyes were very kind. "And I'm sure the job will love you, too."

All at once she relaxed and smiled at Mr. Gaston. "Thank you, kind sir, for reminding me of that," she said. "I have to remember I'm not in Philadelphia any more!"

"You certainly are not," Mr. Gaston said. "All the better for Fairhope."

He had a way with him, this old man, cajoling and encouraging—his ebullient nature embodied all there was to love about Fairhope. He had been making the pleasure and hospitality of Fairhope his life's mission since bringing the first group of Iowans to settle the town over twenty years before, in 1895. His newspaper was a veritable advertisement for the town and what it stood for. She was pleased by the brief exchange and walked the two blocks to the school with a spring in her step.

On her way to the campus she brushed by the derelict-looking man she had seen in town on her earlier visit. He still looked half-asleep, but this time she was close enough to smell the acrid odor of a body that hadn't been washed for weeks. What an anomaly this pathetic man was in the Fairhope she had come to feel was so pure and angelic! His sweat smelled of stale alcohol and he looked like the kind of lost soul one might see in what was known as "the Barbary Coast" of Hoboken—the section of her hometown near the docks, where the cheap saloons were.

A few people had gathered in the front of the new auditorium, teenagers mostly, with the man she had seen there before, Will Hodges, supervising and working along with them. Seeing them was like breathing fresh air—she was breathing much fresher air than that which surrounded the mysterious, scruffy old man.

"Morning, Miss King," Will Hodges said to her. "The meeting of new teachers will take place at the library building, just over there—" his hand directed her up the slope of the campus to a small building in the middle of the block, where she could see people gathering. There were about 15 men and women of varying ages, looking happy and scrambling toward the door. She spotted Avery holding the door as they entered.

"How are you today," Avery said to her, not a question, but a general acknowledgment of a condition of well-being. Amelia, smiling fully now, just nodded and told Avery how excited she was.

"Oh, we all are, as you see. It's the before-school-starts condition."

Just then a few more people walked in and, with them, Mrs. Johnson. "Is it eight o'clock?" she asked a chipper young man at her side. When he nodded, she said, "Well, let's get started then."

Chairs and benches were placed in a circle around the periphery of the room, in front of bookshelves. Amelia found her place on a bench. Avery sat next to her, and Max was next to Avery on the other side.

Mrs. Johnson opened the meeting by saying how happy she was to have her teachers with her, new and old, young and "not so young," and that, for the new people, one of her unbendable rules was that of punctuality.

"I say to my students, and I'm saying it to you too— when necessary, that the two most important *musts* in our school are *being on time*, and *doing one's best*. These are aso basic to me, yet they are both more and more ignored in the modern world. In whatever job you ever have, the very least you can do is arrive on time. Absolutely on time. It's not difficult. It doesn't cost you anything and it is always a plus for you no matter if you're meeting with the president of the United States or your own mother. And with a class of young unfolding minds, it is essential for them to learn the importance this simple habit. *Being on time*."

Amelia immediately thought of the times she had been late for meetings in her life. Why, she had even been a few minutes late for her job interview with Mrs. Johnson, that day she had lingered at the building of the new auditorium! Was Mrs. Johnson thinking of her, was this directed at her slovenly use of time and disrespect for obligations? Her first lesson in the practicality of Organic Education, and already she saw herself coming up short!

"As for the second *must*," Mrs. Johnson continued. "*Doing one's best work under all circumstances.* I know that we have some extremely intelligent children in this school. If you ask the parents, you'll probably hear that every one of them is extremely intelligent…"

Soft laughter rumbled in waves from the assembled teachers.

"There are some who will go to great universities and from there into demanding professions, such as medicine, law—even education—" More laughter here. "But a number of them will be better suited, and happier, in physical work. I tell them, 'Some of you will grow up to be ditch-diggers. But if that turns out to be your job, I want you to be the very best at it that you can. I want you to challenge yourself at every job, *to do the best work you can. Be the best ditch-digger!*

"This goes for their work in class, of course. What they do in school is the best example of the need for personal application. We require that every student apply himself to the best of his ability in every class. He will excel at some, fall short in some, but if he is doing his best, he will be learning. That learning is better than any measurement imposed by any system of education."

There was applause at this, even though those assembled had heard it many times before. They shared a need to hear it again, to have it reinforced as they looked toward their next year of working with the school.

"It is through this educational experience that a child sets his own standard, which will stay with him in every endeavor. The standard is an inner, human one. If the work is suitable and wholesome, and the children delight in it, there is growth, which is the essence of education."

Amelia was fairly reeling with joy at hearing education described in this way. If only she could master this attitude, this basic trust of the nature of the child and eliminate the voice of Miss Pritchard and her elementary-ed teachers in college from her head—her own examples of how *not* to be a teacher—if only she could become the kind of teacher Mrs. Johnson so clearly was and wanted her and all her teachers to be, she might truly become a great teacher. She could do it. She would do it! She would never be late for an appointment again. She would never give less than her own best in her work. And she would spend as many years as it took to learn to teach this way.

Mrs. Johnson spoke for another hour even though it passed in no time at all. Amelia couldn't believe it was time for a break when Mrs. Johnson said, "Now, let's get to know each other better and then I'll talk to you some more. Be back here in 15 minutes."

Everybody got up to stretch their limbs, and wandered out the doors of the building to get some fresh air. A few lit up cigarettes, a few went to the pitchers of water. Their talk blossomed into to full-fledged discussions.

"Are you one of the new teachers?" was the question reverberating around the room. Amelia introduced herself to several people. There was a woman in man's clothes, who apparently taught in the Arts and Crafts department. The voice of Julian Crane, talking of Russian politics, filled one corner of the room. She learned he taught history and geography at the high school level. Crane was rather handsome, tall and white-haired, with a deep voice that carried across the room.

Avery was talking with Maxwell Taylor at the table with the water pitcher.

"I need to find a place to live," she was saying.

"Well, that shouldn't be hard to do."

"Finding the time—and a roommate. That's what I have to do. I'd like to move in as soon as possible."

Amelia was glad to hear Avery talking about finding both a place to rent and a roommate.

"I hope you don't mind my eavesdropping. Don't forget we talked about living together for the school term if we could find the right place? I'd love to give it a try, how about you?

"That would be *great*," Avery said with her eyes alight. "Problem solved!"

"Part of the problem, anyway," said Max. "Finding a roommate is one thing—finding a house that suits the two of you might be a horse of a different color. You can be sure of one thing—you won't find any vulgar house built by the predator rich in Fairhope."

"I should say not!" said Avery.

Amelia looked at them both.

"That's Mr. Gaston's phrase," Max said. "He founded this community to rid the world of real estate speculation, after all."

"One of the points I must drive home to you new teachers—I'll insert it here because I do not want to forget it," Mrs. Johnson began her program. "It is one of those cus-

toms we must not ignore, even though it is easy to slip on."
Now Mrs. Johnson had their attention, and all the teachers
were at attention as if they were learning a battle strategy.

"We refer to each other as 'Miss,' 'Mrs.,' or 'Mr.' In private life, you may call each other whatever you like, but in
your role as a teacher, you are to keep the formal appellation.
There is a reason for this.

"At this school your classes will come to love you, to
respect you, and in some cases even come to think of you as
family. However, you are not their friend. You are the adult
in the classroom. If they hear your common name often,
they will be inclined to use it. This puts you in the position
of being more friend than teacher. This teaches them to pull
down all authority to their level. That could easily lead to
the assumption as they grow up to assume that if their boss
is a nice enough fellow, it is all right to call him George
instead of Mr. Smith. There are not many bosses out there
who take well to this.

"You may have noted that some of us here are referred
to as "Aunt" or "Uncle." There was a big, long laugh at this
from the assembly, all of whom knew that Mrs. Johnson was
universally called Aunt Mettie in Fairhope, and sometimes
Ma Johnnie by the younger boarders at the School Home.

"Now, now. It's true, some of us who have known these
students since the day they were born have been awarded
the honorary title of aunt or uncle. But these too are titles of
authority. And--they are the exception to the rule. Do not
allow your students to call you by your first names under any
circumstances. The best way to assure this is by referring to
each other by titles such as "Mr." and "Miss" in front of them.
This is a hard and fast rule in the school."

Mrs. Johnson talked for another hour, telling the teachers about the unique old bell in the tower of the "bell building," that tolled every 40 minutes to signify the end of a period, giving students ten minutes to get from one building to another for their next class. She felt the walk in the fresh air was good for body, mind and spirit, and helped refresh students for the next class. She told the teachers that there was a piano in every elementary classroom, to be used for singing under the instruction of Edna Campbell of the music faculty. This different educational system required a difference in attitude and Amelia felt she was absorbing it like a sponge.

After the morning session, the group went to lunch at the School Home, a building Amelia already felt warmly about, having had her interview there with Mrs. Johnson.

The big room in the School Home was set with two tables for those attending the teacher- training program. Mrs. Johnson's seat was at one end of the larger table, and at her right was Mrs. Comings. On her left sat a student, the dark-haired boy George Ray Collins, whom Amelia had met at work when she stopped in on the group building the new community hall. He was deferential and spoke in a soft voice, mostly to Mrs. Johnson and Mrs. Comings, but he was holding conversation with some of the teachers he had apparently known from years past.

Mrs. Johnson's plate was adorned with only raw veg-etables—carrots, sliced fresh tomatoes, a green salad, some soaked nuts and a chopped apple. Each place setting had a cloth napkin with a napkin ring, made out of raffia, pine straw from the local long leaf pine, or some kind of natural reed, and with a name written in ink on adhesive tape, the kind from a medicine cabinet, stuck onto the ring. It was clear these napkin rings had been made as an arts and crafts project, either by teachers in the training course or by the students themselves. Amelia found her name and took her place. Everybody was interested in learning who she was and where she had heard of the school. Every one of them, just as she, had heard Mrs. Johnson speak at some point, and decided to pack up everything and move to Alabama. They all found this an amusing common thread.

She sat with Avery and Maxwell Taylor in the break after lunch and before the next orientation meeting was to begin. They were explaining to her that Mrs. Johnson insisted on long lunch hours in her school so that students could—and would—go home to a nice hot meal every day.

"She says that's her contribution to the American family!" Avery said. "I love the way she looks at things."

"But what if they were to take the hour and a half and not go home?" Amelia wanted to know. "What if they were to do something—"

"Unwholesome?" Max said, and the three of them laughed. "Heaven forfend!"

"But seriously—"

"I don't know how to explain it," Max said. "But not much that isn't wholesome takes place around here."

"Don't look so skeptical," Avery added. "You'll see. Contrary to what you might think, Marietta Johnson runs a tight ship."

"There is one person in this town I have to ask about," Amelia ventured. "He could not be counted as 100 per cent wholesome. I spotted him on my first visit, and have seen him already again this morning. He's as filthy a fellow as I ever saw on the dirty streets of the worst neighborhood in Hoboken—"

"Did he smell to high heaven?" Max asked.

"Did he wear shoes?" Avery added.

"Yes to the first question—and no to the second."

The two smiled immediately in recognition.

"You have encountered Luther Beagle," Max said.

"What's his story?" Amelia asked. "He certainly doesn't seem to me to belong here."

"Dunno what his story is," Max said. "But he came with the territory. Just a country boy who happens to be living in this town, the way I see it. No need to worry about him. He's not a single taxer—or a product of Organic Education either."

"Heavens no!" Avery said. "I think there's one in every community. The 18th amendment didn't affect him a whit. His odor is legendary. The boys give him a bath on Halloween every year. In the bay."

Amelia doubted this, but Max said, "It's true—the high school boys drag him to the bay every Halloween and give him a good dunking. Sometimes with soap."

The mental picture of this spectacle was too much for the three of them, who collapsed in laughter. Someone said, "Boys will be boys," but Amelia felt sympathetic to the derelict man at this point.

She and Avery began talking about looking for places to live and agreed they might find a cottage they could share. They decided to meet the next morning and have a look around Fairhope together for "For Rent" signs.

The afternoon education lecture went on for two hours with just one break. It was the teacher's job, Mrs. Johnson said over and over in many different ways, to be sensitive to the individual interests of the whole class. Having had some experience with first graders, Amelia wondered if this were possible. Everybody, after all, was not another Marietta Johnson.

Eleven

AFTER THE EDUCATION meeting, the crowd broke into groups to walk through the town with those who had taught in prior years helping the new teachers get their bearings. They left the campus via Johnson Street, bypassing the main street of town which was aptly named Fairhope Avenue. They passed the post office on Section Street and headed north to the main intersection, where the Crawford store was, and a pharmacy, and the millinery shop next to Crawford's. This part of town was universally referred to as "uptown" in Fairhope, maybe a carryover from the usage in Des Moines, where Mr. Gaston and the original single taxers had come from.

"Is there 'uptown' and 'downtown'?" Amelia asked.

"In Fairhope, no," answered Max. "There is uptown, which is this, and then there's everywhere else."

She saw the Courier office again, and a doctor's office, and a few storefronts and cafés. She could hear the bleat of a goat, and the occasional moo of cows. Chickens scratched about in the road.

A few homes dotted the lanes here and there, and much wooded land in between. The houses were for the most part very small and unimposing, as if that was the best the owners could do. Even the larger homes were without embellishment. Under Fairhope's single-tax system, most houses were modest first homes for young couples who got a break on the land even though they couldn't afford much of a house. A starter home would be just one room, with more rooms added as its owners prospered. Bungalows, so fashionable in the rest of the country, were beginning to appear on the landscape.

"I wanted to see this church," Amelia told Avery as they approached the white wooden structure at the corner of Church St. and an alley. "This must be the town center."

"I would say the school is pretty much the town center, but this is the central church. The Baptists also have a church on this street, and there is a Methodist congregation meeting over on Section Street. Out in the country there's a Friends Meeting House— "

"Really? That makes me feel right at home!"

"Are you a Quaker?"

"No, but I'm at home anywhere there's a Society of Friends..."

Avery smiled, but looked puzzled.

"Philadelphia."

"Oh, of course. Brotherly love and William Penn."

"I have a great deal of affection for the Quakers," Amelia added, thinking of her elementary education at Select Friends School in Philadelphia with her cousins.

"Now that the summer is ending," Avery said, "The focus of the town is about to change."

"How so?"

"There'll be an influx of people, winter visitors and those who want to investigate the school. Since Dewey's book we get a lot of people visiting the school—and most of them stay."

"Really? Most of them?"

"A great number, anyway. You'll see."

They went back to the school for its final meeting of the day. Amelia was weary yet she looked forward to seeing Mrs. Johnson again before the weekend break.

It was a nuts-and-bolts meeting, very brief. They were expected to meet on Monday morning and discuss their plans for the first part of their teaching year. They would be expected to cover a certain amount of required academic work and read from the Oppenheim text and some of Rousseau. Amelia had already finished *The Development of the Child* and the Rousseau that Mrs. Johnson had given her in June, but a few hours of brushing it up over the weekend would be helpful. She thought of looking for a house to rent as a pleasant distraction.

As she called an end to the meeting, Mrs. Johnson made an announcement.

"You are all invited to a special event in Comings Hall tomorrow night. Friends of the school are giving a folk dance party for you!"

Amelia knew that folk dancing was Mr. Johnson's special hobby horse; that she required it of all students, and that in Fairhope folk dancing was often a community enterprise—children together with teachers, parents and old folks danced traditional jigs and reels. Folk dancing was an essential part of organic education. It did not appeal to Amelia, however, and she was not certain it ever would.

Applause broke out across the room, and Amelia joined it somewhat half-heartedly. There was no getting out of it now. Tomorrow morning she would meet Avery and look for a house and tomorrow night she would join the citizens of Fairhope for an activity as exotic to her as deep sea. She was not just a young teacher embarking on a new career; she was in a whole new world.

Fortunately, since she had little appetite, Mrs. Cross's evening meal was meager in comparison to what Amelia had come to expect from her. A bowl of homemade vegetable soup with chunks of beef, a jellied salad and a large glass of iced tea. She was hungrier than she realized and ate what was put before her.

Maxwell Taylor sat at the table, eating heartily.

"I think we're going to have an extraordinary year," he was saying. "Mrs. Johnson is in fine form—she's admonished us, as she always does, to be punctual and creative. And she has arranged to make folk dancers out of all of us!"

"Of course," said Mrs. Cross. "And you're going to love it."

"Miss King became awfully subdued when she heard the news," Max went on. "Her face went white and she hasn't spoken a word since."

"Oh, you!" Amelia said, exasperated with Max. "I may have indicated that I don't know *how* to folk dance, but I'm willing to learn—"

"Game *girl!*" Captain Cross said. "Mrs. Cross and I will be there at the dance tomorrow night and come to your rescue if you find it difficult!"

"Which you won't, my girl," Mrs. Cross said. "It's simple and a pleasure. And very good exercise."

As Amelia pondered this and finished eating, Max told her he was going with a group of teachers to the pier to watch the sunset.

"It's a daily spectacle here," he said, "and even though we go down to the bay almost every day to view it we don't get tired of it. Would you like to join us?"

That was an easy one. It would be not only an opportunity to get better acquainted with some of her colleagues, but she had seen enough Fairhope sunsets to understand their appeal. The panoramic view of the bay as the sky went through an extraordinary range of colors and the sun, bright red and seeming to increase in size as it lowered into the water, created a sunset like none she had ever seen before. She agreed and headed toward the beach with Max.

They passed the two women she had seen months before going into the millinery shop as they walked through town. Again this morning she had seen the one in masculine clothes at the gathering of the teachers at the school. Nothing was said about the couple, who were in deep conversation. The one in the man's suit, with her hair cut short, looked up and greeted Max.

"How are you, Mr. Taylor?"

"Just fine, Margaret," he said. "We're on our way to watch the sun go down."

"Happens every afternoon about this time," Margaret responded, and she and her partner laughed.

"I know, but we wouldn't want to let it happen without us," Max said. Amelia noticed that the couple followed them, laughing still. She was reminded of some young women she had known at Mt. Holyoke, girls who bonded so closely they behaved like romantic couples. Some had continued their relationships through all their college years, and even later moved in to live as roommates. It was not unheard of for same sex couples to form lifelong relationships, but Amelia had never met women in their thirties who had assumed the roles of man and wife so openly. Seeing these two as a part of Fairhope society made Amelia feel very modern.

As they drifted down toward the hill to the pier, they joined three other of the teachers she had seen in the morning, and the group picked up six or seven more, walking toward the same goal. It was a jolly bunch, some white-haired but most in their 20's and 30's. The white-haired contingent included Hal and Martha Etheridge, who had a daughter in the school.

"You'll be teaching First Life?" Martha asked Amelia. Amelia nodded and Martha informed her that their daughter was going to be in her class. "Kindergarten and First Life are in the same building," she said. "All Ally will have to do is cross the hall from her old class! I think you'll love working with Helen and your teaching assistants."

They were near the pier now and the sky surrounded them with shades of pink, orange, red, and a stripe of pale green near the top, where the blue was bleeding into many colors. A chiffon cloud undulated near the sun and glowed with gold as it crossed its path. The crowd was taking in every movement of color in the sky. A pelican perched mournfully on a pylon out in the water, and sea gulls nibbled at crumbs and insects on the sand. Amelia was silent, drinking in the happiness of being engulfed in nature's daily miracle. The bay added the susurus of waves, rhythmically stroking the sand, requiring quiet and contributing to the tranquility of the scene.

"I just want to hug the whole world!" said a voice. Amelia was stunned to realize it was her own.

The crowd laughed an indulgent, grown-up laugh, and a resonant male voice said, "Start with me, honey," and came up to her. It was Julian Crane, the tall, elegant and white-haired teacher she had met in the morning at the school discussing Socialist politics. Tonight he was so warm and appealing that Amelia did not hesitate to allow him to embrace her. After that, everyone in the crowd began to hug one another, beginning with her, and some kissed her on the cheek. Even Max put his arms around her and went to do the same with everybody else in the group.

Someone started to sing.

"There's a long, long trail a-winding, into the land of my dreams…" The crowd joined in, some offering harmonies in the upper and lower registers. Amelia felt as if she were indeed being hugged by the whole world—or the universe, even. The sun dropped into the bay and slowly the clouds went gold, then silver, at last turning grey against a mauve sky. Stars were coming into view and there was a feeling that surrounded them, a feeling that all was right with the world.

How many sunsets would she see in Fairhope, she wondered, and would every one of them be so special? Perhaps, but she knew there would never be a more memorable one, in Fairhope or anywhere in the world she might be in future years.

The crowd trudged back up the hill, some opting for the motorized cable car, but most walking together savoring the fellowship they had begun to feel.

Twelve

L ITTLE BY LITTLE this place was giving Amelia a new sense of security. She felt she was part of a modern movement, a revolution in education and in political thought. She did not dwell on how much she missed the Chapman family. Fairhope itself was becoming her family, enveloping her in the same kind of warmth.

One afternoon Mrs. Cross had sad news.

"Oh, Amelia, dear," she said, shaking her head. "Marie Howland's passed away."

Amelia was sitting in the sunny parlor of The Gables, reading a book Marietta Johnson had given her. When she heard the news, she looked up, put her book on a side table, and then walked across the room to Mrs. Cross.

"I'm so sorry to hear that," she said.

"We're all certainly sad about it," Mrs. Cross said. "But even Marie knew it was coming soon. There'll be a memorial service for her at the library. I think she would have liked that."

The public library, Mrs. Howland's pet project to which she had donated most of the books, from her own collection and that of her husband, had also been her home.

Amelia joined the crowd at the service a few days later. Mr. Gaston sang "Only Remembered by What We Have

Done," a simple old hymn with a bouncy tune, one that particularly suited Marie. The words spoke of seeds which were planted today growing in the future—a metaphor for both Marie's own garden and all the founders' plans for Fairhope.

A graveside service followed in the Colony Cemetery on the northern edge of town. So many of the original Single Taxers were elderly, and they stood at the grave clearly saddened by the loss of their vital old friend. Amelia looked at the weathered faces of Mr. Gaston, Mrs. Comings, the Crosses, and even Mrs. Johnson, who, in her 50s was the youngest in the group, and felt she knew what was going through their minds. Marie Howland was among the first of the idealistic single taxers to die and be buried here. She had always been a presence in the colony and a booster of its mission to save the world through a progressive notion of taxation. Marie had lived a colorful and varied life, finally settling in Fairhope with the firm conviction that it was the place that would demonstrate to the world an idea for its best future. Amelia's eyes were damp; she too had been touched by the spry old lady, so typical of the kind of modern mind that she had confronted in Fairhope.

Young people and little children filled in the crowd. It was a big event, with tributes from all sides and a lot of shaking of heads, "They don't make them like her any more." Despite the gap in their ages, Amelia had had the impression that she was going to get to know Marie Howland much better. Now any hope of that was buried in the Colony Cemetery.

The next day, Avery joined Amelia at The Gables, set to go house hunting. They dressed in very casual clothes, anticipating an expedition through weeds and brush. Not many houses in Fairhope bore "For Rent" signs, and those that invited adventure—which both women sought—were sure to be hidden away. They went down Church Street, around the corner, past the white wooden church for which the street had been named, and saw only a cottage or two, obviously occupied.

They turned in front of the church and followed an unpaved lane down the hill where a footbridge spanned the gully on their left. They turned right instead, to walk toward the views of the bay itself on Bayview Avenue where the houses, modest and all but hidden among shrubs and trees, offered views of the placid, elegant bay.

A sturdy oak stood at the corner of Fairhope Avenue and Bayview. Three children were in the tree, threading through its limbs as if it were extremely familiar territory.

"If we could just find a house to rent on this street," Amelia said plaintively to her new friend.

"Oh, you never know," Avery responded.

They strolled north on Bayview, soothed somehow by the sight of the bay to their left and the wooden two-story cottages scattered to the right. A green space lay on the bay side of the unpaved road, no doubt parkland set aside by the founding fathers of Fairhope. A wooden stair led down the bluff to the beach and there was a huge, sheltering oak near the street. The tall pine trees of the region lined the bluff. A house here and there, mostly on the opposite side of the road from the bay, dotted the avenue southward. Oaks rose over the brush, some draped with the dangling-scarf moss she had seen only in Fairhope. What a pretty village this was!

As they approached the end of the lane they saw a cottage tucked away on the hillside, a light green-grey house, the color of the lichens that grew on the side of the oaks. There actually was a sign at the driveway that read, "For rent. Inquire within."

The house was so typical of Fairhope, simple, covered in sage-green shingles, seeming to Amelia to offer all sorts of intimate acquaintance with pines and sea.

"Ask, and ye shall receive!" Avery said, a little too soon, a little too exuberantly.

"Oh—you know we won't be able to afford this," was Amelia's response.

The inhospitable yard covered their legs with sandspurs, but they refused to be deterred. Nobody was home, but they glimpsed though the French doors to see a generous well-proportioned fireplace in a rambling living room that struck them both as perfect. French windows—many of them—a corner window seat and an open staircase added to the attractiveness. It did not look luxurious, but well-planned and comfortable, in a way that Amelia expected here. A few threadbare overstuffed Morris chairs and a table that looked to be in Stickley's style sat solidly in the living room.

"Do you want to look at the house?" A man's voice came from behind them as they peered through the windows. "I can show it to you."

The man, introducing himself as Sam Bradley, said he lived next door, his sister owned the house, and he had permission to show it. The young women, feeling certain it was out of their price range, could not resist walking through the cottage, if only to dream. Bradley was muscular and of medium height, his brown eyes and salty-looking hair giving him a pleasant look, even though his clothes looked rather shabby and worn. Work clothes, typical of Fairhope, Amelia thought.

The house, Mr. Bradley told them, had had something of a past. Years before it had been a gristmill. Then, when it passed into disuse, someone appreciating its fine lines and sound timbers had moved it onto the bluff, adding porches, a bathroom, and kitchen, and covered the whole with gray shingles thereby assuring it a most satisfactory old age.

"This is so perfect," Amelia said. "All it needs is gray smoke curling out of that chimney!" But the matter of rent had not been discussed.

When the neighbor finally told them that they could have it for the rest of the season for twenty-five dollars a month they accepted the bargain at once. They later discovered why twenty five dollars was reasonable but just then it appeared to be a very special miracle.

The cottage had its own furniture and all they needed, really, was a little assistance in carrying their trunks of clothes.

The excitement Amelia was feeling was tempered by Avery's almost-cynical sense of humor.

"Don't you love the house too?" she asked her new friend.

"Of course I do—but I don't want to anger the house gods by being too sure of myself," she said.

Anger the house gods? Amelia was beginning to love the way Avery expressed herself.

They told Mr. Bradley they would be back with a deposit and sign the papers before sunset. He told them to knock on his door and he would be ready with the key.

"Most of us don't bother to lock our houses around here," he said to them, "But you'll want your keys just in case."

As they trudged back to The Gables, they chattered about the house and about not needing to lock it. They sat for coffee with Mrs. Cross and asked her all about it.

"Mr. Bradley was right that most of the houses hardly get locked," she said. "But two beautiful women living alone—well, you'll certainly want to lock it at night. You can decide for yourselves whether to lock it every time you leave."

Being city girls, they could not imagine leaving a house open when they were gone, but in time the relaxed atmosphere and safe small-town feeling would put them at ease with the custom, among many others they had not encountered before.

They could probably move their things in the next day, but this afternoon was all about gathering their clothing and re-packing it into their bags. Mrs. Cross said there were a few teenaged boys she could enlist to help them with the move. Avery mentioned George Ray Collins, who stayed at the School Home and was always willing to help.

"And, don't overwork so much that you miss the big dance tonight," Mrs. Cross reminded them. "You said you were going to be there, and so you are," she reminded Amelia, who had not thought of folk dancing this day.

"It did slip my mind—"

Somewhere in her heart she had hoped to be let off this duty.

"Oh, we'll be there," Avery said. "You're going to enjoy it, Amelia—much more than you think."

Avery went to the School Home to start her packing and to see if George Ray was available to help with the move the next afternoon, and then joined Amelia for a walk to their new home. The friendly wood-frame houses seemed to smile at them as they walked together, two brilliant young women beginning an adventure together.

Mr. Bradley was home, as he had said, and he was waiting for them with two sets of keys. They walked through his house, which smelled of coffee and cats, and sat at the kitchen table where they gave him a money order for their deposit and first month's rent on their house.

"It's all yours, ladies!" he said, and told them that if anything needed fixing he would help.

Amelia could hardly wait to move in and she looked forward to the life in her cottage. The two young women walked the path that joined the two houses and unlocked the back door to their new home. They wandered the rooms, exclaiming at the views everywhere, and then went upstairs where two bedrooms shared the bathroom.

"Avery—there's something missing here," Amelia said from the bathroom.

Avery squeezed into the room with her.

"A bathtub?"

"I don't see one, do you?"

"At least there's a toilet!"

"Well, yes, there's that…"

They dissolved in giggles, finally finding a copper pan that looked about the size of a washtub. There was a drain in the floor.

"Well, that's something," Amelia said. "Look, there is always the bay if we need a full complement of water—"

"Sure, that's what most of the locals use," Avery said. "Everybody bathes in the bay. We won't be alone out there."

Amelia wanted to ask about the nudist camp, but decided to let the matter rest for now. She was not averse to bathing in the bay, and the little pan would do for mid-week splashes. They were not to be dissuaded in their love for their own place, and both were quite giddy as they made their way back to ready themselves for the folk dance party.

Avery said that she had caught up with George Ray and he said he could find a friend or two to help them move their things.

"He's an extremely helpful kid, one of Mrs. Johnson's 'almost' adopted children. She befriends the needy children in town, and he's been one of hers since he was just a tyke stealing watermelons, apparently. He was a problem child, but a few years under her wing and he's now a model citizen."

"Marvelous," said Amelia.

"See you in a couple of hours—don't be late now! Everybody who is anybody will be there. Oh—and no matter what you're wearing, wear tennis shoes. They are *de rigueur* in Fairhope for folk dancing."

"Tennis shoes? With socks?"

"Of course with socks! You don't want to get blisters, do you?"

"I'm not even sure I want to dance!"

"Got no choice about that—everybody dances in Fairhope!"

Thirteen

AMELIA CHOSE A frock that wasn't fussy or pretentious, she thought. A plain middy-look that was really a dress, although it appeared to be two pieces. Simple pearl earrings, and white tennis shoes with socks. She felt a bit foolish when she descended the stairs.

When she got to the parlor Captain and Mrs. Cross were there, already decked out in casual dance attire, including white tennis shoes with socks. Down the steps came Maxwell Taylor. He had on his same beige slacks, a white shirt—and tennis shoes with socks.

"Shall we go together?" Max said.

"Why not?" Captain Cross said. "Might as well arrive early and get a good place."

Women were setting out food when they arrived in Comings Hall. Most of the dishes contained salads, bread, and a few plates of ham and beans. People brought their own plates and utensils from home, and most contributed to the array of food. A young lady was warming up the piano with rambunctious music, and Esther, Mrs. Johnson's niece and secretary, was chatting with her. Amelia had not noticed before that Esther was in maternity clothes now. She was standing near a short, agile man who must have been her husband. She smiled at Amelia and signaled for her to join them.

"This is my husband, Paul," she said. "He is one of the folk dance teachers."

"A good man to know," said Amelia.

"Paul, this is Amelia King, who will be teaching First Life this year," Esther said.

Paul Frederick made his greeting brief and then went on talking with the piano player. "I want to start with easy dances tonight," he said, "But the students will do a short demonstration of some of the things Mr. Rabold has taught us after the dance has been going on a while."

"After we break for dinner?"

"Good idea," Paul said.

The large hall was filling up fast. Amelia loved its high ceilings with exposed rafters, and noted a few children climbing up there like monkeys, agile and unafraid.

Marietta Johnson entered the room. If possible, she was more energetic and downright joyful than ever as she circulated and spoke to everybody who was there, winding up at the piano and saying to Amelia,

"How are you today, young lady? I hear you've found a home!"

Avery had obviously wasted no time spreading the word.

"Yes—it's a dear little place! I'm sure Avery and I are going to love it. So close to the beach, with beautiful views—"

"I think I know the cottage. Yes, it's charming. I'm sure you two will have great times there," Mrs. Johnson said, and then she went to Paul Frederick's side and took him a few steps away, obviously discussing the evening's program.

"My name is Piney!" said the piano player. "You must be Amelia King—so glad to meet you!"

Piney had an open, happy face, elongated, with a fine long nose and a ready smile. She played as if she loved nothing more than hitting those piano keys and laughing with the people who surrounded her. Amelia knew at once that she wanted to get to know her better.

"I'm only playing for the first dances," Piney said. "Augusta will play after my break—and I'll get to dance!"

"I wish I could share your enthusiasm for folk dancing," Amelia said.

"Oh, when you learn to do it, you'll love it," Piney said. "It's easy."

Amelia surveyed the room and saw many faces she recognized. The tall white-haired man who hugged her the evening before at the pier was talking with Avery. Max was in conversation with a couple of teenaged boys, George Ray and Wallace Hodges, whom she had been introduced to on her first visit, working on the hall when it was still under construction. It looked as if the whole town had turned out, from little ones to the elders. Mrs. Comings was arranging bowls and platters of food on a long table, and children ran freely in the hall. Some women even had babies in arms.

"What a brilliant turnout," said E.B. Gaston as he stepped up on the stage. "So glad to see old friends and new ones here! I've been asked to say a few words in introduction of Marietta Johnson—"

As soon as he said her name, the room swelled with applause, stomping, and even whoops of joy.

"Now, that's enough, friends," Mr. Gaston went on, signalling by waving his hands downward that they should quiet down. "This is not a night for speeches anyway. I'm here to present the lady who clearly needs no introduction—Marietta Johnson!"

Mrs. Johnson was already beside him on the stage.

"Thank you all for coming," she said. "I'm happy to see you and hope you're as excited about the beginning of a new school year as I am." There was applause at this remark, which Amelia found a bit astonishing. Never had she been in a community so truly excited about the start of school. "I'm glad to take this opportunity to announce that Charles Rabold, the eminent musicologist and expert on the folk dances of England, is going to join us here in Fairhope—" This was met with much applause.

"Before the end of the year—to be on the faculty, teaching folk dancing to the students in junior high and high school. So tonight we need to warm up, with the help of Mr. Frederick, who has worked with Mr. Rabold at our facility in Connecticut. But as Mr. Gaston said, this isn't a night for a speech, even from me. I just wanted to say welcome to you all. This is a night for dancing!"

Amelia understood the importance of the announcement in a school that in many ways revolved around folk dancing. She had not heard of Charles Rabold—the name sounded like the word "rainbow" to her, a mistake that would be made by generations to come in Fairhope. But it would not be long before she knew Charles Rabold well.

As soon as Mrs. Johnson made the announcement, there was thunderous applause again, and, as if prepared for it, Piney began to bang out a happy tune on the piano and Mr. Frederick started to call out: "Choose partners for a nice easy one. Children and old-timers and everybody in between—join in! 'If All the World Were Paper'!"

It sounded like a command performance, so Amelia accepted when Will Hodges stepped out of the crowd and took her hand.

"This is a fun one, Miss King," he said. "We'll get you through it."

His callused hands felt rough holding hers, and she was self-conscious about her ignorance of the simple dance, but, as he said, the group was eager to share the simple steps. This dance had a song that went with it, "If all the trees were bread and cheese," that sort of thing, and by the time they had gone through it once of twice she was singing out with the rest of them.

"This is a good one for First and Second Life," Hodges said.

It was exhilarating—skipping, singing like children—and actually *with* children—and she was enjoying herself. Clearly this was a dance her First Life class would be doing!

Next, a dance called "The Black Nag" was announced. Piney played music, the demonstrators danced, then the room began dancing all at once, just as instructed, bouncing happily—even Marietta Johnson. Amelia was among the happiest. How easy folk dancing was going to be!

The last figure of this dance is called the "Hey," which both sides of the set dance in a figure eight, boys with boys and girls with girls. Avery faced Amelia and said, "Do a figure eight!" as she skipped down the set. She and the little girl understood the instructions but Amelia was flabbergasted, and tried to find her way around the floor until the music was over. To "do a figure eight," apparently, meant to weave through the other dancers forming an 8 on the floor. Some of the younger dancers were outstanding, but the activity was so much enjoyed by all that nobody got special attention for doing it well. Amelia could not help thinking that in spite of Mrs. Johnson's determination to call this an egalitarian approach to physical education, certain people were genetically inclined to excel at it.

When the dance was over everybody was laughing, and Amelia said, "What on earth were you talking about?" to Avery who said, "In the first place, you weren't doing a figure eight!"

"I certainly wasn't," Amelia said.

"With a little work, that one will be wonderful," Mr. Frederick said. Let's take a break and talk it over, then we'll try it again."

He asked if anybody needed special help, and Amelia was among the large crowd of newcomers who practically swamped him. In ten minutes he had walked them through the unknown parts of the dance and they all emerged feeling like they knew something.

"That was great, people," Mr. Frederick said. "Now let's have something to eat. Don't overeat; it isn't good to dance on a full stomach!"

The crowd converged on the tables of food like locusts. Immediately after heaping their plates they milled about, talking. The white-haired man introduced himself as Julian Crane, teacher of high school history and English, and Avery was talking with Will Hodges.

"Having fun?" said Max Taylor behind her, and Amelia turned to him.

"I certainly am! I can't believe I never knew about this before."

"Folk dancing? Ah, folk dancing and organic education are the hope of the world," Max said, spooning potato salad onto his plate. He gave her a sidelong glance.

"That may be a stretch, Mr. Taylor," she said.

"No, I've discussed both with Mrs. Johnson, and she knows, you know. She is in the camp that believes folk dancing should replace ballroom dancing and all that other vulgar gyrating that young people like today. If they folk danced, on the other hand—"

"Really, Max!" Amelia couldn't tell for sure if he was kidding or not.

"No, listen. If they all folk danced, we could do away with the Fish-Walk and the Turkey Trot tomorrow!"

"And replace them with "The Black Nag!" she said, incredulous, but laughing.

"I'll make a note next time I'm in Philadelphia," Amelia said. "If there is a craze for folk dancing, and ballroom dancing becomes a fading fad, we'll know that Fairhope has won the battle!"

After the meal Mr. Frederick introduced a special treat, a demonstration of a Morris dance by two of the high school boys. This dance, "Jockey to the Fair," was a two-man challenge dance of jumps, kneels, lunges and hops, with both the boys wearing white handkerchiefs tied to their fingers. One boy did the complex steps, then stopped while the other did the same dance moves. Both boys were very accomplished, and watching this "challenge" was quite breathtaking and beautiful.

Everybody applauded.

"By the end of the hour, you'll all be dancing like that," Mr. Frederick said, and the crowd laughed.

After this brief exposure to folk dancing, Amelia could see why it was central to both Fairhope and the school. It was good exercise, to be sure, and the students at the school took it seriously and certainly excelled in the coordination and grace it required. Having to dance herself now, Amelia had seen it was a mental activity as well as physical one—learning steps and figures, thinking ahead, and holding hands in friendship all the while. It was structured and wholesome, and it even related to the cultures it represented.

The party came to a close with the first verse and chorus of "Fairhope," the song that reverberated through town at the drop of any hat. Strains of the chorus—about the roses blooming and the waters blue—wafted in the air as she, the Crosses, and Max Taylor began their stroll to The Gables, just a bit weary but happy at the same time. Max walked beside her, feeling his heart throbbing in his chest.

Luther Beagle lurked on the corner just outside the hall, drinking from a clear bottle what appeared to be the home brew known in the South as moonshine whiskey. Alcohol was strictly illegal in Alabama as it was in every state, but this did not stop those determined to find a bottle, even in remote reformist enclaves.

The air was cooler tonight, promising crisp days to come. Tomorrow she and Avery would move to their new home.

Fourteen

I T WAS A bracing, sunshiny day. Amelia would learn fall came gently and late in the deep South, not with the blazing color of trees against the bright royal blue of sky, as in the Northeast, and not in October as she was accustomed to. By the end of November in Fairhope you could definitely call it fall, but the weather was only occasionally chilly and most of the trees didn't turn. Fairhope was a land of evergreens. Today, the second day of October, was clear, bright, and not really hot, although it would be in the 80s before the end of the day. And it was sure to feel hot with all the moving she would do.

Avery showed up with two boys. Joe Cyrus, the boy from the trolley on Amelia's first day, carried her large trunk with the help of George Ray, Amelia felt a jolt of joy and excitement. Avery carried two suitcases herself.

"We decided to stop here first since it's on our way," Avery said.

"I'll take one of my suitcases and go with you!" Amelia said, unable to contain her excitement.

"Well, I'm not lugging that trunk by myself," Max said, but I can help with some of the bags. This is going to take at least one more trip." To Avery he said, "Do you have anything more?"

She didn't, but Amelia had two suitcases as well. She carried one, and Max carried one of hers and one of Avery's all the way to the Bayview house.

Max had brought his friend Jim Holloway, who taught shop and music at the school. Jim was tall and had a distinctly Southern accent, and seemed to be fond of telling tale tales and jokes. Avery seemed as happy as Amelia to be getting into their cottage.

"It's an old house," Avery announced. "You'll see when we get there."

"And the old need love to survive," Amelia added.

"And the young need strong backs," Max said.

The group saw the wooden steps leading to the bay.

"Let's leave the bags on the bluff and go to the beach," Jim said. "I feel like swimmin' nekkid."

The boys laughed.

"Not today, at least not yet today," said Avery. There was a large oak with a low-lying limb hardly above the ground. A teenage girl lounged on the limb reading a book. She looked up and saw the group approach.

"Hey, Miss Buchanan, Mr. Taylor," she said and looked back down at her book.

"Hi, Georgia," Joe said to the girl.

"That's where I'd like to be right now," said Max. "Reading a good book up in a tree."

"You can do that when we finish," Amelia said.

"Slave driver," Max said. "We all should be up in trees, reading."

"Maybe I'd like to be up in a tree," said George Ray. "But I prob'ly wouldn't have a book with me."

They arrived at the house.

"So is this your 'Blue Heaven'?" Max asked.

"It is *not* blue," said Avery.

"It's lichen colored!" said Amelia.

"Oh, I should have known that—lichen colored! You don't find many lichen colored houses."

"Lichen covered?" said Joe, looking surprised. They all laughed.

"Colored, colored—lichen *colored*," Max said. "It remains to be seen when it will be lichen *covered!* There may come a time."

"My room is upstairs, the one on the right," said Avery. The little room had a lumpy looking bed in it and a chest of drawers. A painted chifferobe for her hanging things stood against the wall.

The boys put the trunk on the floor just inside the door and Avery and Jim Holloway put her suitcases on the bed. Amelia went straight upstairs her room, putting one of her suitcases down on her bed. Max stepped in the doorway and put the other suitcase on the floor.

"All right, men!" he said. "Back to the Gables for the rest of Miss King's things!" Amelia and Avery stayed in the house and unpacked as they waited.

Amelia had claimed the room that had an actual closet because she had brought more clothes than Avery. There was a little wardrobe in the other bedroom that Avery thought would be fine for herself. She unpacked the suitcases, including the books Mrs. Johnson had told her to read, putting them on top of the chest of drawers.

"Home at last!" she said.

"There's no place like home!" called Avery from her room.

"Home is where the heart is!"

"Be it ever so humble—" said Avery.

"You tried that one."

"The chorus, not the verse. How about 'Fairhope, Down by the Waters Blue'?" Avery asked. She burst into the refrain, "Down where the roses are bloo-oom-ing..."

"Please, not now. I'm already a little tired of that one."

"Don't let Aunt Mettie hear you say that," Avery said. "Blasphemy!"

"Oh, it's sweet, I agree. And so beautiful to have a town song—"

There was a brief pause.

"But?" Avery stuck her head in the door.

"Well, you know," said Amelia.

"A little goes a long way?"

"I would say so, yes. But I haven't gotten my fill of Fairhope yet."

"Let's take those stairs to the beach as soon as the boys get here with the rest of your things," Avery said.

"I can hardly wait!" Amelia said.

Max, Jim, Joe, and George Ray soon appeared and hauled the heavy trunk up the stairs. Mrs. Cross had packed a picnic basket for Amelia and Avery for their first night in the new house.

"No doubt full of sweaters, coats, and blankets!" Max said as he struggled to help the boys with the trunk.

"More than I'll need, I'm sure," said Amelia.

She and Avery had agreed to give each of the boys a dollar for their work, but were stumped about what to offer Max and Jim.

"Don't mind us," Max said as he saw the women giving dollar bills to the boys. "Jim and I expect you to have us over for dinner a time or two until we work this out."

They shook hands with the boys and with Jim, bade them goodbye, and each gave Max a quick hug.

"Ah, on second thought, that's almost as good as a free dinner," he said, and walked down the lane with Jim, Joe and George Ray.

"Now let's see what we can find on the beach," Amelia said. "Unpacking can wait."

"And grocery shopping."

Amelia had almost forgotten about grocery shopping. They were neophytes at independence, and had a lot to learn. A look at their new neighborhood topped their list of priorities for the day.

They took their picnic down the wooden stairs and strolled the beach for almost an hour, sitting on one of the unoccupied piers to eat their supper. They left a sandwich for breakfast. Their light repast dispatched, they walked down the beach, picking up pieces of driftwood and watching the sun tinge the sky with red and orange. They shared a joy at their new reality—the opportunity of seeing such glorious sunsets every day, their sweet new home, all the parties they'd give, the children they'd soon be teaching, and the wealth of interesting people at every nook and cranny of Fairhope.

"I feel like I've lived here forever," Amelia said.

"I hope Fairhope lives forever," Avery said softly. There was a pause while they listened to the crickets and tree frogs. "I wonder what will become of us all."

After seeing the sun do its swift dip into the bay, they walked up the steps—counting sixty of them—and up the dirt road which was called Bayview Avenue to their lichen colored house. Fireflies flashed their tiny flickers among the trees and there was enough moonlight to cast a glow on everything.

❧

The house would provide Amelia and Avery with many adventures. After the first night they realized the beds had mattresses made for heavy sleepers. Amelia's was lumpy and uneven, but she soon learned to sleep on the lumps in such a way that they were tamed, and after a few nights and she was able to manage a full night of sleep.

Avery's lumpy mattress, on the other hand, caused her to steer a varying course through the night. After a brief survey of topographical conditions on its surface, she arranged herself in a northeast and southwesterly direction bounded on either side, she said, surrounded by what she termed "lumps of high altitude." Her description of this constant battle was the highlight of many of their parties and much of her conversation about the house.

One of the first things the two young teachers did after moving into the house and securing groceries was to descend the steps to the beach with a large wooden basket. They were off to collect driftwood for a fire and making a meal.

The abundance of firewood on the beach astonished them. They could easily make fires with it. They were to make such fires on the bluff overlooking the beach many times to come at sunset with the peaceful vista at hand. They loved the total experience of these campfires, cooking light suppers there and talking as the twilight rose around them, bringing out the flash of fireflies and the emergence of stars. They would go in when real dark set in and mosquitoes arrived in numbers to disturb their serenity. The smoke kept insects off for a time and the girls refused to acknowledge they were being bitten until they got inside and counted respective welts.

"The ability to make a fire here takes no skill more than knowing how to strike a match," according to Avery, playing authority. "Pitch pine—even wet—burns with a quick flame."

The redolent odor of pine burning, the sputter and bubbling of the resin as it burned out of the log, the delicate green flame of the driftwood, the white fingers of fire around the oak backlog—these smells. sounds, and images formed the background for many evenings to come, and provided Amelia with an unforgettable vignette in her collection of memories of life in Fairhope.

The two began having parties right away. A few days after their arrival, they had Max over for a dinner they actually cooked for him, a pot of Boston-style baked beans and some fresh lettuce and tomatoes they had bought from a truck just on the edge of town. They didn't try to bake the beans, having only the big oil stove and no real knowledge of how to use its oven, but they soaked some navy beans the night before and simmered them in a sauce that had molasses and ketchup in it and at least looked like the genuine article. Max was mightily impressed with this feat in the kitchen, or at least he said he was.

"We have to have a party," Maxwell said to them at the end of the evening. "Everybody can bring his own bacon and we'll have a fire on the beach…"

This sounded like such a wonderful idea that Avery and Amelia took to it right away. They began making a guest list and deciding what to do.

"Not a formal affair," Amelia said.

"Certainly not! This house would never countenance such a thing," Avery added. "Come as you are and bring your own bacon!"

The first of their get-togethers was a bonfire on the beach, with Jim bringing the art teacher Sarah Kitwell, with whom he was romantically involved. Sarah was a beauty, but she looked for arguments with almost everybody about almost everything. Hal and Martha Etheridge came, and Piney Gaston and her husband James, the son of E.B. Piney and James brought their baby Jimmy, who slept the whole time in a basket. Everybody brought some food to cook on the fire. They sat on driftwood logs on the sand to watch the fire die down, its light fade and turn to embers. By then it was dark and the stars were out above them. It was so relaxing, hearing the waves of bay gently fall one by one against the sand, watching the fire burn slowly down, and talking easily of many things. Amelia told them all about the Chapman family, and Avery revealed her first meeting with Mrs. Johnson at the teacher training program held in Greenwich, Connecticut.

"I was in awe of her after the first class," Avery said. "I was wearing a white skirt and shirtwaist, with a purple scarf at the neck, quite stylish, I thought.

"That afternoon Mrs. Johnson came up behind me and said, 'Where'd you get that outfit?' She scared the life out of me."

"And?" Piney asked.

"I told her. I got it in Boston."

"'Looks cute!' she said. "I felt wonderful after that. I loved her from that moment on—and after that I loved the outfit even more!"

They all had a few stories about Mrs. Johnson. Piney and James called her Aunt Mettie, and the other asked what it took to be allowed to do that.

"Oh, everybody pretty much calls her that," James said. "I think she loves it."

"I'm not ready for it," Amelia said. "I'm sure when the time comes I'll know it."

"You seen them little critters flyin' around here with lights on 'em at night, Amelia?" Jim Holloway said, out of the blue.

"Fireflies," Amelia said, and gave him a questioning look.

"Some call 'em that. Some call 'em lightning bugs," Jim said. "They's parts o' Kentucky where they call 'em moondust."

"Why is that?" Max asked, knowing his friend was about to spin a yarn.

"I was thinkin' somebody might ask that," Jim said, his mountain accent thickening as he warmed to the tale.

"It started in the hills years ago," he said. "There 'uz this widder woe-mn with three chilren she had to keer for. She had ta move 'em 'round the valley when the weather got too cold or the storms came. She had nine cats that had all lost their tails, and her chilren didn't have food for to eat. She cried for help after years o' this, and the moon decided to help her out.

"'Widder Staples,' the moon said—the moon knowed her name—'There be a place jes' over that thar hill whar thar h'aint too much wind nor too much nair too little undergrowth.'

159

"Ole moon gives her a bag o' moondust with which to git the tails back from a ugly ole witch who had taken the tails from the cats and sewed 'em up in the hem a her petticoats. Moon tells the widder Staples to throw moondust at the witch and cut the cats' tails out of the petticoats while she be looking the other way.

"Widder done as she was told, the old witch fainted dead away, and Widder Staples and her chilren and her cats found they had broke the spell for good. They moved to the clear side a the hill and played in the flowers there til they was all growed up.

"Even the moondust was fruitful and multiplied and filled the air with specks of the moon forever after."

"Aw," said James Gaston. "So that's how those little bugs got their lights."

"On that note, I'm ready to take my little light home," Sarah said.

Max and Sarah had heard the tale before, and Sarah, always ready to be the first to leave a party, stood up and brushed sand from her skirt. It was one of the many tall tales Jim Hollaway was to tell, and it would not be the last yarn he would spin at one of their parties. He knew a wealth stories from the Kentucky mountains—tales of moonshiners, revenue officers, and magical animals of all kinds. He and Piney often discussed music at these parties, both of them being big fans of Wolfgang Amadeus Mozart.

Max hung on Jim's stories, and often added one of his own—a yarn by Mark Twain or Ambrose Bierce. His rendition of "The Celebrated Jumping Frog of Calaveras County" was a classic.

Sarah's temper sometimes put her at the center of arguments that might have been more for show than actual substance. Everybody let these conflicts pass by just saying, "That's Sarah." She loved to talk, but always seemed a bit on edge. Amelia sensed insecurity that might have been based on a feeling of jealousy. Sarah was very possessive of Jim, while at the same time making his life difficult. Avery said to Amelia, "It's hard not to like Sarah—until she opens her mouth."

Fifteen

Amelia started the first day of school with eager anticipation. This would be a far cry from her experience at Fernwood. She had selected a few favorite books to read to the class, and she planned to take her students outside for nature study and games.

Edna Campbell was scheduled at nine to teach some songs and simple folk dances.

Most of her class, she discovered, had been to the kindergarten just across the hall and were not the nervous, neatly combed and polished children she had seen on the first day of school all her life. They came to the class eagerly and were at ease with each other and their new teacher. The class had tables and chairs for moving about. No desks were screwed to the floor.

Amelia was in charge of three five-year-olds, 11 six-year-olds and two seven-year-olds. The five-year-olds would turn six before Christmas and all the six-year-olds would turn seven before the year was out. Amelia still thought of First Life as "first and second grades," but Mrs. Johnson insisted upon regarding the children as individuals while providing a wide array of academic options to the whole class. Many of their studies would come from the children themselves and be based on questions that came from the class.

"Good morning, everybody! I'm Miss King." Amelia smiled see the looks of anticipation on the young faces. "I'm going to call the roll. Does anybody know what that means?"

Curious looks on their faces.

Ally Etheridge, daughter of Hal and Martha, was the kind of child who never allowed a question to go unanswered.

"That means our *names*," she said.

"That's right. The roll is the name of everybody en-*roll*ed in this class." Here Amelia held the list for them to see. "I don't know your names yet, so I need you to tell me. When I call your name, say, 'Here!' and I will put a mark by your name to show that you were in school today."

She went down the roll and saw that she had full attendance. Sixteen. It would not take long to sort them out. They were all participating and they were all pretty vocal. They already loved school. It was up to Amelia to nurture that feeling.

The five- and six-year-olds would not be allowed to read. This was a hard and fast rule. Some of them, however, had already been taught by their parents, and a few others were beginning to pick up the knack of it just by memorizing the books that were read to them frequently. The challenge was to eliminate reading as a goal at this age; Mrs. Johnson's own special subject was botany, and Amelia thought she was quite correct in saying that plants and the world outside the classroom were more compelling to children of this age than words on a page. However, if they already knew how to read, so be it.

The next morning Mrs. Johnson ventured across the campus to the south end, where the kindergarten/first life class building was. Kindergarteners were wading and splashing in the shallow pool at the side of the building, with Miss Lucille and her two assistants, both teacher training students fresh out of the Organic graduating class of 1921. Amelia's class was spending recess climbing in the thicket of vines and bushes on the southwest corner of the campus. It was an exciting place to explore and play. They climbed the low-limbed trees and were already creating playhouses in the vines.

At one point Amelia was transfixed by Patsy Blalock, playing off by herself, talking out loud to the air, in conversation with people who weren't there, yet were answering her. Patsy was truly in her own world. The sight of her reminded Amelia of her days behind the closed door of her room in Hoboken at the age of five, saving her bear from the fires of hell and acting out her own psychological fear as put in place by Miss Pritchart. The similarity took her breath away, but she did not hear fierce anger in Patsy's tone as had been in her own all those years ago. Patsy played happily on her own, creating scenes with imaginary friends.

Amelia had set up a game of "Village Store" at the edge of the thicket, and, as the children grew curious, they would wander out of the bushes where their attendant assistant teachers kept a watchful eye on anyone who might venture too high in a tree, or come upon a snake or other animal. Amelia learned early Fairhope was home to a few non-poisonous snakes.

"What have we here, Miss King? A retail establishment in the forests of Arden?" Mrs. Johnson asked, beaming.

"Exactly! As they get interested, I show them the cash register and what goes in and out of it. They get another ten minutes or so in the thicket, and then we'll all play store."

The cash register was a cigar box with coins in it and a few dollar bills. The game of "Store" was designed to teach basic arithmetic and the names of the coins and their value at a real store.

"Ah—that sounds like a good idea," Mrs. Johnson said. "I like to alternate the academic with the creative. And where possible, to do the two at the same time."

Just then three boys burst from the woods and ran in the broad open space.

"Beat ya to the *tree!*" one of them shouted, and all three squealed at the top of their voices. They ran to a nearby pecan tree, all three of them slapping it, almost at the same time, and then they collapsed in feigned exhaustion onto the ground.

"That's what I like seeing," Mrs. Johnson said. "Little boys are just puppy dogs. Let them run until they can't run anymore and they fall into a heap. When they get up, they'll be interested in learning something. You can be sure of that."

Watching Mrs. Johnson with children was a revelation for Amelia; she had a way of conversing with them that made them aware she took their concerns seriously. Her intercourse with them wasn't so much adult-to-child as person-to-person. Each child felt valued and comfortable with her. Here, in her own school, exploring life with the youngest of her scholars, she was in her element.

Sixteen

From the people who attended their parties Amelia learned of other factions who vacationed or visited Fairhope. There were the physical culturists who loved the privacy of Fairhope for their nudist and physical exercise routines. You could occasionally spot families at either end of the beach, in the nude, swimming and picnicing.

Some of these people went out to the nudist camp in nearby Montrose every weekend, and some just used the bay for their baths. They were harmless, happy people, with their own ideas of how to change the world. Some had lived for a time in Bernahrr MacFadden's physical culture colony in New Jersey, or Kellogg's in Battle Creek, Michigan, the one which promoted high grain diets as the path to better living. Some came from Chicago's community of artists and writers. That contingent—a motley assortment of anti-establishmentarians who spent their free time in Chicago at a raffish club called The Dil Pickle—found Fairhope a hospitable climate for the winter.

Whatever their origins, iconoclasts and outsiders added a dimension to the already offbeat atmosphere in the village. Many were writers, some were artists and gallery owners in big cities, but in Fairhope they were on vacation from any responsibilities. A few stayed on to enroll their children in the Organic School.

In some families the wife had a different name from her husband. These women were known as "Lucy Stoners"— called so after the Feminist leader who refused to take her husband's name after marriage—but some of them were living together without benefit of marriage license, even though they had children. This might have caused something of a scandal in other communities, but was hardly an issue here. If E.B. Gaston knew of these gadflies, he was not bothered by them.

Sometimes Mercedes Morehead came to Amelia and Avery's parties. She was always busy, her hands fluttering, always looking elegant no matter how casually she was dressed. She tended to don capes and medieval looking hats—and she managed to look grand when just in her riding jodphurs and a classic white button down shirt. She spoke with Jim Holloway and Piney of classical music, of trips to Europe, and was always eager to get into matters of philosophy. Amelia was somewhat in awe of her at first, but found her to be very likable and down to earth. She was a practical woman and a lover of animals. She followed her heart, and her presence was a force field in Fairhope.

Margaret Fisher, who wore men's clothes, and her partner Jane Whitlock, who sometimes did, came several times. They always brought casseroles, which were Jane's specialty and certainly added dimension to the meals, usually nothing more than weiners or bacon on rolls. Margaret and Jane made their own wine and occasionally brought a bottle. Margaret Fisher and Jane Whitlock were so omnipresent in Fairhope, and always together, that they were often referred to in singular, as "Fishlock."

One night two guests from the Philadelphia area were in town, the artist Wharton Esherick and his friend Sherwood. Esherick had taught in the school the previous year, with his wife, who had come to Fairhope to learn from Mrs. Johnson. He and Sherwood, who had lived in Fairhope the previous year as well, had no trouble getting invited to Avery and Amelia's get-together. The two men brought wine with them, and enjoyed drinking most of it themselves. Sherwood was Sherwood Anderson, a writer who would later go on to achieve fame, but when he joined Amelia and Avery that night he was just another seeker of the truth around a Fairhope campfire.

Sarah Kitwell was on fire herself that night, eager to engage Esherick in a debate about the school. She had worked with him teaching at the school the previous year and was less happy than ever now with the school's approach to art.

"I'm not sure all children should be required to be artists," she said, beginning a war of words that went on for most of the night. "Some of them have no talent for it—and even less interest."

"I talked that over with Mrs. Johnson," Esherick said. "She allowed me to teach art as I saw fit, as long as the students were not put in competition against each other."

"That's just it," Sarah said. "I think competition is at the crux of learning!"

All the assembled teachers and parents cried out at that. They spoke at once, as if the voice of Organic education—stating that learning must be based upon each child competing only with his own best work.

"But there is good art and bad art," Sarah insisted.

"There is good and bad art, but that is not what this school is about," Amelia shot back. Her most tender nerve had been touched. "This school is about exposing every student to everything he wants to learn, and letting him find his own reward in doing it well."

Amelia sensed unhappiness in Sarah, a smoldering, unaddressed anger with everything life offered, the good as well as the bad. Probably the simple fact of the matter was that she was teaching in the wrong place. She made Jim Holloway's life very uncomfortable with her demands, and the way she set herself up against people exacerbated her bad humor.

The group then hashed out the value of Organic education, of art education, of the abilities and nature of children. It was a broad and lively discussion, but it was clear the topic would not be exhausted in one evening. Esherick told of his days teaching at the school, when he had had an interest in integrating the Negroes of town into the school.

"This was met with unqualified negativity," he said. "I was told that the town was not ready for it."

"What do they have against the blacks?" Sarah, from Chicago, asked.

"I had many discussions with Mrs. Johnson about it," Esherick volunteered. "She does not seem to be a racist, but she complies with the conventional wisdom of the other town fathers," he said. "That is, she felt that it would stir up too much controversy to engage the black community in school activities. I wanted to teach them art, and Mrs. Johnson said I could do so—only after school hours, off campus, and if I kept it quiet."

"And did you?" asked Maxwell Taylor.

"Damned right I did."

This reminded Amelia what she had observed of blacks in Fairhope. She thought of the look on the face of Sadie, the colored girl at The Gables, whose downcast eyes and discomfort with conversation with guests at the hotel appeared to hide a deeper hurt.

"The Negroes have to abide by a curfew," Avery said.

This was the first time Amelia had heard of the custom.

"They must be in their homes, on the other side of the gully, by sunset every day."

Amelia felt a shudder. She had heard of Jim Crow laws in the South, and had noted there was a very small black population in Fairhope, but had no idea this idealistic enclave had such regressive laws.

Jim Gaston cut in.

"My father and the other founders didn't think it would help the cause of single tax if the community integrated the black population into the Colony. The memory of the Civil War was still fresh in the minds of the locals in the area in 1895. It was the purpose of the Fair Hope Industrial Association to establish a single tax demonstration and they focused on that, however they might have felt about the treatment of Negroes in the South. Nobody could think they were unaware of the situation or unsympathetic to the Negro population."

Evidently, from the response to that remark, many in town did think the Colony should have also worked for the equality of blacks, but the people at the party were not of one mind on this—or any other—subject, on this night. They enjoyed taking both sides on all topics and relished the thrill of disagreement.

Amelia was disturbed at the information about the curfew. She didn't want to think about it, but she was beginning to see a dark side of this picture-perfect community.

Julian Crane, the resident Bolshevik, could not let the evening go by without a challenge to the single tax theory.

"The boys from Iowa—" his term for the Fairhope founders who did come, for the most part, from Iowa— "didn't go far enough when they set up shop here. They had every intention of changing the world, but how could they think just one remote colony espousing the principle of a single tax on property would change the world? What is needed is what the Russians went through—a complete revolution!"

Here he, Jim and Piney Gaston, and others wrangled about whether the single tax theory was revolutionary enough. One side loved it and saw it as the wave of the future—paying only one tax to the colony, for all practical purposes a rent for use of land on which to build a house.

"It is a winning proposition for all," Hal Etheridge said. "The town gets enough revenue to provide basic services, and the colonists get the use of the land for 99 years, which should be long enough!"

Crane felt that citizens should share everything and that government should provide more than basic services. When he got on his soapbox it was clear that he would one day leave Fairhope and move to Russia, where he expected to find his ideal life.

"You know what I think?" Max asked.

"A rhetorical question," commented Julian Crane.

"I think we all come to Fairhope looking for something, all of us different things."

"I think we're all figments in the imagination of E.B. Gaston," Hal said.

"No—of Marietta Johnson," Amelia put in.

"Possibly Fairhope is a figment of all our imaginations," Max said. "It's a mirage."

"It's a place people come to find themselves," Avery said.

"And then they leave," said Piney, ruefully, looking as if she had known all too many interesting people who come to find paradise, gave Fairhope a try, and then had moved away.

Silence descended as all of them contemplated different things. They all turned over in their minds the various quests that had brought them here. Amelia told them she thought she had come to the peaceable kingdom of Edward Hicks' paintings but was finding it not what she had expected.

"It's better, as a matter of fact," she said. "It's more human and more earthy than I had thought Utopia would be. I'm finding a personal peace, but there are some lions around! And they are not the solemn, stately lions of Edward Hicks' peaceable kingdom paintings."

"We roar," said Julian. "But we seldom bite."

She pushed aside the notion that he might not be right about this.

The group always lingered, reluctant to leave these parties, and on the night Wharton and Sherwood joined them Amelia and Avery walked down the path with their guests and stopped by the gully to get their breath of the heady, strong fragrance of night-blooming jasmine.

"Nothing like that smell," Esherick said.

"What is that anyway?" Sherwood asked, looking confused and clearly feeling the wine. "Flowers?"

"Something Southern, I would say," his friend answered.

The two of them laughed as if this was the most brilliant wit they had ever heard.

"You two!" said Piney Gaston, and she and James put their arms around their shoulders to lead them back to The Gables, where they were staying. Little Jimmy had learned to sleep through grownup laughter and talk, and Piney shifted his basket to her left hand while her right helped steady Wharton Esherick.

"We'll take care of them," Piney said to Amelia, "And thank you for another wonderful evening."

"Yes, indeed," said her husband, with an arm around Sherwood Anderson's shoulders, leading him and his friend down the lane.

A few clouds gathered in the sky, but the moon was bright, casting glow over the neighborhood as the group broke up and Amelia and Avery ambled home, hearing raucous laughter from the group going down the lane in the other direction, toward The Gables. It was more humid than usual that night; Piney and Jim said that was a sure sign of upcoming rain.

As they got into the cottage they heard ominous rustling from every room. They had come to know that this came from their archenemies in the house, the large chocolate-colored cockroaches that had lived there for generations and apparently needed only a little food in the kitchen to awaken them into action. When the house was gone dark and quiet, the little monsters stirred, with total abandon and the apparent freedom of primogeniture.

These were not the frail, pale insects the young women had occasionally encountered in cities in the Northeast, mincing along slippery kitchen sinks in otherwise spotless apartments. This big, dark creature was his sturdier country relative who had not felt the ravages of an effete civilization. He lived in wood, roamed in sand and wandered into kitchens only when baited by food.

Amelia and Avery took the whooshing rustle which flooded the house as a signal to arms, and made battle with their foes, the offending cockroaches, in a whirl of determination and merriment. Avery's weapon was a pancake turner, which she found in a drawer, and Amelia's—a long-handled scrubbing brush. Like all warriors in the heat of action they never paused to consider justice or the rights of small bodies for self-determination. They proclaimed themselves loyal patriots, protecting women and children and acting as the chosen committee of the Almighty. It would not do to hesitate.

The valiant schoolteachers, temporarily transformed, waged war madly for several thudding minutes, cleaned up the battlefield, and collapsed in laughter on the lumpy, threadbare furniture of their adopted home, and then put away their battle equipment and went to bed.

How effective their attempts at pest control were was a moot point, as the opposing troops, although depleted, always rose again at the next opportunity in numbers that were still alarming.

A gentle shower that night softly lulled the town to slumber, but when the teachers awoke Amelia noted puddles dotting the floors throughout the house. She and Avery discussed it in the morning, and concluded it was a one-time occurrence and the puddles would be dried out and not return any time soon. But the first heavy rain, some time in the next few weeks, was to prove them wrong.

Amelia awoke one night to find rainwater drenching one side of the bed. She leaped out to move it, only to hear a steady drip on her pillow. She leaped from her bed and ran into Avery's room for help. The two of them spent most of the night setting up pans and bowls to catch the rain, which had somehow found its way through a leak in Avery's bedroom floor straight to the kitchen. They found it necessary to set up a temporary shelter over the oil stove, using a piece of canvas they found on the back porch.

After the first heavy rainstorm they named the house "The Sieve," and vowed to get Mr. Bradley to repair the roof. Apparently engaged in other projects, he did not do so at once, so they learned how to cope with the leaky eccentricities of the cottage; how to tangle with the infestation of their enemies in battle, and how to accept the vicissitudes as well as the enchantment of their chosen home. The two were enduring interruptions in their creature comforts together almost to the point of learning to enjoy them. Amelia saw how much sheer fun it was to have a companion to laugh with when things went wrong.

One afternoon after work when Amelia was home alone, reading, Sam Bradley appeared. He had with him a man Amelia didn't know, but one she had seen around town, the odd tow-headed man with the curious half-smile on his face. She had first seen him on that afternoon of her job interview with Mrs. Johnson, doing some work in a dark corner at the new community hall.

"This is Curry Cumbie, who's gonna help me with the roof," Sam said.

Amelia managed a smile, as she was genuinely glad someone was going to take care of the sieve-like properties of the house, perhaps before the next rain.

"How do you do, Mr. Cumbie," she said, and he just said, "Ma'am," and nodded his head.

She couldn't get past feeling there was something dangerous about this Cumbie. In Philadelphia or Hoboken, she had seen such men, men whose menace smoldered just below the surface, lurking in marginal neighborhoods when she chanced off the main, well-lit streets. There was a roughness about him, like a criminal—one that a well-bred girl was taught to shun on sight. She wanted to be modern and to accept him because he was in Fairhope, but she couldn't. His eyes looked hollow and ringed with the dark circles of a person deprived of sleep. The shadows on his face intensified the pale blue of his eyes. Incongruously with his shady, untrustworthy look, he had a woman's lips, curled up at the corners and a distant, distracted look as his eyes avoided hers.

The men said they would be working in the morning, and then they left.

Amelia tried to describe Curry Cumbie to Avery, but it was hard to put in words how the benign look on his face emphasized a sense of danger about him. She didn't know if she was imagining things. But it was so unusual to meet someone here with a dark side that she couldn't help but read some meaning into her instinctive reaction.

"He has pale blue eyes, and lips that look like a smile—curled up at the corners—"

"What could be bad?" Avery said.

"Oh, I don't know. There's just something about him." Amelia shrugged and decided she was being silly.

"All he's going to do is patch the roof!" Avery reminded her. And it was true, Amelia knew. He posed no danger at all. It was just a feeling she had.

Seventeen

Living in Fairhope again was not all that different for them from being with Curtis and Lou Ellen, but Ernestine Cumbie kept hoping it would change Curry. She was glad to be in walking distance to the School Home, where she worked five mornings a week now. Curry got jobs at the lumber mill and helping Will Hodges with handyman work. She was pleased he was learning electricity, as they both thought it might be the kind of thing more and more people would need and knowing about it might provide more steady work for him.

But his mood was not really any better than it had been six months before when they first moved back. He had always been one to mistrust people and to feel put upon that he couldn't get ahead. Some people, she thought, must just be born to argue with life itself, and to point a finger at others when things go wrong. Curry never enjoyed it much when things were all right. He was even moodier and meaner now that they were away from Curtis and he complained about Fairhope just about all the time. Most nights he did his drinking at somebody else's house and she had a little peace at home.

They were able to earn enough between them to pay $500 for the house on Single Tax Colony land and pay the yearly rent to the colony. It wasn't much more than a shack, really, but it had a bedroom and a little bit of yard at the back. She and Curry had planted some collards and squash and they had a few chickens too. In some ways she would rather be with Curtis and Lou Ellen and not just Curry, but it was good to be in Fairhope proper and be closer to things. Being alone with Curry all the time was like living life walking on eggs and hoping the shells wouldn't break. With Lou Ellen to talk to every day at least she had some relief.

She was at the School Home Monday through Thursday from seven in the morning until two, helping with breakfast and then doing some cleaning. She worked for Mrs. Myhers, whom everybody called "Auntie Co," and some days Ivy, the colored girl, came in. Ernestine had no problem with Negroes as long as they stayed in their place, and Ivy was quiet and a very good worker. Curry hated them all and didn't even like that she had to work in the same place with one, but he knew they were a fact of life in the South and usually he kept his mouth shut.

After the breakfast dishes were done, her job was to clean the big room in the School Home. That meant dusting and sweeping it out every day and mopping every other day, and helping in the kitchen before and after dinner and getting everything ready for supper before she left for home.

Once in a while Ernestine would see Miss Esther, who would soon have her baby, working for Mrs. Johnson, and some days she would see Mrs. Johnson go into her office. There was always a lot going on at the School Home, with the boarding students and the work in Mrs. Johnson's office. The boarders were required to keep their own rooms clean and to help out in the kitchen and with chores. Classes in cooking were held in the kitchen for the high school students, boys and girls alike, twice a week.

Ernestine had never thought of boys or men doing any cooking or housework, but that was part of the program at this school. When she told Curry about it, he snorted so loud it startled her. But deep down she didn't see anything wrong with it and thought it might even be a good idea. Some of the boys and even some girls made furniture which was used in the School Home. It was a nice place, real homey, and the boarders on the whole were pretty good kids, although some were snobby and some deserved nothing so much as a spanking. She was aware they were not likely to get one here.

More often than not Mrs. Johnson was out of town, making talks to schools and teachers all across America about her ideas of education. Ernestine and Curry could not believe that anybody would take Mrs. Johnson's school seriously after what had happened to Alice Ann. Even though they sympathized with her and Curry, everybody sided with Mrs. Johnson.

After the accident there had been no more school trips to the gully, but the very idea of learning outside a schoolroom still made Curry mad, and he thought everybody would agree. Alice Ann's death should have been proof. But as Ernestine saw it, the school still flowed with nice people—smart people even—who Curry said should have been able to see what was right before their eyes. Letting kids run wild was dangerous. He looked at it as Satan's playground, yet Ernestine was at peace here.

In lots of ways she was happier working than she was at home but she didn't think about that. The reason she gave herself for working was always that it was helping her and Curry pay for their house and pay the rent to the colony for the land. She didn't make much money, but you didn't need much money in Fairhope. People were always giving you things—sometimes she was allowed to take home leftover food from the kitchen and it was better than what they would have had at home. When she did think of Alice Ann, Ernestine remembered the fact that she had loved going to school here. She couldn't help but think if the child had lived longer, she might have grown up to be as happy as the other children.

The real reason she didn't mind being at work was that life with Curry was more difficult than ever. She had to steel herself against his quick temper at all times. It was hard to predict his stormy moods, or know what to do when he went for days without talking at all. Sometimes he would drink too much and she knew to expect him to hit her on some pretext or other. It was easier when he would just yell at her for not keeping the house just the way he wanted it.

They had gotten through the school year right well so far. Mrs. Johnson had made a trip to the North already, but she was in town now and would attend the Halloween party the school put on in Comings Hall.

Eighteen

THE SCHOOL YEAR 1921-22 was moving almost too fast. It was soon time for the big Halloween Party, and, by the second semester, the new folk dance teacher would be on campus. There was much more excitement about folk dancing than Amelia ever would have imagined.

In the meantime, Mrs. Johnson had already made one trip to Greenwich, where her summer teacher training school was held, and met in New York City with the "Fairhope Educational Foundation" who gave fund-raisers for her school. When she traveled she was always invited to speak in neighboring towns, and she took the opportunity to encourage them to employ Organic methods in their school systems. She never returned to Fairhope without a family or two following her, to see her demonstration school at work. Most stayed and enrolled their children. There were over 100 students, many of them boarders.

All the students were excited about the Halloween party they would hold in Comings Hall. The older students organized projects to make the party fun—a costume contest, cakewalks, washtubs of water full of apples, and booths surrounding the rim of the hall with games. Everybody in school would be involved in decorating the big, empty hall. They envisaged the event as a massive fund-raiser, even though little money exchanged hands. They would charge for a wheel of tickets, and every game and contest would cost a certain number of tickets. The parents got involved with refreshments—a bake sale, plates of ham and potato salad, lemonade and punch. A large urn of coffee would be on hand. Mothers baked cakes for the big cakewalks which would be held periodically during the evening. Mordecai Arnold, father of Louisa and five other Organic students, had for several years volunteered for the job of calling the cakewalks, which featured himself standing in the center of the circle while Piney Gaston played her enthusiastic brand of piano, stopping suddenly, and calling a random number for a handful of cards handed him by Mrs. Johnson. Whatever cakewalker—man, woman or child—was standing on the square marked with that number, was the winner of a homemade cake! This age-old party game always had currency in Fairhope.

The school event would be on the Friday of Halloween weekend, meaning that most of that day was taken with preparations for the party. The high school emerged as organizers, painting the floor with the cakewalk circle, putting up posters all around town, and decorating Comings Hall with festoons of crepe paper and huge handmade posters of witches, black cats and jack-o-lanterns they had created in their Arts and Crafts classes. The older boys were in charge of the Fun House, which was set apart on the stage with the curtain drawn. Behind that curtain they had created a maze of reconstructed cardboard cartons, a crazy mirror, the tunnel to a barrel that would roll its occupant some ten feet, and an exit on a slide down the steps to the main floor. The boys guided their charges, mostly kids their age or younger, through the labyrinth to the exit. If a child entered who was clearly not able to make his way, he was given an abbreviated tour.

Five cakewalks were scheduled during the evening, and one big costume parade. Sarah looked astonishingly beautiful in a gypsy skirt and blouse with golden hoop earrings. Paul Frederick, Jim Gaston and Maxwell Taylor were judging the costumes. This was a wrench for Max, who had a hankering to win with his Mad Hatter costume, but he had recused himself from the competition to lend his expertise as a judge.

All the town, Amelia reckoned, showed up for the party, and in fancy dress too. Captain and Mrs. Cross came as Tweedledum and Tweedledee from Alice in Wonderland; E.B. Gaston came as a wizard in a high pointed hat with stars on it, and his wife came as Mother Goose. Mrs. Johnson felt she should have come as The Old Woman Who Lived in a Shoe, but she didn't know how to articulate that as a costume, so she settled on a ghost costume, which didn't fool anybody for long.

The women of Fairhope had spent weeks making these costumes, sometimes going against their better judgment when asked by their children to create such outlandish disguises. One boy gave his mother the task of designing a Headless Horseman costume. She accomplished this by taking a hatbox to cover his head and shoulders, attaching a tin can to the top of it to provide a neck, covering the whole thing with construction paper and cutting slits in the box so he could see. He made a head for his horse, and the head he would carry under his arm, out of papier-maché in his arts and crafts class. The horse's body was a broom. Fairhope children rode brooms as horses all the time.

One of the school's big families, the Arnolds, came as the ragged, shipwrecked Swiss Family Robinson, taking the idea from a book they were reading together. Their oldest four children were boys, with Ezekiel ("Zeke") being a senior in high school, and the others, stair steps on down in size. The two youngest girls took part with Louisa playing Jenny, the English girl who appears at the end of the book. The toddler Bonnie dressed as Knips, the monkey.

Hal and Martha Etheridge, and their daughter Ally, came as a family of French poodles.

Avery and Amelia decided not to tell each other what they were working on for costumes. Avery's was quite unusual, Amelia could see that—at its base a black, body covering leotard, such as worn by circus performers. She peeked one afternoon as Avery assembled all the components of the costume, but Avery shooed her out as soon as she saw her.

"This is ART!" she told her roommate. "I need my solitude to create!"

Amelia stood outside the bedroom door like a curious child. "It doesn't look like art to me," she called. "It looks like black underwear!"

But it did look rather like art at that. She knew also that there was a lampshade involved. Amelia would dress as a scarecrow, in bedraggled men's clothes with a floppy straw hat and bunches of hay sticking out of her shirt cuffs and pant legs. The girls agreed not to see each other dressed until the party, so Avery put on her costume at the School Home, which was chaotic with children getting into costumes. Amelia dressed at The Sieve, and walked to Comings Hall in full scarecrow attiree. It was still daylight. She might scare a few crows on her way. The party started at 5 P.M. and she didn't want to be too early or too late.

She was hardly prepared for the pandemonium. She watched in awe as the hall filled up--little kids were literally climbing in the rafters, and the crush of partygoers in bizarre modes of dress was impressive. Jim Holloway was Abraham Lincoln, and it turned out Avery was a floor lamp, complete with cord and plug. She had cut out eyes in the lampshade so she could see. She was quite a figure. Jim took one look at Amelia in her scarecrow attire and said, "Who are you? Luther Beagle?"

Moments like this made Amelia wish she had the kind of quick wit that Avery did. She said, "Who are you? Charlie Chaplin?" It got a laugh, but she wasn't sure it was really funny.

She and Jim were having their ham dinners when the first cakewalk was called. They put their plates aside and took part in the walk which was made more fun by the running commentary by Mr. Arnold, describing the costumes and chanting, "One, two, three, four, keep walkin'," and Piney, in a witch costume with a long black gown and a pointed hat, played a variety of tunes, from "Alexander's Ragtime Band" to John Phillip Sousa marches—and the walkers fairly strutted in time creating a kaleidoscope of color and contrasts.

"And the first cake goes to the gentleman without a head!" he announced as one of the mothers beamingly presented a cake to the headless horseman. The boy had to pass the cake to his parents so he could continue to enjoy the party. Without a head he couldn't bob for apples, but he remained headless to the costume parade.

This would be the climax of the party. At that moment the milling, chattering crowd of fantastical characters circled the hall in a slow-moving, serpentine extravaganza of color and flash. Disparate characters talked with one another, a circus of incongruity. The four judges, just as extravagantly attired, were making notes and conferring with each other about what they saw. One by one contestants would be tapped on the shoulder by a judge and asked to form a smaller circle in the center. Clearly these were the finalists: The Crosses, the Headless Horseman, the floor lamp, Abraham Lincoln, and one four year old in a fairy costume that looked as if it came from a road company of A *Midsummer Night's Dream.*

Max showed his theatrical side in announcing the inner circle of winning looks. How different he was in his role as a theater director! His voice boomed, and he exuded the confidence of a circus ringmaster—which he was for the night. His replication of the Mad Hatter in the Tenniel drawing was complete with a lopsided top hat that had a tag tucked into the ribbon, saying *In This Style 10/6.* He added a dramatic flair to his announcements. Amelia had never noted the rich baritone timbre of his voice before.

"The floor lamp with the astonishing hourglass figure is runner-up Number Two!" Max bellowed. Applause from the crowd. Not that Avery had the kind of figure called an "hourglass" by previous generations, but her female shape definitely showed in the black body stocking. She may have been embarrassed by Max's description, but if she was blushing it was hidden under a lampshade.

"Tweedledum and Tweedledee agreed to have a battle—" he said, "But they won't have it tonight, because together they are the First Runners Up!"

It was clear how much everybody loved the Crosses. There was a wave of applause and whistles.

"And the winner of this year's Best Costume Award..." Jim in his Abe Lincoln get-up looked as if he thought he would surely win, and the little girl did a fairy dance in the most modest way she could.

"The Headless Horseman of Sleepy Hollow!"

No one was surprised or disappointed when the headless horseman won the contest. His prize was a handmade pottery jack-o-lantern, made with some artistic flourishes by Miss Kitwell. It had been glazed bright orange in the kiln, and filled by the high school students with homemade fudge.

After the presentation of the prize, the crowd began to mill around, forming random patterns of colors and patterns. There were enough witches to add a dash of black among the contrasting splashes of bright color. The oversized bow around the neck of the mad hatter was blue with big gold polka dots and the Swiss Family Robinson were mostly in white and gray. There was Julian Crane as Father Time, a grim reaper with a sickle and a dingy white robe, accompanied by his wife in sparkling white as the evangelist Aimee Semple McPherson. Abraham Lincoln had his arm around the waist of a beautiful gypsy girl and was gazing down into her eyes. Mr. Gaston, for the night a wizard, possibly of the dark arts, approached them with his peaked hat—sparkling with moons and stars—slightly askew. Mrs. Johnson, well concealed under a ghostly sheet, strode around the room, as if she assumed she had anonymity in her village for a night. Amelia realized she was truly anonymous; her scarecrow costume included a hooded mask, and she was new, so not that easily recognized. The phantasmagoria of costumes disguised the usually reserved, scholarly reformers, teachers and parents, and it was as if the town had actually become inhabited by their doppelgangers.

The floor lamp came up to her and said, "Well? What do you think? Does this group know how to put on a party or not?"

"I never saw anything quite like it," Amelia responded. "I'm beginning to understand the concept of the surrealist movement."

"I think it's about time to leave this cacophony of color and go home," Avery said.

The party was winding down as people gathered up their things and told each other goodbye until tomorrow—which would be the day they would get together to take down the decorations.

When they got home Avery went straight upstairs to get ready for bed, but Amelia went to the kitchen to make herself a cup of cocoa. She needed to unwind. When the milk was hot she stirred it into the cocoa powder and sugar, thinking of the party. She heard noise from next door, as if maybe Sam Bradley might be having his own gathering. She walked out to the back porch to see what was happening.

"Hell-FAR and damnation!" came the boom of a man's voice. A chill went down her spine as she strained to see who making the racket.

It was clear in the dim light from Bradley's back porch that he was ejecting someone from his house.

"The devil take 'em all!" The man was screaming.

Amelia had not heard such language in Fairhope. She was riveted to the spot, squinting to see who it was. Bradley's voice was low, as if trying to tame a wild beast.

"I know how you feel, but we can't do nothin' about this," Bradley was saying. "It's time you went home to cool off."

"They're all goin' to HELL anyway."

Just then the cursing man wheeled away and started to stumble up the path to the street. She had a glimpse of his face, distorted in rage but eerily smiling. After a moment she recognized Curry Cumbie, but Amelia was thunderstruck with remembered fear.

She thought of the wicked witch causing danger to her teddy bear. She heard her own voice warning her cuddly toy of hellfire and damnation. She began to understand the source of her mistrust of this man, and once the connection was made she would carry it with her the rest of her life. Miss Pritchart.

❧

The real Halloween, October 31, was Monday. The date was known as a night of mischief. A few high school boys let livestock loose on the streets, not doing real damage. Some threw a few eggs into the trees on the streets of homes they knew well—basically their own and those of friends.

The big event was taking Luther Beagle to the bay and giving him his yearly bath. Luther protested, as usual, but he was light in weight, so that two boys were able to subdue and lift him after he realized that fighting was futile. He had gone through this for several years by now, so he knew well that protesting would only postpone the inevitable. Usually he tried to hide from the boys, but his cunning was long gone and he could never successfully avoid his yearly dunk. It was a rite of passage for the older teenaged boys in Fairhope to abduct the old derelict, in his fit of mostly feigned outrage, and haul him off to the big pier, late at night, every Halloween. They claimed it was the only bath he got all year.

Nineteen

AMELIA DECIDED TO spend Christmas in Fairhope. She would miss the happy chaos of a family Christmas with the Chapmans, and felt a twinge of regret at not making a perfunctory trip to Hoboken to see her parents, but she told herself it was important to be in Fairhope and experience a whole school year her first year there. Maybe she would not return to the school next year. It was only right to give the school and the town her full attention now while she was here.

But if she were to be truthful with herself, she would admit she was looking forward to a Christmas without snow and all the inconveniences it brought—and to finding out what the holiday was like in Fairhope.

Soon after the Halloween party, the student body began preparing for a big Christmas pageant involving all classes from kindergarten through high school. Max had prepared a script from the story "Why the Chimes Rang," and Jim and the other music teachers rehearsed all the classes in Christmas carols that carried the story along. The setting was Anglicized a bit so that English Christmas music would fit, but music from France, Germany and even the Latin *"Dona Nobis Pacem"* was included. The story was about how a village which is home to a church with a set of magical bells, long broken and unused, tries every year at Christmas to reactivate the chimes by presenting gifts on the altar. The chimes have not rung for years, maybe a century, but year after year the townspeople lay their best offerings—gold, silver, and handiworks—on the altar. On the night of the story, a boy places a coin on the altar in the true spirit of sacrifice and love of God, and the chimes ring for the world to hear.

First and Second Life were to play village children. Amelia and Lillian Rifkin, the teacher from Second Life, worked together on learning a few songs and dances for their classes to do in the town square scene. The music teacher, Edna Campbell, took the little ones under her wing and taught them the round, "Christmas is coming/ The goose is getting fat/Please put a penny in the old man's hat." They learned to sing it in parts and after a few weeks it was quite charming. Then they learned to skip in a circle singing it, with George Roy Collins, from Avery's Junior High class, playing the old man—getting up from a sleep and holding out his hat in the middle of the circle. The children took turns tossing coins into the hat. The one to do it on performance night would be chosen at random at the pageant. Maybe they would draw straws.

The premise of casting an all-school pageant at the Organic School was to give every child in the school a line or two and avoid having any star performers. Three narrators told the tale, all with equal size parts, all from the senior class in high school. Teachers selected students for the leading roles—such as Peter, the boy who gave his brother his humble gift to place on the altar—at random, or at least not because they were more beautiful or appealing than their classmates. Amelia remembered Mrs. Johnson's interview question, "Do you love all children?" and thought this democratic approach to the pageant to be evident in all school activities.

All the school, students and teachers, were engaged in building and painting sets and costumes for the pageant. Amelia heard beautiful carols ringing from the music building, many she had never heard before, some with intricate harmony and in minor key, as she walked to the building with her class of moppets. She was so impressed with the high school students; they attacked all their work—creative and academic—with equal fervor. This music was unforgettable.

It wasn't particularly cold that December. The temperature dropped into the 40s for three nights in a row, but by noon all three days it was in the high 60s. Transplanted northerners like Amelia found it difficult to think of it as the Christmas season; however, decorations went up all over town and the spirit radiated throughout Fairhope even without bitter temperatures. Amelia was now aware that boots, overcoats, and snow were not essential for Christmas.

When the pageant night neared it was obvious they would have to have two performances to house the crowds. Many would attend both nights—even if they didn't the hall would be full to bursting. Ham and potato salad again, and a buffet of homemade Christmas cakes and candy on the side.

The pageant itself went off without a hitch. Max had worked with three narrators, two girls and one boy, dividing the parts. One of the readers was Emily Wilson, sweet Chauncey's older sister. There was not a lot of narration, but it anchored the unwieldy cast so they remembered where they were in the script.

When the night of the first performance arrived, there was excitement in the air. Max was confident, and reminded the students this night was basically a dress rehearsal with an audience. Children ran up to him for approval of their costumes and makeup, and ran back to their home room teachers to be herded into groups for their entrances.

"Good Lord," Max said out of one side of his mouth to Amelia. "Everybody in town is in this play. Who's going to be in the audience?"

He needn't have worried. Although many parents were being employed helping keep the kids in line, plenty were available to attend the show—along with Mr. and Mrs. Gaston, the town doctor, the constable and his wife, the Crosses, Mme. Morehead, and on and on until the hall was quite full.

Amelia enjoyed the pageant as much as she could, but didn't relax until the "Christmas is coming, the goose is getting fat," number was over and her students were gathered in the corner of the hall to watch the rest of the play. Max and Jim's staging was very clever. They used the stage itself for the inside of the church scene, while everything in the village took place on the floor in front of it. Tables and chairs were arranged for the audience around the room. A public address system was set up so that the chimes would have the right magical effect at the end of the pageant.

The Christmas pageant was just one step toward the beginning of second semester. Amelia had never envisioned an academic environment in which neither the students nor the teachers looked forward to the holiday break. In Fairhope the school year was all of a piece with the rest of the activities in town: Meetings of the Wednesday Forum, The Progressive League, The Library Review Club, The

Women's Henry George Society, German Club lectures, the Fifth Thursday Club, the Arts and Crafts Club, and Mrs. Johnson's gatherings of the Mothers' Round Table, and informal musicales continued every day except Christmas Day, which was on Sunday this year anyway. The National Holiday was declared for the following day.

The Crosses had invited Amelia, Maxwell, Jim and Avery to join them at The Gables for Christmas dinner. At this point it was no real surprise that Sarah Kitwell would not be returning to teach after the Christmas break, but Jim was distracted over her imminent departure.

Captain and Mrs. Cross realized sadly their old friend Marie Howland would not be with them this year, but Lydia Comings would drop in over the holidays, and maybe even Mrs. Johnson making her rounds. There was a circle of places to go in Fairhope on Christmas—and The Gables, with its large, fresh cut cedar as a Christmas tree, was on everybody's list. They would then drop in at each other's homes, and to the Colonial Inn.

Fairhope's citizens made Christmas decorations from the local evergreens, from smilax to giant green leaves of magnolia trees and red berries of holly branches. They tacked festoons of greenery to the bannisters on porches and staircases, and attached red oilcloth bows onto them. Every home had a tree, fresh cut from somewhere nearby. The town did not miss these trees as there were plenty more where they came from and those sacrificed for the holiday were soon to be replaced with cedars and pines. Roses, the redder the better, were the flower of choice for Christmas in those days, and those gardeners in Fairhope who were able to cultivate them in the moist climate made great use of them, especially in winter.

They chose camellias for table decoration. It was the time of year for them, pink and white, and the housewives placed them in low bowls on tables spread with long-leaf pine branches. Many stuck to holly for the traditional colors.

The Gables had a fireplace. Everybody who dropped in said how lucky it was that it was cold enough on Christmas Day to light it and simulate a familiar Christmas atmosphere. Being English, Captain Cross preferred a good roast of beef for the holiday, and this was much appreciated by his guests.

Some, of course, went to the pier for the ritual of watching the sun go down on another Christmas Day, another day in Fairhope, an end of a season and the beginning of another.

School was to open January 9, with a fresh start—and a new folk dance teacher. Amelia met him on a visit to Mrs. Johnson's office during the week after Christmas, when the school was still having holidays. Mrs. Johnson had summoned her to her office in the School Home to talk about how her classes were going. She maintained her composure throughout the interview even though it was very exciting, as always, to be talking about education, in theory and in practice, with Marietta Johnson. Mrs. Johnson revealed that she knew each of the children in Amelia's class, and their siblings and parents. Amelia really wanted to discuss some of her students.

"I saw Patsy Blalock at the edge of the thicket, playing by herself," Amelia told Mrs. Johnson. "She was in a world of her own making, talking to people who weren't there, as if she were in a play. It reminded me of myself at her age."

"I'm not surprised," Mrs. Johnson said. "Patsy needs her dreams to escape to. Her father left town a few years ago and her mother is a very complex and moody person. We are not certain what the child is exposed to at home.

"Imaginative play is good for all children, and not to be discouraged. It is more natural to children than the study of academic subjects, and, if I may say so, every bit as important. If one cannot find time for dreaming in childhood, when will time be found for this accomplishment?"

"Exactly," Amelia agreed. "It was lovely observing Patsy in her private world. It reminded me of the days with my dear teddy bear Nicodemus!"

Mrs. Johnson was charmed at Amelia's ability to regress to her own childhood and relate it to the children entrusted to her care. She was interested to hear about the Chapman family and suggested that they all belonged in Fairhope. Amelia agreed and said she would bring them down for a visit one day. She told Mrs. Johnson about her own parents, and even mentioned the nanny Miss Pritchart, who was her first example of how *not* to be a teacher.

"I loved my grandfather," Amelia said. "He took time with me, which my parents didn't do. He would take me to the parks in Hoboken and tell me the names of the flowers and trees, and his memories of growing up there as an immigrant boy."

"I sometimes think I'm a bit of a grandma to some of my students," Mrs. Johnson said, fairly twinking. "Especially George Roy Collins, whom I volunteered to look after when there was some danger of him being sent to a reform school. I plan to take him with me on my next trip to Greenwich, to my summer teacher training program.

"He's never been outside of Alabama—bless him, I don't think he's ever been out of Fairhope!" Mrs. Johnson said. She thought about it for a moment and then realized her mistake.

"No, that's right—he's been over the bay to Mobile!" Then she laughed. "And as he gets older we'll send him off to Greenwich to help Mr. Rabold teach folk dancing and Mr. Holloway to teach woodworking. But to get him started I'll take him to New York and Connecticut with me, as a bodyguard!"

The two of them laughed at the thought of this gangly teenaged boy being a bodyguard for anybody, but the picture of George Ray at Mrs. Johnson's side in New York was a sweet one, not unlike what was seen on the school campus every day.

They had talked for nearly two hours when Mrs. Johnson rose from her chair behind the craftsman oak desk.

"Time for a walk, don't you think?" she asked, and Amelia happily agreed. She would have walked across the county with this woman.

They opened the office door and went out to the big main room.

"Oh, Mr. Rabold!" Mrs. Johnson summoned the pleasant, balding man at the stairway. He immediately stopped his ascent and came across the room.

"I want to introduce Amelia King, our First Life teacher," Mrs. Johnson said. Amelia was taken by the warmth in Mr. Rabold's eyes, and his soft hand as she took it.

"Charles Rabold," he said in a quiet, well-modulated voice.

So this was the great musicologist and expert on English folkways! He had been a student of Cecil Sharp, the eminent English chronicler of the folk dances, songs, and stories of England, who had worked with Mrs. Johnson on developing a folk dance program at her school. Mr. Rabold had begun teaching folk dancing at Mrs. Johnson's summer teacher training program in Connecticut. Mrs. Johnson made no secret of her admiration for the man.

"Welcome to Fairhope!" Amelia said, and realized this was the first time she had uttered the phrase she heard so often in her first days in the town.

"Thank you very much. I don't know how many times I've heard that since I arrived."

"Considered yourself welcomed, then," said Mrs. Johnson.

"Well welcomed indeed," Mr. Rabold said.

"I'm a recent convert to the discipline of folk dance," Amelia said. "I didn't know anything about it until I came to Fairhope in the fall."

"I understand that Mettie has turned this into a dancing town," Mr. Rabold said.

Amelia liked this fellow right away and felt certain he would fit into the motley assortment of characters in town. He was a gentleman of the old school, yet young enough to relate to high school students.

"Miss King and I are going to take a walk," Mrs. Johnson said. "This would be a good opportunity to show you around town, don't you think?"

Mr Rabold's brisk step reminded Amelia of the way people walked in the North. The three of them strode out the door, passed Comings Hall, and turned west to go toward the bay on Fairhope Avenue—a wide, unpaved boulevard with a wooden water tank in its center where the two main arteries of town intersected. The ground was well worn in the street, making it easier to walk on than the paths. A wagon rumbled by, then someone rode past them on a horse. Even a pedestrian or two approached them and spoke.

As usual, there were children in the trees, some hanging upside down like monkeys, and a few townspeople about. At Crawford's store a family stood on the porch with cloth sacks of groceries, apparently awaiting a buggy or motorcar to pick them up. Customers in millinery shop regarded them through the store window as they passed.

"This is the center of town," Mrs. Johnson announced.

"So I see."

"Let us go to The Gables and take tea with Captain Cross," Amelia suggested.

"I would love a little tea, Marietta—do you have time?"

"I'll make time today. I want you to meet Captain Cross and Idella."

Moments like this were rare for Mrs. Johnson. She was always busy—composing correspondence, engaging new teachers, working on speeches and, as often as not, boarding yet another train for a speaking engagement in California, Chicago or the Northeast. She sincerely wanted Charles Rabold to be comfortable in Fairhope and in the school, so she made that her priority for this day.

They walked past The Courier office.

"Ah—*The Fairhope Courier!*" Mr. Rabold remarked. "I have had a subscription for some time now."

"We'll meet with Ernest later," Mrs. Johnson said. "I know this is the day he has to finish his weekly editorial."

They were reaching the corner of Church Street, with The Gables just ahead. Captain Cross sat in a rocker on the porch, with a cup of tea at his side.

"Hallo—the Organic School contingent," he said as they approached. "So happy to see you, Marietta! And Miss King."

"And this is Charles Rabold," Mrs. Johnson said quickly.

"Ah, Mr. Rabold—Mettie has talked so much about you."

Mr. Rabold walked onto the porch and shook Captain Cross' hand. "Please call me Charles," he said.

Mrs. Johnson and Amelia shared the glider while Mr. Rabold made himself comfortable in one of the rockers.

It wasn't long before Mrs. Cross heard the voices and joined them on the porch.

"So good to see you, Marietta—and you, too, Amelia, of course. Will there be three more for dinner?"

Mr. Rabold was duly introduced; Mrs. Johnson begged off joining them for the meal, and Amelia basked in a feeling of family that she so enjoyed in Fairhope.

"Are you sure, Mettie?" Captain Cross said. "We can find a carrot or two if need be," and they all laughed, including Mrs. Johnson. Her raw foodist and vegetarian eating habits were well known in town.

"Charles and I will be eating at the School Home today. We just stopped in on his tour of Fairhope."

"And I shall have a sandwich at home," Amelia said. "I didn't realize the time."

They talked a few minutes more and then Mrs. Johnson decided it was time to head back to her office before the meal would be served at the School Home.

"It's been delightful," Mr. Rabold said. "I look forward to many such visits in the future."

They parted ways, and bade goodbye to the Crosses, who stayed on the porch watching them leave.

᳍

Charles Rabold did fit right into the school. He was a fine dancer and excellent with the students. Mrs. Johnson marvelled at his grasp of conveying his knowledge and inspiring students, especially high school boys, to want to dance more and more complicated figures. He had imported his protégé, Hannah Bottstein, from New York, to play the accompaniment to the dances, but he hit it off well with Piney and Miss Megehan, both of whom had been playing for the dances at the school in the past. In no time he was working with the students to have a spring festival of dances and songs, early in May, demonstrating the techniques and steps of the English Morris and other folk dances.

Charles taught country dances, court dances, and Morris dances—the showiest and most theatrical. The country dances required precision and teamwork, being walking and running dances, usually in a circle, with very English names like "Oranges and Lemons" and "Christchurch Bells." The music was infectious.

For demonstrations, the boys wore bands of bells on their calves, and baldrics and lanyards—like a military ribbon across the shoulder and down to the waist. The style came, Charles told her, from the ropes used by sailors to carry their knives.

The Morris regalia all looked very symbolic—some of war and fighting, like the wooden "swords" (handmade by the boys in shop) in the Kirkby Sword dance. This was to be the finale of the festival, a dance with six high school boys clashing wooden swords and weaving them into the shape of a star, holding the star aloft as they danced off the field.

Mrs. Johnson insisted on all programs being gender neutral, but Charles Rabold balked at allowing girls to do the Morris dances because it broke with the English tradition. A compromise was reached: They were not taught the two-person challenge dances or the sword dance, but participated in all other dances on an equal basis.

The program was to be held outdoors "on the green," the space between Comings Hall and the library. This green space was just the right size, about 50 x 100 feet, and grass was planted, soon to be a green carpet. The boys would wear white pants and white shirts, and the girls were to have floral jumpers with white blouses underneath. Everybody would be in tennis shoes—a fact which still made Amelia laugh.

Twenty

I T WAS ONLY March, but Fairhope was already in the full bloom of spring. The days were sunny, and the sky was light blue with clouds here and there. Flowers opened their faces on footpaths, roadsides, and in the trees. The first blossoms had burst on the redbud trees, providing tiny splashes of mauve against the new green leaves. Dogwoods stood here and there, their layered branches now shelves for their white four-leaf blooms.

Years before, the locals had gathered in a civic group to plant azalea bushes around the perimeter of Knoll park. At at this time of year the big, raggedly uneven bushes came into bloom all at once, as if blanketed in pink. Large azaleas in white accented the color. Shades of pink bloomed in sequence, finishing with the deep, almost red shade known as "Pride of Mobile," which had newly come into vogue.

A wisteria vine, planted on a magnolia tree adjacent to the school's library, broke into a cascade of lavender blossoms, which seemed to breathe a heady sweet fragrance into the breeze. The vine actually connected two trees and would one day grow big enough to climb on; already it provided a seat between the trees, and the flowers opened with a sweet, springtime smell that was to be unforgettable to generations of Fairhope children.

Although the temperature usually hovered in the low 80s, humidity was not so high as in summer months. One could almost inhale spring itself. The air had a lightness to it that transferred to the mood of people.

More and more often, Jim Holloway was a visitor to The Sieve. With Sarah out of his life his relationship with Avery grew more intense. Amelia found herself avoiding being alone with them as they clearly enjoyed their growing intimacy. Amelia left the cottage to them and went alone to watch the sunset on the pier, or take a walk around town. Sometimes she took a book, sometimes a notebook to write down ideas for class projects. Some evenings she spent at The Gables, talking with Captain Cross, who could answer many questions, particularly about history. He recommended books to her, and lent her his copy of Tolstoy's short stories.

This night, when Amelia came into the parlor at The Gables, Idella Cross presented her with an envelope, with her name on it, in Maxwell Taylor's unmistakable handwriting.

"Mr. Taylor asked me to give this to you," she said.

"Max? How strange!" Amelia said.

"Oh, I wouldn't think strange," Mrs. Cross said with a sly smile which was lost on Amelia and walked into the kitchen. Practically everybody in town had caught on to Max's feeling for Amelia except for the lady herself.

"My Dear Amelia," read the letter. "I must talk to you. Please meet me at the northeast corner of Knoll Park, Magnolia and Bayview, at 8 P.M. Maxwell Taylor."

Amelia was somewhat anxious reading this. There could be some bad news that Max wanted to reveal, or some personal situation. Perhaps he was going to be called away for a family emergency, or perhaps he was in some sort of trouble at the school. It was half an hour before the appointed time and Amelia could do nothing but bide her time at The Gables until then.

Captain Cross was working on a Mozart sonata on the piano, and she had a Rousseau book to read about the nature and needs of the child. She chose her favorite chair in The Gables' main room, a threadbare old carpet rocker which had the smell of years of musty dust to it. All the same, the book was hardly relaxing, and Captain Cross' struggle with Mozart did little to ease her tension.

It was hardly a five-minute walk to the spot designated by Max's missive. He would be coming from the cottage at Bancroft and Pine Street where he rented a room. She decided to walk down Fairhope Avenue to the Knoll Park corner. It was dark now, a night not unlike when she and Max walked this way to Marie Howland's, when she got her first look at Fairhope illuminated by southern moonlight.

Max was standing near a dogwood tree at the edge of the park, full of white blooms. When she got close enough, he said, "Good to see you."

"Hello, Max."

What was he going to tell her? Tree frogs were deafening for a moment.

"I see you got my letter," he said, with a smile curling one corner of his mouth. His smile was awkward, uncomfortable, as if he had forgotten how but was giving it a try. He fixed her with his eyes, although they trembled in a strange and inexplicable way. All she knew to do was look back at him firmly, hoping a steady gaze would relieve the anxiety he clearly felt.

"Yes, although the postal service might be disappointed at the loss of revenue," she said.

"I never thought of that."

Again there was silence but for the frogs.

"I thought this would be a nice place to meet."

"And so it is. The night reminds me of our first meeting, walking Marie Howland home."

He nodded, and clearly began to think about that night.

"This is different," he said after a pause. "That was before I loved you."

"Oh, Max!"

"Now let me speak."

She took a breath and nodded.

"I've given this a lot of thought. It was not something I was seeking. 'It' found me instead. I'm kind of a solitary person, pretty much independent and I've always been happy with that—depends upon what you mean by happy, I guess. I was content with it; I didn't expect more—this damned *town*—"

"Maybe it's all these flowers," she said.

"Flowers and springtime, is that what you think?"

"I don't know what to think."

"Well, let me tell you something then. It's not flowers and springtime! It's—it's a wistful scarecrow at Halloween, a pair of lovely eyes glowing in the reflection of light of a campfire, the music of a laugh at a folk tale…"

He was warming up now.

"It's camellias and roses for Christmas on a warm day. It's sunsets on the pier. It's the passion to embrace the whole world after a chorus of 'A Long Long Trail A-Winding.' It's the accidental grasp of a hand doing an English country dance. It's the scent of pine and wisteria in the breeze. Yes, it's this damn, irresistible Never Never Land of a town—but most of all it's you, my beautiful Amelia. Oh, dear God, let me repeat that." He paused.

"My beautiful Amelia. Okay." He paused and took a breath. Then he launched into an imitation of Ethel Barrymore. "That's all there is."

"There isn't any more?" Amelia picked up on the imitation, as everybody liked to do, picking up the exit lines in a play the actress had spoken years before but echoed in common usage for years afterward. Maxwell at his best was all about the theatre.

"No?" he said after a long pause, making it a question, imploring her to understand that he meant far more than he had said.

"That's a great deal, Maxwell."

"Yes. It's profound. Not so deep as a well, maybe, nor so broad as a church door—"

"Now you're quoting."

"Well, at least I quote from the best."

"I liked when you were being original."

"You did?" He looked at her, hopeful for the first moment.

"It's like being in a play."

"There are times when life is," Max said. Now he was staring at her, trying to fathom her soul.

"This is new to me," she said. She was not sure how to capture in words the conflicting feelings that swept over her. But she knew she had to say something.

"Dear Max."

In an instant he stepped over to her and put his arms around her. Amelia did not resist. She knew he was going to kiss her and that she would not resist.

The world of sunsets and wisteria blossoms and firelight and tales of moondust came crashing about her as she responded to his gentle, long kiss. The chirping of tree frogs crescendoed when he stepped back at last and looked into her face, still with his arms around her. She was unsteady on her feet. Caught in the moment, she could not speak. Her mind was flooded with confusing thoughts and she felt stirrings and tingling sensations throughout her body that she had not known before. The books she was carrying slid from her grasp to the ground.

All at once Max was laughing.

"You dropped your books," he said. He picked them up from the patch of grass. "Ah, Tolstoy!" he said, looking at the top book. "How appropriate!"

"Can you blame me?" she said. "About dropping them I mean, not about the books. I feel—a little foolish."

"Ah no, not foolish, I hope. I did my best—"

"I didn't mean that. You did very well."

"Yes, I know," he said.

"I think you are more accustomed to being in plays than I," she said.

"This isn't a play."

"What is it, then?"

"It's real life."

"Please, Max," Amelia said. "This is going to take me some time."

"Oh, 'please,' yourself," he said. "Don't think so much. Do not make this a problem. I kissed you in the park, I said some things. You liked it."

"Yes."

"I shall walk you home now," he said. "And then I'll dance all the way to my own humble abode. Then tomorrow…"

"Tomorrow?"

"That's the one one-word question to which there is no answer," said Max.

The two walked up Bayview, through the big old oak trees, both of them moved by the moon as it shone through the Spanish moss. Fireflies glittered in the trees. He held her hand. The excitement of this night, and the thought of his kiss, completely eclipsed Amelia's memory of the only other kiss she had known—an awkward, unmoving kiss from her college beau. What to make of Max in this new role she did not know.

As they approached her cottage she felt she had to tell him something.

"Avery and Jim are at The Sieve," she told him.

"That's good, I think. They are at The Sieve, there's a little moondust in the air, and you and I are walking down the street. Life goes on."

She wasn't sure if Maxwell understood the significance of Jim being with Avery.

"They are a couple."

"Well, yes, I had hopes. Jim has had his eye on her for months, even before the departure of the volatile Sarah."

"I hadn't seen that," Amelia said.

He said nothing.

"I shall drop you at the door," Max said. "I don't know that I'm able to take any more excitement tonight."

She turned to him as they reached the door and he leaned down and kissed her cheek.

"Promise me," he said, "that you won't think too much."

"Not an easy promise to keep," she said.

"Sure it is. If your mind races, just insert thoughts about Tolstoy and Rousseau."

"And Marietta Johnson?"

"Well, Marietta Johnson too—but I think the distant gods are more comforting than those close to home."

As she climbed the stairs, Amelia heard his voice in her head, repeating, "Tomorrow is the one-word question to which there is no answer," and she felt the memory of the kiss suffuse her body with tingling hope. This was so different from her only previous experience with a man, a few dates and one sterile, stolen kiss from Robert Harding, a young divinity student who had sought her out when she was in college. She was in a different world now, yet she could not grasp why.

When she got into her bed a few minutes later, she had not noticed whether or not Jim was still in the house. She wrapped her arms around her spare pillow and wished for her old teddy bear.

Twenty-One

IN THE MORNING Amelia heard voices downstairs in the kitchen and she could smell coffee brewing and bacon frying. Her dreams had been of Philadelphia, where she told Althea and Lettie about the flowers in bloom in Fairhope.

"We know you like it there," Althea had said gravely. "But what about this man Maxwell?"

"He's very nice…"

Althea and Lettie were giggling at this, and burst into laughter that they couldn't quell, and by the end of the dream Amelia was laughing with them, so hard that she woke up, thinking she might be laughing out loud. But she was not. She felt warm and happy—as if she had had a real visit with Althea and Lettie—but her mind was still confused with new emotions involving Max. That there was coffee and company downstairs was a relief. It was Saturday. She put on her most comfortable clothes and went downstairs.

"Good morning, Ma'am," said Jim, in that Southern mock-courtly way Amelia had become familiar with since the first morning she encountered it from Will Hodges, as he was working on carpentry in Comings Hall.

"Morning, you two," she said. "The smell of bacon and coffee is the nicest way to wake up."

"Jim is going to honor us with battercakes," Avery said.

"Pancakes?"

"Something like pancakes," Jim said. "Kentucky version. You Yankees can have your pancakes, but I'll allow as you never had cakes as good as these." He had a big bowl of batter and a skillet full of the grease from the fresh, hot bacon on the stove.

"I could do with some nice scrapple about now," Amelia said, thinking of her dream of Philadelphia.

"Scrapple? That's a new one on me," said Jim.

"Oh, we occasionally get scrapple in Boston," Avery said. To Jim she said, "It's made of all the leftovers of the hog, ground together with spices and filled in with corn meal."

"Now that sounds like something we'd sure enough like in Kain-tuck!" Jim said, licking his lips. "You are makin' me want to go to Philadelphia. Scruh-apple, huh?"

"You eat it with maple syrup," Amelia added.

"Sure you do!" Jim was entranced. "That sounds mighty good." He was pouring rounds of batter into the bacon pan and watching it carefully.

Amelia took a crisp piece of bacon from the stack draining on a plate at the back of the stove and sat at the table with Avery.

Jim poured coffee for them all. He took his black, but both the girls wanted sugar and cream. There was no way to discuss the previous night, even though Amelia was fairly bursting with it. Later, when she and Avery were alone, she might confide to her, but this morning was for battercakes, bacon and the easy camaraderie the three enjoyed. She was sure to see Max before Monday.

Fresh cane syrup was the choice for pancakes in Alabama. There were times when Amelia yearned for the caramel tang of maple syrup, but it was not to be found here.

Jim was piling the cakes into stacks on their plates, slipping pats of butter between the cakes and putting slices of bacon on the side. She was content with the cane syrup and very impressed with Jim's creation, which tasted of buttermilk and corn meal.

"Just what I need today!" Amelia said. "Something new and delicious."

"Jes' between us, ain't them better than pancakes?" Jim asked in a pleading voice.

"Yes," Avery said.

"I wasn't asking you," Jim said to her.

"You want my endorsement, then?" Amelia said, "Well, of course. Best battercakes I ever had!"

"Left-handed compliment, we call that in Kentucky."

The three ate heartily until all the batter was gone from the bowl, the whole rasher of bacon consumed, and they were all sufficiently fed and awakened.

"In a little while, let's take a walk," Amelia suggested.

"Good idea. When we're up to it," Avery said.

They stretched out on the sofa and easy chairs, seeing the bay out the window. Amelia walked to the porch and watched a sailboat out on the water.

"Wonder who that is this morning," she said.

When she got back into the parlor, the two of them were supine on the sofa together.

"Spooning, at this hour?" she said.

"I was thinking maybe it's time for a nap," said Jim.

Amelia and Avery exchanged knowing glances, and she watched the two of them stand together and start toward the stairs.

"I'll take my walk then," she said. "I need some exercise—the kind you get alone!"

Amelia felt a twinge of resentment at how close Jim and Avery had become, how proprietary he was with Avery, and how ubiquitous Jim was about their house now that they were a couple. Amelia had become fond of Avery, and, although she enjoyed Jim's company, she could not help feeling he was taking her friend away. Maybe he was.

Her emotions overcame her when she got to the beach, quiet but for the whispering waves. She stared out at the bay and its lone sailboat. She was thinking about change—Avery changing, Jim changing, and last night Max changed, at least in her mind. These were forces beyond her control, just things happening, and all these would likely transform what she had come to accept as her life. She wanted so to be modern, to be a New Woman, armed with courage and conviction and the self-confidence that eliminates self-doubt.

She did not know whether she was in love with Max. She had never been kissed like that or regarded in the way he seemed to think of her, as far as she knew. It would be difficult to reject him in any case. She was not ready to think of that. She asked him for time to think and he said he wanted her to, but something in the way he talked to her last night suggested he was urging her to allow her emotions to rule. She was not able to do that. All right then, this morning was the time for assessing her emotions. She had great fondness for this odd young man, felt companionship and admiration when she worked with him and saw him guiding the older students at school. She could talk to him; he always had wonderful insights when she had questions for him. Yet falling in love, from what she understood of that state, should be easier than this. She thought it should be spontaneous, and ideally it should be of mutual impact. She could not say she understood Max's declaration. It came as a surprise to her. She couldn't sort out her emotions or quite believe his either. She had no doubt he was sincere, that he had spent a great deal of time debating whether to speak up, and if so, where, when and how. He had selected that romantic spot in the moonlight. It was almost as if he had written his own lines, but no, she did not think he had done that. He spoke too haphazardly, too charmingly for that. "At least I quote the best," he had said. "You are a warm Christmas," he had said, or something to that effect.

She turned the evening over in her mind, knowing she was in a transition of some kind in her own life now, and not knowing how to handle it. Unlike the organization of her days before moving to Fairhope; unlike the gentle flow of events in her life since arriving—this was a night that stood out. She listened to the waves hitting the beach and silently wished as hard as she could she would be wise enough to handle the events that might come next.

※

Maxwell did not dance home to his shabby room that night; it was as if he did not feel his feet touch the ground at all. He had heard the expression "walking on air" but until he kissed Amelia he did not think of that as a literal sensation. All the way home that balmy evening he hardly felt he had feet at all.

He could find her today, but sensed that would not be a good idea. She had been ambushed already—not only by him but also apparently by her own responses. A wise man would leave her enough time to come to him on her own. He knew she would probably be down at the bay by now, and if Jim was with Avery she would be alone, but much as he would have liked to surprise her, he was sure this gentle girl would likely bolt like a doe in the woods if he appeared. It was not easy for him to stay away from her, and indeed a lesser man would take the opportunity to force the issue. But he had work to do in blocking *The School for Scandal.* He had to design a workable set for it. He was better off letting her contemplate her own feelings today. He could not stop himself from turning the scene the previous evening over in his own mind.

Had she actually said, "I like it when you're original" as if she preferred his words to those of Shakespeare? He thought of the look on her face when she said, "Dear Max." He had known damn well that that look said, "Come over here and kiss me," and he had done so. And—she dropped her books!

Kissing her was better than anything he had dreamed of. Her lips were soft and she allowed him to part them a bit with his own. She had felt so warm and pliant in his arms that he had thought of nothing else all night long. An owl spent the night asking him WHO and he said at one point, "You know damn well *who*, you knothead! My beautiful Amelia—and she let me call her that!" Then came another WHO and he gave up. He decided he would sleep in the land of WHO and talk to the creature there. At last he did fall asleep, but if he dreamed it was simply the same scene he had at last enacted with the love of his life, the beautiful Amelia. He could not tell for certain if he had been asleep or not, the whole night.

✲

Amelia walked back to The Sieve late in the afternoon. Jim was gone and Avery was working at the kitchen table on a project she would start with her class on Monday, a science study of the local plants. She pulled up a chair at the table.

"Hi," Avery said. "Did you have a nice walk?"

"I had a lot to think about."

"Oh?" Avery looked up. "I hope Jim and I aren't making you uncomfortable."

"No, not exactly. I've just got a lot to learn."

"Learn?"

"About myself. Life."

"Life. Oh, that," Avery said, beginning to smile.

"I'm wondering if you're going to want to move out."

"What? Leave this gorgeous palace? Whatever for?"

"Oh, for Jim, maybe."

"Oh, heavenly days—have you seen where he lives?"

"Yes. Maybe he'll want to move in here, then."

"Certainly not. At least it's nothing we've talked about. You are rushing us, Amelia. All I think about this place is that we need to get Sam Bradley back on the roof."

"With his horrible henchman," Amelia suddenly remembered the strange man with the feminine mouth and the hooded, evil eyes.

"Oh—you make too much of that fellow," Avery said.

"I can't get that frightening face out of my mind."

"Well, do. He's not so bad as that, I'm sure. Works around town all the time. His wife is that obese woman who works at the school home."

"That makes it worse!"

"Amelia, what's bothering you?"

"Everything is changing."

"That's what happens. You know that. You always struck me as a very flexible person. Otherwise, what would you be doing in this crazy town? Teaching at this crazy school?"

"It's something else. It's Max."

"Oh dear."

Now Amelia gathered her thoughts. She had truly hoped for an opportunity to discuss this with Avery, but now she wondered if it was the wrong thing to do.

"We had a talk last night."

Another pause. Avery's eyes were riveted on hers. She didn't say anything.

"He left a note for me at The Gables, 'Meet me at Knoll Park, Northwest corner, Bayview and Magnolia, 8 P.M.'"

Avery was suppressing a laugh now.

"Don't laugh!"

"Sorry, sorry—I know it's serious. I mean, it's scary, is what it is."

"Well, yes. I didn't know if maybe he'd been fired, or was in some kind of trouble, or what."

"And was he?"

"No. He wanted to tell me…that he's in love with me."

"Oh, my *gosh!* How dramatic of him! I can't imagine Max—"

"Maybe you shouldn't try to imagine it. I mean, what he said to me, what he did—"

"What did he do?"

"He kissed me."

"Be still, my heart! I'm sorry, Amelia, I just can't believe this!"

"I can't either!"

"Did you like it? Was it a good experience?"

"Of course it was! I loved it! I fell to pieces! I dropped my books on the ground!"

Avery slung the papers and books from the table to the floor. "I am too—I'm dropping my books here!"

"Oh, stop it! Don't make fun of this!"

"No, it's wonderful. It's crazy! I don't know what to think!"

"That was my feeling exactly. I still don't know what to think—what to feel! The only other time I was kissed it was different," she said.

"When was that?"

"In college there was a young divinity student. We went to concerts together, he was very good-looking, but also rather dull. My mother had hopes…"

Avery was hanging on her every word.

"But I knew then I wasn't interested in getting married, and certainly not to him. He kissed me at the last dance of school. He asked me to marry him. But it was not this kind of kiss."

"Is it too early to have a little drink?" Avery said. Her cure for emotional outbursts was often some wine from the cupboard.

"Let's do it," Amelia said.

Avery was up and opening a bottle of homemade wine Fishlock had given the two for Christmas.

"This should be perfect for the occasion!"

Avery poured the red wine into the nearest glasses in the cupboard.

"Keep in mind, Amelia, that this is not marriage," Avery said. "This is just another step in life."

"Marriage is not on my agenda," Amelia said. "But I'm interested in taking steps forward in life."

"I'll drink to that!" Avery said, offering to clink glasses.

"Promise me you won't talk with Jim about this," Amelia said.

"You think Maxwell hasn't yet?"

"If Maxwell had told Jim about it, he would have enshrined the whole story in a Kentucky folk tale by now."

"You're probably right. I'm sure Max is not going to share his experience until he's sure you're really committed to this."

"Until we publish the banns, you mean?"

"Well, that's going a little far."

"Oh, dear," Amelia said, "My whole life is passing before my eyes." Then she took a long drink.

"Do yourself a favor, Amelia. Don't make plans; don't worry about this."

"You sound like Max."

"Why, what did he say?"

"Not to think about it."

"I agree with him, then. Jim and I don't know what's going to happen with us. We haven't any plans for the future. Look at him—three months ago he was in love with Sarah. I think he just needs a woman."

"And you're it."

"For the time being."

"Maybe Max and I will be like that."

"Whatever happens, you crossed a line last night. There's no going back—"

"Gosh, don't say that!"

"No, listen to me. You won't go back to what you were before last night. Why would you want to?"

"What will become of me?"

"For God's sake, Amelia, listen to yourself. You were kissed. You liked it. How bad can that be?"

Twenty-Two

MONDAY SHE SAW Max at school. She was surprised at her emotional reaction to him now, and she felt self-conscious about it. He was a transformed man in her eyes; no longer odd or awkward, but virile and confident. He even seemed almost good-looking.

"Good morning, Miss King," he said. His speaking voice was somehow more resonant and well-rounded. He was not trying to pressure her, nor was he assuming the posture of a victor. He was simply happier.

Amelia was beaming in spite of herself. This silly fellow now looked like a catch! And maybe it was she who was the victor. Or maybe it was not a battle at all.

"Good morning," she responded.

"Beautiful weather we're having," he said. He was clearly pleased at her smile.

"Spring is definitely here."

"I passed the wisteria vine earlier," he said. "Its fragrance was the essence of springtime in Fairhope."

The wisteria reference was an allusion to his speech to her. Or was it?

"The scent of wisteria and pines on the breeze?" she said.

He blushed in a way that told her he hadn't actually been thinking about that speech, but was thrilled to be reminded of it.

"And how are you doing today?" he said.

What an odd conversation this was—as if the two of them had begun to create a code by which they could convey thoughts beyond their words. Amelia found herself willingly carrying the game further.

"I haven't dropped my books today," she said.

"That's good," he said. "Tolstoy should be held firmly in hand."

Then he said, "I want to see you again."

"Of course."

"What I really want to do is sweep you up in my arms and carry you off to my room, and, and—make a cup of coffee for you!"

She was laughing out loud now.

"Really, Sir!" she said, in mock Victorian outrage. "What a vile suggestion!"

"You don't like coffee?"

"Well, I've never had *your* coffee."

"That's quite true. You have to try it to know if you like it. How about Saturday?"

Amelia had to think about this. But she answered before giving herself time to break the mood.

"Saturday it is. I'll probably be in your neighborhood on Saturday morning—say, about 10 o'clock?"

He readily agreed.

Saturday came in a flash, after a week of reading to her class, supervising play in the thicket, and, on Thursday morning, a visit to her classroom from "Aunt Mettie" who brought with her a cocoon she'd found and left it for the class to observe in its metamorphosis.

On Friday Amelia decided to take in a few minutes of Mr. Rabold's folk dancing class with the high school. She left her class with Helen, her very serious and competent young assistant, abetted by Joanie, by the high school girl in teacher training. Helen would probably take over Amelia's job one day.

From outside Comings Hall, Amelia could hear the sound of the piano playing the absolutely beautiful folk dance music, played with heavily-accented rhythm by Hannah Bottstein, the accompanist Mr. Rabold had brought with him from Connecticut. This style of playing made it easier for the dancers. When it came to a demonstration, Miss Bottstein could ease up and simply play the music, but for folk dance practice her style was perfect.

"Watch your lines!" Mr. Rabold was saying.

When Amelia got into the hall she saw two sets of girls doing "Step Stately," a challenging country dance that required mental as well as physical agility. It was a beautiful dance to watch, and Charles had decided to "give it to the girls," as he said, since so many of the showier dances were for the boys only, following English tradition. "Step Stately" was an intricate dance and the girls really threw themselves into getting it right.

"Good morning, Miss King—would you like to give it a try?"

"Oh, no, not yet." Amelia would have been terrified to try such an advanced dance. "Maybe in the future. I'm just here to observe this morning."

The girls took the dance from the beginning one more time, and, although Amelia thought she saw one mistake, the dancing was graceful and impressive. It was followed by the boys doing a "stick" dance, with broom handles cut short and clattering together.

When the bell from the Bell Building tolled time for classes to change, Maxwell came into the hall with his cast to rehearse *The School for Scandal.*

Max was clearly pleased to see her there, so she decided to stay for a few minutes of his rehearsal.

"If you don't mind, I'd like to watch a bit," she said.

"That's fine," he said. "Just don't try to direct."

The cast hooted at this and began to mill around until he told them to find their places for Act Two, Scene One. It was the scene in which Lord Peter Teazle admonishes his young, extravagant wife to rein in her spending—hardly a scene which Fairhope teenagers of 1922 would normally have known much about. Sir Peter was played by Ronson Marshall, a slightly overweight boy from Connecticut, who boarded at the School Home, and the bossy Bessie Fields was extremely aptly cast as Lady Teazle.

They went through the scene twice, and Amelia was very impressed with Max's total absorption in his work. After the second run-through he said to the boy, "I'd just like to see a little more pomposity," and bounded up onto the stage himself, taking over just a few lines. All his class delighted at seeing him do this—through a few movements, gestures, and the use of his voice he transformed himself into the corpulent Sir Peter—and when he'd done this briefly, he handed the scene back to the actors. Ronson's interpretation, a dandy imitation of Maxwell, was much improved. Max called for a break when they'd finished, and Amelia told him she would reluctantly have to go back to class.

With a look in his eyes that said he couldn't wait to see her the next day, Max said, "Can't take any more of this?"

She said, "I loved it—but if I don't get back to my class, I may be tempted to run away and go on the stage!"

When she left she wondered if Max had been showing off for her, but his way of working with his students was so effective she shrugged that thought off. There was no question he was a good teacher—but now she realized he was a good actor too.

✺

The next morning the sky was overcast. Not a breeze stirred the air as Amelia left The Sieve before breakfast, taking a ham sandwich with her on her walk to the bay. Jim and Avery were there but she did not want them to have a hint of where she was going later in the morning. It was to be a breakfast without coffee, because Maxwell had promised to make coffee for her.

The birds sang happily and the flowers brightened the grey day. Reflecting the color of the sky, the bay was not always blue, like the ocean or the lakes of the Northeast. In fact it usually was brownish, sometimes the exact color of a muddy river. To Amelia it was as if the bay had moods—excited moods, crystal moods, and, rarely, moods of storm—heavy, thrashing moods. When its mood was peaceful, like this morning, the sound of the bay's waves, combined with an occasional squawk of a seagull, were comforting and gentle, like some eternal lullaby.

She could smell the blossoms from the satsuma oranges—a beautiful portent of the citrus fruits to come, underscoring the promise of this morning. She felt independent and powerful, even though she was a complete novice at the undertaking she faced. Maybe this was what it meant to be a New Woman, really, the ability to make a choice and not be daunted by its risk.

She knew where Max lived, in a room at the back of a stucco cottage on Bancroft Street, not that far from the campus. She might be seen by someone who knew her as she headed that way, but she really didn't care. This was not a town where she would be thought of as a brazen hussy for such an act—after all it was a Saturday morning, and she and Maxwell Taylor were known to be friends. He had invited her to join him for coffee, and that was what she was doing.

She didn't see anyone in the neighborhood. The only one she would have been chagrined to run into would be Marietta Johnson herself, but even she would probably have been wise enough to look the other way. Amelia knew very well if Mrs. Johnson saw her coming or going from Max's digs she would take her aside and explain her feelings about the situation, perhaps in somewhat humiliating detail. If she could duck inside without being seen perhaps her secret assignation would not mean the loss of her reputation.

Max opened the door before she knocked. He had probably spotted her coming up Bancroft, and wanted to spare her the embarrassment of standing at the door too long. They didn't speak, but she swept inside and he closed the door behind her.

"I'm sorry I can't provide much of a breakfast," Max said.

By then she was kissing him. She didn't care to make idle conversation.

When she pulled back, he said, "Did you want coffee? I can do coffee…"

"Not yet," she said.

His room was small, with a hot plate at one end and a bed taking up almost all the rest of the space. There was an open door to the bathroom and a door to what must have been a closet. Amelia did not take the time to survey the surroundings, but there was not much to look at.

She kissed him again, and he pulled her to him and she felt a decided firmness in his pants as he held her. It was her first experience with a man and his erection.

"My God—I'm dropping *my* books now," Max said.

Amelia laughed, feeling the full force of her power over him, and simultaneously of his over her. They sat on his bed and he put his hands on her breasts. Her nipples grew hard as if shot as if with electricity, and she felt goosebumps rise on her arms under her blouse. She had not aware that any of these things would be likely to happen, at least she had not thought of it beforehand, but the sequence of sensations gave her a sense of her own role. She felt like a slave at the same time that she felt like a master. She felt a melting sensation all through her. She became more aggressive, kissing him over and over.

"You're damn good at this, you know," Max said as she was unbuttoning his shirt.

"No, I don't know. Tell me." By now she had made her way to his bed and he willingly threw himself and her upon it. She heard something different in his voice this day. It was rich and modulated, comforting, masculine. She basked in the sound of it.

"You're damn good at this."

"You said that."

Now he was undressing her; she was unbuttoning his shirt, and they were lying on the bed scrambling to get their own and each other's clothes off, and they were laughing, euphoric, passionate, each trying to get close to the other.

"I want to look at you," he said.

"I want you to," she said.

"Isn't it funny how it works out that way?" he said, and they laughed again. She was responding to his overflow of emotion. It was palpable, in the air almost, and her own desire fed off his in a crest of shared euphoria, domination and surrender. It was as if he transferred his great emotion for her and she simply drank it in. They were caught in it and became one—greater together than the sum of their emotions.

When he entered her she experienced a sharp sensation, not pain exactly, but in that instant of sharpness she was fully aware that everything in her life had changed forever.

"I'm sorry, this isn't going to take long," said Max, and she didn't know quite what he meant. In reality his meaning was quite literal—that he was sorry that it wasn't going to take long. It was just a few seconds, and he was done and he pulled out of her and rolled to the other side of the bed, as if exhausted.

"I—uh. I'm sorry," he said. "I was just too excited."

"That's nothing to apologize for," said Amelia, confused.

"Well, dear, it's not supposed to go that way."

"Not?"

"I'm supposed to give you pleasure."

"And you think you didn't?" she said.

He gave her a questioning look.

"I've never had more fun in my life," she said. She was at a loss to express her sense of victory at being vanquished so easily.

"Well, that's a promising beginning anyway." He still wore a quizzical expression. "It will be even better in the future," he said quietly.

He lay by her side for a few minutes, and then he sprang up and darted to the bathroom.

"Just stay there, lie still, just a moment," he told her. He closed the door and she heard the sound of splashing water. She felt the enormity of her actions today. How simple it all was, really, when you surrendered to the love of another.

Then he came back into the room, wearing a towel wrapped sarong style around his waist. He had a small towel in his hand, which he gave to her.

"I suggest you put this under you," he said, and she did. Now she was lying on a towel, and the wetness they had created was captured in its fabric. She would always know, from that moment, to find a towel nearby before the act. She would never know how unusual this was, as it was her introduction to the act of lovemaking, and she would take for granted that finding a towel first was part of the procedure.

"I thought some coffee might be in order," he said.

"That would be nice." She sat up straight, like a school-girl at a public school desk, except that she was naked, sitting on a towel. Maxwell Taylor melted with pleasure when he saw her like that.

"Good. You did come here for coffee, did you not?"

"Of course—coffee. What else?"

"I thought perhaps something else. But I shall make the coffee now."

He had a blue enamel percolator, which clearly had been used for many breakfasts, putting coffee in the basket and water in the pot. He turned on the electric hot plate and the two of them waited.

"I expected to enjoy this morning coffee," Max said. "But not quite this much."

She was sitting on the towel now, completely nude, not sure what to say.

"I came here determined to win my credentials as a New Woman."

"You've achieved your goal."

Max was smiling fully now, but not looking at her, looking at the coffeepot. It began to perk and he jumped up from his place beside her and turned down the knob on the hot plate.

"Won't be long now."

When he poured the coffee he said, "Your coffee."

"Here's to New Women." She raised the cup in a mock toast.

She knew this coffee would be black—he wouldn't have cream or milk in the house—and she knew it would be strong. But this was too strong and too black to consider drinking. She only had a sip or two.

"I do have sugar!" he said and presented her with a sugar bowl. She added two spoons of it and sipped at her cup but she had no intention of finishing it.

"Taking a break, we call it in the theatre."

"I've heard that," she said.

"I would say you are well on your way to being a New Woman," he said.

"I would think so," she said.

"Maybe not quite," he said, finishing his coffee and taking her cup from her.

She opened her arms to him, and he leaned down over her on the bed, unfastening his towel and kissing her. This time he kissed her face, her ears, and she relaxed while he touched her gently and stroked her shoulders and breasts. He put his hand gently into her, moving it while she just looked at him, close up and with wide eyes. He knew how to do things she had never known about, to get her ready for intercourse, and this time he waited until she responded with involuntary sighs before he entered her. This time he took more time in the act. He completed his pleasure once more, this time with Amelia responded with moans until she cried out in full pleasure herself. Afterward the two of them lay together for some time.

They had dropped into sleep when he leaned over and kissed her again, waking her and saying, "That was one hundred per cent astonishing, but I'm not sure it will replace food."

"A meal? Really? Is it lunch time?"

"Just about. We must think about doing something else today—although for the life of me I don't know why."

"I'll be among the missing if I don't show up at The Sieve soon," Amelia said. "Avery will send out alarms for the volunteer fire department!"

"Can't have that," Max said. "We must be discreet. You'll want a splash in the tub, and then we must get dressed and go."

"All the while hoping not to be seen coming out of this hidey-hole together."

"That would be embarrassing, yes. But if anybody sees us, the story is that you came here to help me with blocking."

"What on earth is blocking?" Amelia asked, making her way to the bathroom.

"It has to do with *The School for Scandal*."

"Oh, well, then I'd be happy to help."

His tub was equipped with a little rubber hose with a spray head for showers. She climbed in, sprayed, dried herself with a nearby towel, put on her clothes and came out. The ordinary act of dressing took on a new significance in this place.

"Hey, you look just like that new teacher at the Organic School," said Max when she emerged.

"I hope so."

"Well, she certainly wouldn't be in a place like this."

"If anybody asks, she wasn't," said Amelia.

Max had slipped on his pants and shirt. Now he looked tousled and flushed, and not like the awkward fellow she had met in September. He seemed to have more poise, more maturity. He was more interesting. What had looked like cowlicks in his hair before as he tried to tame it into the sleek, slicked-down fashion of the day now simply looked like curls, casually covering his head almost like the tresses on a Greek statue.

"I think we should go out separately. I'll meet you at The Sieve in half an hour, and we can decide where to have a bite of lunch."

It was with great caution that the New Woman emerged from the lair of the wolf, trying her best to look casual, as if perhaps she had gone in the door by mistake and only stayed for a moment. But the elation she felt at her liberation and the discoveries she had made about herself brightened her step toward her cottage where she would soon be met by her man.

Twenty-Three

THE ARDOR OF their first sexual encounter cooled somewhat as over the next few weeks Amelia and Maxwell reached something of an understanding. He was very involved in play production, which was much more demanding than Amelia could possibly know. He stole every possible minute he could to be with her and she found herself anticipating those moments with joyous excitement. They reached an agreement with Avery and Jim so that each couple had time alone at The Sieve on a regular basis. What had become at least as important to them both was that they could and did talk about everything now—she told him her story, all about her life in Hoboken, in Philadelphia, her teachers and her first meeting with Mrs. Johnson.

He talked of his experiences in the theatre, in college and in Baltimore, the greats he had seen and what he wanted to do in his life after Fairhope.

"Life after Fairhope," Amelia said, trying to contemplate it.

"I've got a lot to do," Max said.

"I have too, but much of it is here."

It was as if she hadn't spoken, she realized. He wanted to talk about himself, his plans, his commitment to the theater, and he had a way of ignoring her when she talked about her own plans. Fairhope was just a stop on his journey; to her it was an essential training ground and a place to try her wings.

He told her about Sarah Willard Hiestand, the Shakespearean scholar from Chicago wintering in Fairhope, and how the two of them were going to produce a Shakespeare Festival involving the whole town in early summer. Mrs. Hiestand had dreamed up the project as a celebration of Shakespeare's birthday. She coached everybody in town with the verse, helped the local seamstresses to "build" costumes, as she and Max put it—speaking in theatre jargon that was becoming well known in town. She helped Max with The School for Scandal as well.

Mrs. Heistand did not expect English accents, but it was her job to rid the locals of sloppy speech.

"Roll on, Thou Deep and Dark Blue Ocean, Roll!" she would bellow at the front of the class, demonstrating the diaphragmatic breathing necessary to project the voice to the back of Comings Hall from the stage. They had lazy lips, these Southerners, even if most of them had a basic General American accent. She had lip exercises, facial exercises, and any number of tongue twisters to keep their minds and mouths busy.

George Ray Collins, Mrs. Johnson's special charge, had a minor role in the play and worked earnestly with all the instruction Max could give him on speech, movement, and stage presence. He was the kind of boy who normally hung in the background, and being onstage terrified him so much he made an extreme effort to learn the ropes in hopes his discomfort didn't show when the audience was there.

Mrs. Johnson hoped taking George Ray with her to New York would awaken the young man to greater possibilities than he might have known before she took him on.

A few years before, he was a lad in trouble, with an alcoholic father and a longsuffering mother who had learned to live on very little. George Ray might had gone to reform school had Mrs. Johnson not vouched for him with the county judge. Since moving to the School Home, he had become her shadow, and he took on any project she designated for him. She thought of him as one of those pure and power-less children who needed a hand up and out of the poverty and desolation into which they had been born. He had not disappointed her. His work at school had steadily im-proved. He was a marvel in woodshop—Franklin Johnson had taken the underweight nine-year-old under his wing to nurture that interest. He showed a real gift for it. In ad-dition, George Ray seemed to intuit that it was up to him to help others, particularly the new students who resisted the methods of Organic Education. Both the Johnsons had impressed upon him the all-important tenet of doing one's best in all things. "If it's worth doing," Mrs. Johnson would say to him again and again, "It's worth doing well."

George Ray was 14 now. Franklin Johnson was gone. But George Ray and his Ma Johnny had soldiered on, with both of them feeling that the spread of Organic Educa-tion was a project of worldwide significance. Her own son Clifford Ernest, now in college, had put the school behind him and probably would not live in Fairhope again. Mrs. Johnson, as if in anticipation of this, had cultivated a cadre of youngsters who dedicated themselves to proselytizing for her cause.

Most of the girls in high school aspired to be teachers. They wanted to be like Marietta Johnson and they wanted her to know it. Many of them were enlisted as assistant teachers in the lower grades and some exhibited a natural ability to work with children, teaching them as they had been taught. Mrs. Johnson worried about some of them. Young Bessie Fields was energetic and vivacious and had had many talks with "Aunt Mettie" about the possibility of her becoming a kindergarten teacher. Marietta Johnson was adamant that this would not be an appropriate place for her—Bessie was high-strung and a little loud. In Mrs. Johnson's opinion this type of personality could be disturbing to pre-school children. The personality of the teacher, particularly a tense teacher, had a carryover effect to very young students who tend to emulate what they see. Such tension had no place in a kindergarten classroom. Over and over Marietta explained this in the best way she could, but Bessie was determined not to agree.

Their talks bordered on arguments, until at last Bessie agreed, with great, overblown angst, that she would not continue to pursue this particular dream.

"Bessie," said Mrs. Johnson. "Believe me, you are going to find work that you can do better than anyone else. This is your time to survey all the opportunities you have, to test all propositions, to look inward and get to know yourself better. This is the time in your life to do just that."

Bessie flounced out of her office just as Esther was coming in. Esther said, "Excuse me," to Bessie just as Bessie was in the process of making her dramatic exit. When she was gone, Marietta said to Esther, "Never pity the martyr. He is having the time of his life!" It was one of her favorite sayings.

"In this case, 'she,'" Esther said.

Charles Rabold fit right in with the student body, just as Marietta had known he would. One of the boys christened him "Everybody's Friend," and whenever he joined a group outside the folk dance class, somebody would use the phrase. He didn't mind at all. He liked the pleasant, cooperative attitude he found in this school, and he had engendered an outright love of music and dance in the students. He told Mrs. Johnson he would like to join her and George Ray on their trip to New York, but only as a fly on the wall to see how the boy took to the lights of a city he could not have imagined. George Ray struck him as an angel on earth, a true innocent, perhaps a naif. It was impossible not to like the boy. He also was a very good folk dancer.

The fact was Rabold was advancing his classes into the finer points of folk dancing—a little backward step here, to take advantage of extra music, the importance of keeping lines straight, the way to hop higher when doing a caper. His attention to such details made them all better dancers and produced dances that worked like well-oiled machines. Mrs. Johnson and Cecil Sharp had conferred about the benefits of folk dancing from a young age, and they were right that its mathematical precision kept minds alert and bodies coordinated. Her educational theory involved alternating strict academic disciplines with dance and handwork; it certainly worked in subtle ways to keep her student body committed to everything they did.

Maxwell Taylor was reaping the rewards of this attitude. His play would require a style that these students knew nothing about—the clever if stilted dialogue was a challenge for their voices and tongues, and 18th century movement, in costumes that were totally unfamiliar to them, would have been a great if not impossible challenge to any other school in the South. But it was just another learning experience here. The way he approached the play was as contemporary as possible, suggesting to his young actors that they take the characters of Sir Peter Teazle and Lord Sneerwell as people they might know, and play them sincerely. They were cartoons, but so were the teenaged actors portraying them.

He told Amelia of every detail of the production. She tried to be interested, tried to contribute to the conversations, but he did not have a lot of patience with her stories of the plays she had seen in college and in Philadelphia.

"Look, this is big stuff these kids are doing—" Max said.

"I think it's very ambitious of you," Amelia said.

"Oh, you don't know the half of it! They are my own experiment."

"I thought they were Mrs. Johnson's—"

"Well, hers too."

Amelia was preoccupied by her own emotional arousal. As their intimacy increased she noted that she and Max were not like Avery and Jim, cuddling everywhere they could. With her and Max most of the communication was intellectual and enlightening—and based upon neutral things they both found amusing. She treasured the memory of the first night he kissed her and the explosive morning when they consummated their relationship. His touch now thrilled her. She no longer thought of him as odd. Now she knew how to connect with him in a deep way that softened them both around the edges.

Once she tried to engage him in a conflict she was having with the parents of a student.

"There is some trouble between them, and I think that carries over in her behavior," she said.

"She is a young Hamlet, a young Ophelia—"

It was frustrating to have a conversation with him about the things that interested her—the very real workings of human relations, and the development of children through healthy activities. Max always found an excuse to turn the conversation to the classical theatre, and he had an annoying tendency to misinterpret what she said.

She sincerely wanted to discuss child development, and this child in particular, but he was holding forth on some point in Shakespeare.

"There is a moment in Lear when he says to Cordelia, 'Strive to be interesting. What can you say to draw a third more opulent than your sisters. Speak.' And she says, 'Nothing, my lord.'"

Amelia could not see a permanent relationship with a man whose obsession was the world of art and make believe. She could draw no comparison between her student and Cordelia or to Hamlet, or to Ophelia. It looked as if he were just looking for an excuse to expound on his own great knowledge of Shakespeare.

Max had given her a path to herself as a New Woman, and perhaps that was all she really wanted from him. She enjoyed him, yes, but she felt his affection for her was built on his image of what she was, which was quite different from the modern, self-sufficient educator she strove to become. She avoided conflicts with him, enjoyed intimacy as his friend, but she did not give him her heart. She could feel herself holding back and wondering about their relationship. Was this what marriage was for a woman—the constant checking of her own thoughts against his, the need to let him prevail by agreement with his notions and opinions? No matter what she contributed to the conversations they had, he seemed to be in a world apart from hers.

He didn't see the distance between them. His need for her to need him was so strong that he believed he saw it although it wasn't there and she never pretended it was. She wondered whether she was misleading him or if perhaps he simply had a greater capacity for fantasy.

"We'll move to New York," he was saying. "While I take the American theater by storm you can teach in one of the progressive schools there."

He was busy with plans for his life and could not think she would not be a part of it. She could see no point in her telling him her plans.

Twenty-Four

MARIETTA JOHNSON WAS readying for her trip to New York and Connecticut with George Ray Collins. They were to leave on April 8th and return on the 22nd, which would give her enough time to meet with The Fairhope League of New York City on the 11th and spend the rest of the time at Greenwich. The boy would only miss one week of school as the Easter recess was the week of the 10th. The Fairhope League was a fund-raising group for the school that was planning a debutante ball in her honor in late June. This kind of activity was anathema to her but she had long since learned that to raise money for your cause, you simply must go where the money is. This club had persuaded John Dewey to visit her school and write the critique that had started her on the road to great success. They could not be taken lightly.

George Ray would benefit from broader horizons. No doubt he would live in Fairhope all his life, and almost certainly would one day be in the employ of the school, but he did not have family or others to take him outside the narrow confines of his location.

He would not believe that it would still be chilly in the North when they got there; the temperature had been in the high 80s every day since the end of March in Fairhope. Marietta looked forward to showing him the Museum of

Natural History and taking him to the great library on Fifth Avenue. One of the Fairhope League members had offered to shepherd him for a day and take him to Central Park. She was intrigued to get his reaction to life in the city.

She would take him to meet Walter Damrosch, the great music scholar who was popularizing classical music and music theory via the radio, and who had agreed to come to Fairhope in the fall to teach a music appreciation course for all the Organic students in Comings Hall. She had met Mr. Damrosch the previous summer when he had visited Edgewood and they had struck up a lively friendship based upon a mutual interest in education—music education in particular. He agreed with her that the more everybody knew about music, the better their lives would be. He taught by explaining the complexity of music in simple everyday terms. His skill, knowledge and easy manner would be of utmost value to her school. She was excited about seeing him again and working out a schedule for his classes.

She noted that the school was at a high point this year. New boarding students had flocked in, including the sisters of the noted anthropologist Margaret Mead, the son of the writers Heywood Broun and Nancy Hale among them. She hardly noticed the people around her these days as she did so many big jobs with gusto and the sense that her school demonstrated a breakthrough in education, just as she had always known it could.

Her niece Esther gave birth a few months before to a boy named Paul for his father. Workers in the School Home were in a better frame of mind than usual—happy even. The morose and heavy Ernestine Cumbie was losing weight and was in a better disposition. There was no way of her knowing that Ernestine was more concerned than ever about Curry, who was slipping into severe melancholia and behaving more erratically every day, refusing to bathe, and growing a wild and untrimmed beard.

The situation in the Cumbie household would have distressed her, but Mrs. Johnson was focused on matters in her own life, all of which she was optimistic about. Money was still tight, but the townspeople were supporting her efforts in full force, and families continued to relocate to Fairhope just to enroll their children in her school. Truly, she felt, if this trend grew, she could take the concept of organic education to the public schools, where it was most needed, and rid traditional education of its adherence to testing and grading children.

Ruminating on these thoughts, she felt the stirrings of a speech. It had begun to dawn on her the night before as she played her game of Patience at the end of the evening, after the students had gone to bed. She spent most evenings with her deck of cards, unwinding, and letting her thoughts come to her as she gently dealt out red queen on black king and so on. Nothing relaxed her so much as a game of Patience, and often her best ideas came to her as she played.

The previous night she thought of how the warriors of history, portrayed as great men by historians, were actually cases of arrested development who would have benefited from an education that emphasized equality and cooperation. Whenever she read the histories of Napoleon or even Julius Caesar, she was entirely uneasy with the interpretation of their exploits. Could or should these men be seen as heroes, even hundreds of years after their deaths? Were they any better than schoolyard bullies who took what didn't belong to them—in fact were they not far worse, taking the lives of hundreds and thousands of innocents in their own unstable quest for power? What was this insane quest for power but the product of an unhappy, negative childhood? Would it not be possible to improve the state of the world by establishing a system of education that did not offer rewards, victories, and punishments, but instead encouraged free access to information and skills for living a better life in body, mind and spirit?

Marietta knew these were strong words, words that most men might find fault with, yet she did believe in her heart that she was right and that she had hit upon the best possible defense of her educational system. It was her habit to try out her radical ideas in the open air, with a captive audience of a cross section of merchants and citizens of Fairhope. As this particular big concept took hold in her mind, she felt the need to work it out in a practice speech, portions of which she could weave into talks she would have on her trip to New York.

She got up from her desk and crossed to the door, telling Esther she would be gone for about an hour.

"I have to work on a speech," she said, as if Esther did not recognize the symptoms from the many times she had seen her aunt in this state. Esther nodded and smiled and went back to her typewriter. Marietta Johnson strode out the door of the office, through the main room of the School Home, across the porch, past Comings Hall, and into town. She stopped in the pharmacy, where she told one and all, "I'm going to Knoll Park to practice a speech," and she was followed by the three women who were there making purchases, the lady behind the counter, and Mr. Ellerbe, the pharmacist, who followed his patrons and locked the door behind himself as he walked to the park to hear the speech.

This scene was repeated in the shops and cafes all down Fairhope Avenue, in the Courier office, and in Dr. Beatty's clinic near Church Street. Capt. Cross saw the crowd from his rocker on the porch of The Gables and called to his wife. The two of them joined the procession. Soon some 30 people were in step behind Mrs. Johnson as she entered the park and went to her favorite peak of the hill. Mme. Morehead, on her horse, was in the group.

"Thank you for joining me," Mrs. Johnson began. "I feel like making a speech."

It was an easy crowd. Fairhope was always kind to her, and she had come to expect it. This time she had some new ideas. She wanted it to be the most astounding speech she would ever make, even though it would never be heard in exactly the same way again. She challenged herself to come up with the right words, and never forget them or the moment they first came to her, here on a hill in her beloved Fairhope, surrounded by intelligent people who wanted to know what she had to say.

"I know that Organic Education is the way to bring an end to arrested development. You've heard me say that many times. *False values* and *arrested development.* The pursuit of power is one of the gods of mankind today. It can only be stopped if we change the way we look at children and childhood.

"The child is more individualistic than the adult can be. He owns the world and frankly views the whole universe from self as the center. Boastfulness and egotism in a child is quite normal and delightful. He takes the largest apple because he wants it. If he offers the best to others, it is because he has learned he may gain something by *appearing* to be unselfish.

"To push the child, rather than seeing to his own growth at his own pace, is to arrest his development. This may seem to be a paradox, yet it is at the heart of real education—education which seeks to know the needs and nature of the child and not impose adult expectations based on generalities.

"Fighting is a fundamental impulse for a child. It certainly needs no encouragement. Neither should it be too severely discouraged. It must be seen for what it is—a part of the growth process. A baby will go into hysterics if held against his will. Children also resent injustice. They fight for their possessions and to secure their way. This impulse is for the preservation of the individual. The perversion of the fighting impulse, however, is not only destructive to the individual, but to the entire race.

"It is perfectly normal for the child to fight on the physical plane. He uses whatever weapon comes to hand to attain his ends or in self-defense. If he is allowed to grow normally he will outgrow this form of aggression and will use only intellectual and spiritual means.

"The righteousness of one's cause is the only defense a developed individual needs. This will also be true of nations when armies and nations disappear, and the only defense is truth and justice."

"What was Napoleon? What was Julius Caesar? Did they possess greatness or were they merely examples of unmet potential for greatness, cases of arrested development? Schoolyard bullies allowed to run rampant over whole societies, leaving thousands of innocents dead and maimed in their wake."

The audience grew silent. They had not heard Mrs. Johnson speak so boldly in these terms before. They had

MARY LOIS TIMBES

not thought of the men of history in this way. As she looked at the crowd she could tell that the women were in accord with her views, but the men were a bit skeptical. Because she was who she was they were considering her words, but with doubtful looks.

"Why does history speak of these men as great at all? They changed history, to be sure, but they were not good. They may have been brilliant. They may have been extraordinarily talented leaders, but for what did they use their gifts? Is the world a better place for their having lived in it?

"The glory of war has been sung because of the self-sacrifice, consecration and heroism which is sometimes developed through war. The degradation of the soul and the destruction of ideals in war are not usually emphasized. When we commemorate our fallen heroes, we should humbly beg to be forgiven for permitting such sacrifice and should pray for wisdom and strength to find a better way of settling problems."

Here she could tell she held her listeners in thrall. There were tears on the cheeks of some of the women—some of whom she knew had lost sons in The Great War—and one or two of the men. All were listening for her to explain how a better educational system would lead to a wiser, more spiritual world.

"We do not need to destroy our fellow man in order to be heroic. We must as a society learn to honor as much the man and woman who does good—ministering to human welfare—as the warrior-hero. They are called upon, and answer the call, to develop the finest spirit of self-sacrifice. They are needed to establish health, to remove disease, to abolish poverty and to establish universal well-being. This sort of heroism, endured on the cross and espoused by the best of mankind every day in large and small ways, surpasses the murderous impulses of waging war."

She had to find a wind-up.

"The teacher should see to it that every child has an opportunity to develop leadership, as he exhibits the ability to do so. Children may not be ready to return good for evil, but the adult can show the evildoer that unhappiness follows wrongdoing. The injured child can learn to forget his desire for revenge.

"Love is the law of life and the universal solvent of all problems. The child's growth should ensure the development of the ability eventually to use this power."

The small crowd around her was stunned into silence for a few moments before they burst into applause. Some of Mettie's sentiments had been expressed before, but she was on her best game today. She was forceful and inspired, and she had made points about the nature of childhood and the nature of arrested development that she had not stated so clearly before. When she rounded up a Fairhope audience, they knew she wanted their honest reactions, but not necessarily at the moment after the speech. First off, she wanted to know if they had learned anything. Later she would ask them, in a personal setting, what points she might need to clarify.

Lydia Comings, who had spotted the gathering as she took her afternoon constitutional, was among the listeners who could find no fault with the speech, although she knew her friend would want to hear the worst. She approached Jack and Idella Cross.

"I've never heard her do better," she said.

"Did you think it a bit too hard on those of us who claim arrested development?" was Captain Jack's rejoinder, and the two women laughed. His wife swatted his arm with a fist.

"Not a moment too soon, I'd say," Lydia said. "I thought she might have been a little hard on Napoleon and Julius Caesar, however."

"What they deserve," said Idella Cross. "But I've never thought of them that way, I must confess."

"I didn't agree with that part," said Captain Cross. "But I'll admit it's an idea I must conjure with. I have my war heroes. Parting with them, or even seeing them in this light, will take time."

"Maybe a lifetime," his wife said to him.

Mme. Morehead was one in the audience that morning who had been the most moved.

"If only the rest of the world saw things as you do, Mettie," she said fondly to Mrs. Johnson.

"If only they'll listen, maybe they will," Mrs. Johnson answered.

The three stood together tossing around some of the ideas they had just gotten from Marietta Johnson's test speech as the crowd began to disperse. A few went to Mrs. Johnson to express their enthusiasm for the speech. No doubt this particular talk was a really good start for a lot of the discussion that would spring up around town. Mrs. Johnson would get feedback, to be sure, and would hone the specifics of the talk to specific audiences. The general reaction she got to the comments about Napoleon and Julius Caesar were just what she expected—astonishment and some opposition. She had intended for this particular talk to create some controversy, particularly among the males in the audience, so she suggested that her listeners take it home and talk with their families about it.

The gathering remained, talking among themselves about Mettie's theory of how her school might affect world events in the future. None of them were for war, and they were all set on changing the minds of the world, either through the economic theory of single tax putting an end to the profit motive behind land development, or through an egalitarian school system as Mrs. Johnson had started here. What the world needed, they agreed, was ideas like this.

Outside her listening audience there were those who were not reachable and those who unknowingly ignored her. One such citizen of Fairhope, lost, depressed—deranged, even—was shambling on the edge of the group, unaware of the profound insights that so stirred the nucleus of Fairhope's intelligensia. Near the park, Curry Cumbie made his way toward his house where Ernestine would have his dinner ready.

He saw people at the eastern edge of the park and wondered what the fuss was, until he recognized the figure of the woman he despised most in the world, talking innocently with other old ladies and shaking their hands as if she were some kind of preacher. He paused a moment to regard the scene from a distance. He had just come from some roof work over at the house Sam Bradley was renting, and to get home he had to walk by the park. He gave the assembly a few minutes to break up while he lit a cigarette, which helped him relax, although not nearly so much as the beers would do when he got home.

He didn't hear the speech; he didn't even know there had been a speech. He would never know that much Mrs. Johnson said that afternoon was about men who, deprived of childhood, suffer from what she regarded as "arrested development." Had he heard it he still would not have recognized that this very lack was at the vortex of his own swirling emotions.

Twenty-Five

EVIL HIDES BEHIND a mask of good. It may look shiny and bright but it is from the heart of Satan. God wants it eliminated, put down like a mad dog or a mindless duck or turkey. Mankind will be better when the madness is stopped. The one who stops it will have a special place in heaven for saving the world and will sit at the foot of the Throne of God forever. Heaven awaits him who takes matters into his own hands and avenges evil on this earthly plane with whatever means he can.

Curry's mind was whirling and swimming, thoughts tumbling over thoughts, emotions building as at last he understood that he was the one chosen by the Almighty to stop the Dark One on his earthly mission to change the world by deceit and the taking of lives of innocents to further his Satanic ends. It had to be done and if it meant the end of his life on this plane he was prepared with the strength of a hundred warriors.

He had taken a room at Mrs. Baker's boarding house on Royal Street in Mobile the night before Mrs. Johnson was to take the train to New York. He signed the register as Joe Smith so as not to be discovered. He made his way to the train terminal that Saturday morning. Luckily there was a crowd that day and he would not be seen or detected. He was invincible, invisible; he was all powerful. His Colt

45 was concealed and he was skilled in its use. He put his hand on it now.

"Baby, this is the day you and me is gonna do great things," he said softly, feeling the cold metal on his fingers. He hadn't eaten breakfast but he felt a need for coffee. He had a beer before he left Mrs. Baker's; it was the last of the bottles he had brought with him. It was warm but he didn't mind that this morning. The beer was a comfort to him, relieving the pain in his head somewhat, and giving him the sustenance to do the work he had to do. He had not slept that night, but lay on the cot in the boarding house with his eyes open almost the whole night. There were demons in the room and he had to watch for them.

Dawn broke and he rose from the bed, not having changed his clothes or moved an inch in the night. He focused on the task he had to do. No stray thoughts would distract him.

※

April 8 was a Saturday. Mrs. Johnson had helped George Ray pack his few things, encouraging him to travel light as she always did. So much of her time was spent in trains going across the country that she had become something of an expert in packing, and she wanted him to temper his excitement so that he would benefit more from the trip. He was a sensitive boy, and she had no doubt he would feel homesick for Fairhope, but it was vital that he develop a tougher skin for many things; travel and exposure to a broader range of people and ideas than could be found in Fairhope was an important step for him.

She helped him select the best outfit for traveling, which in his case was a pair of corduroy knickers. He protested at first, saying they were winter clothes but she knew it would not be too warm for corduroy in April in New York and Connecticut. He looked very spruce, she thought, really a rather handsome lad for a country boy, and she would be proud to introduce him in Connecticut and New York City as a product of Organic Education.

He carried her bags and his to the railway car that went down the hill. He marched with his back straight and a firm step like a slender soldier, or, as Mrs. Johnson saw it, as a slender Morris dancer. All the way on the boat ride he chattered, first to her, then to other passengers as he made his way around the deck. Mr. Pilcher was aboard, congratulating him on his journey, talking with him about the wonders he would soon be seeing. He also saw others from Fairhope and was compelled to bend their ears about his trip. Miss King and Miss Buchanan were together, taking a trip to buy stuff for their classes. He made sure to explain to them where he was going and how long it would be before he returned. Fairhope was going to be different without him and it was important that he inform all the residents that he would be back soon and tell them of his adventures in New York. He was not a braggart, but he was clearly proud to be a companion of the great and famous Marietta Johnson.

Two hours later the boat pulled into the docks in Mobile, and Mrs. Johnson and George Ray were on the way to the train station by the jitney bus that shuttled people between the two destinations. Even this ride was an adventure for George Ray; Mrs. Johnson worried how he would be able to contain himself when he saw the traffic of the city. She took him to the line for the tickets and once that was settled she directed him to the line to check their baggage. There was a clot of people between them and the counter, and George Ray was standing close by her, either to keep from getting separated from her or to protect himself from what seemed to him to be a mob, she couldn't tell. She would have to think for both of them until he got accustomed to being in crowds.

They were at the station in plenty of time. The train would go through Birmingham, Atlanta, and then on to the North—all of which were exotic to the boy. He sat beside her in the waiting room, stiff as a poker, looking out at the crowd as if he didn't know what he might see.

Then he saw something he could never have imagined—Curry Cumbie, with a full beard, wearing a jacket in this weather, stepping out in front of the crowd. George Ray knew who Curry was; he knew his wife who worked at the school home, but had not seen much of Mr. Cumbie, and now here he was, looking like a madman or a monster, there was no doubt of it. Cumbie was looking right at Ma Johnnie with a face the likes of which George Ray had never seen. Instinctively he knew this man meant to do harm to Marietta Johnson and could do so in an instant.

He saw the flash of the revolver as Cumbie drew it out of his vest. Without thinking the boy threw himself in front of Marietta Johnson. He heard the report of the gun and he felt the fire in his chest as he shielded her. The look of sheer horror on the face of the monster was the last thing George Ray Collins ever saw.

In the instant after he had pulled the trigger, Cumbie realized what had happened. He had not seen the boy with Mrs. Johnson and thought he had a clear shot from where he stood. Then the face of the kid turned to him in the instant that the gun went off. He saw his own intention thwarted and he saw the look on the face of that child, much as his own Alice Ann might have looked when she realized her life would be over before she had time to live it.

A woman screamed and the crowd scattered, running this way and that around the terminal. It was chaos, which would only get worse. He knew he had killed a child and he could not tolerate the thought of living another minute himself. He turned the gun on himself, shooting himself in the head. He fell to the ground.

Marietta Johnson hadn't seen the man in the crowd until it was too late. George Ray had acted instantaneously and heroically and now two people lay dying, one of whom was trying only to save her and the other in an unthinkable attempt at murder. She felt as if she herself had been hit. She was numb, sitting with the boy's head in her lap with tears flowing from her eyes, very still, like a statue on the station bench with people rushing about her, screaming and running in all directions except toward her. At last a policeman appeared along with some medics in uniform. She said, "It's no use," when one of the medics caught her eye. George Ray lay still with his head in her lap, his blood on her clothes. The medical man responded to her patiently, indicating that she was right, yet he went forward with his work of removing the two bodies to stretchers. A kindly man who introduced himself as the chief of police, although he was in plainclothes, was helping her to her feet as she said, "We were—going—to New York," and he said, "That's all right Ma'am," sensing that she was in shock. "You won't be taking that trip just now."

They took her to the hospital too, to a room where she could rest, they said. The nurses cleaned blood off her, put her in a hospital gown, and gave her a glass of water. The police asked her a few questions about the man who had the gun and the boy who died. Everything seemed to be moving slowly, especially her own thoughts. She had trouble answering the simplest questions. Words just wouldn't come.

※

It was still the Lenten season in heavily Catholic Mobile, which meant Amelia and Avery might expect a more somber attitude in the city than had been the case the previous weeks during the Carnival, when the streets were clogged with parades and revelers.

Yet stores were open today for brisk business. The streets were busy.

"Let's get the mundane out of the way first," Avery said. They ventured off Bienville Square to a section of Royal Street that held small retail establishments selling novelties and school supplies like scissors and maps. They had their favorites among these, and fairly bounced into one to browse and place their orders. A gray-haired man behind the counter dourly explored the cabinets until he found exactly what both young teachers wanted. They carried large handbags, the kind women used for storing large items they bought.

"Now to Hammel's!" Amelia said, glad to have the business of the trip behind her and ready to venture into Mobile's premier department store.

"Onward!" said her companion. "But only if you promise that Three Georges" –their favorite candy store—"will be next!"

"I think some candy will be in order after I pick up a few colorful and stylish scarves," Amelia said. "Let's have lunch at The Tea Room too."

It had started off as an ordinary day, even a good one, but this day was to be one of the most terrible in the lives of the young schoolteachers. They simply did not know it yet.

On their way to Three Georges they passed the office of the Mobile Press Register, where the afternoon paper screamed a headline with the terrible news.

Murder-Suicide at Mobile Terminal; Marietta Johnson In Hospital.

The girls hurried, anxious for information, into the newsroom to find out how and where Mrs. Johnson was and what could possibly have happened. They picked up a copy of the paper at the front desk to read the harrowing story of the shooting at the train terminal.

Avery stopped the first man they saw who looked as if he might be in charge.

"Where is Marietta Johnson?" both girls asked at the same moment.

"Mobile Infirmary," the man in the newspaper office said, rolling down his shirtsleeves in deference to having ladies in the newsroom.

"Is there some reason you young ladies want to know?

"We work for her," Amelia said. "We are teachers."

"We just happen to be in Mobile for some shopping," Avery added. "Do you think she's in any condition to see us?"

"I don't think she's doing too well, but if you want to go there, take a bus, and see if they'll let you visit." He saw the obvious concern in their faces. "Prob'ly will."

There was a bus stop on the corner of Government, just outside the Press Register building, and they waited with unspoken anxiety until a creaky old city bus rattled toward them and heaved to a stop.

They were quiet on the bus ride to the hospital, expecting the worst and unable to picture the usually dynamic and vital Mrs. Johnson in such a vulnerable condition.

"This is going to be all right, Amelia," Avery said to her friend. Amelia glanced at her but could not return Avery's uneasy smile.

"I think we're going to get there and find out it isn't so bad. Mrs. Johnson has been through a lot in her life, and she can handle this," she continued, trying to keep the ball of conversation in the air and alleviate her friend's obvious anxiety if she could.

"Handle it?" Amelia said, almost as if she didn't understand the words.

"We all know she has the strength, if anybody does," Avery said.

Amelia's fear was so deep that she could hardly respond. She tried to concentrate on what her friend was saying but she was almost overwhelmed with fear that it may not be true and they would find Mrs. Johnson injured or traumatized. Everybody in Fairhope knew Marietta Johnson had a weak heart.

When they got to the hospital they were sent to the lobby on the wing where she was being held. Avery kept chattering and Amelia tried to listen and nod in appropriate places. She was again feeling her childhood emotions of fear and insecurity—feelings she thought she had conquered. Contemplating life without Marietta Johnson to consult on matters large and small just was not possible for her.

A handsome doctor with graying hair came over to them.

"I'm Dr. Blake," he said. "I understand you are here to see Mrs. Johnson."

"Yes, yes!" said Avery, while Amelia just nodded her head.

"She's had a terrible shock, as I guess you know," Dr. Blake said.

They both nodded and searched his face for some indication of what to expect.

"I've spoken with her doctor—Dr. Beatty," he said. They nodded. They both recognized the familiar name of the Fairhope physician. "He tells me she has a heart condition. I don't think she should be moved until tomorrow. Dr. Beatty agreed and will come over to help her go home on the morning bay boat."

That sounded good. Surely Mrs. Johnson would benefit by medical attention and the chance to rest in the hospital overnight.

"May we see her?" Avery asked.

"I think that would be all right," Dr. Blake said. "I don't know if she'll be able to talk to you, but I think just seeing familiar faces may help jar her back to normal."

This was the first hint Amelia had that Mrs. Johnson herself might be injured in some way. She really didn't know what to expect now—Mrs. Johnson was her model of well-being and good cheer. When they saw her in the hospital bed she was stone-faced and looked confused.

Avery attempted to behave as normally as possible and to keep as lighthearted as she could. Amelia could sense her doing this, but she simply could not. She faced Mrs. Johnson with an unnatural look on her face, trying to hide her fear with a forced smile that looked more like a grimace.

"These young ladies have come to see you," Dr. Blake said.

Marietta Johnson did not move, but her eyes turned to them and she looked as if she were trying to smile.

"Do you know who they are?"

"Hello, Aunt Mettie," Avery said. Mrs. Johnson brightened a bit. Amelia raised her eyebrows, as if that were a way to ask a question.

"Can you tell me who they are?" the doctor asked again. But Mrs. Johnson only said, "I know, yes, I know who they are."

"Of course you do," Avery said.

"But I can't think of their names," Mrs. Johnson said, almost angrily. "I do know."

"That's all right," the doctor said. "We know you know. It will come back to you soon. Just be easy on yourself now."

Then he turned to the young women and said, "I think that's about all the company she can take today. We'll see that she gets some rest, in hopes that she can get to Fairhope tomorrow."

The nurse herded the two teachers out the door of the room. When they were in the waiting room she spoke to them softly.

"She is in a state of shock, you see," the nurse said. "Memory loss is common in shock, and it's usually temporary. Be patient with her, and try not to worry about it. We'll help her rest for now."

Amelia could hardly believe she had seen Mrs. Johnson in this condition.

"I think I'm in a state of shock too," she said to Avery as they made their way to the nearest bus stop.

"Well, that was pretty awful," Avery said when they waited for a bus at the door of the infirmary. "You do look bad, you know—as if you'd seen a ghost."

"I have," Amelia said. "The Ghost of Christmas Future."

Amelia had a great deal to think about, but she couldn't seem to focus her mind. Instead, she was assaulted by random memories, unrelenting and out of her control, as she felt more and more disoriented and frightened. To calm herself she bore down on one thought—at least Mrs. Johnson had survived. They said at the hospital that she would be better tomorrow.

The bus lurched toward the docks where they would get on the boat for the two-hour ride home.

"Here, now," Avery said. She straightened herself. "Our vessel awaits. The good ship Bay Queen."

Familiar faces, some also looking stricken, swarmed around the boat, some speaking to each other, some staring out at the bay as the boat pulled away from the dock. They all had heard the news and were in various states of coping with it. Some carried the newspaper. Mrs. Johnson was the rock they all leaned on, really the center of the community. Her losing one of her students, so beloved and full of promise, in a sudden and violent way, might be too much for her. There was also the unreal aspect of the murderer being one of them.

Avery and Amelia chose to stick to each other, away from the crowd. Avery kept up her strategy of bolstering Amelia by changing the subject. The calm bay waters and the murmuring crowd were beginning to help her calm down. The monkey-smile on her face relaxed to a normal appearance.

Avery took a deep breath, seeing her friend revert to her familiar, former, more comfortable self.

"I liked that doctor," Avery said.

Amelia almost smiled. Avery was always susceptible to a good-looking man.

"I mean to say, I trusted him. I think she's in good hands."

"I think so too." Amelia said. After a pause she added, "I never expected anything like this."

"How could you?"

"I have this awful feeling, that I could have done something—that I should have prevented this," said Amelia, almost as a confession.

"I hate to tell you, but that's always the way people feel when such a thing happens. My uncle was killed in a riding accident, and to this day I don't think my mother has stopped saying, 'If only I hadn't let him go out that day...'"

"I didn't feel like that when my grandpa died," Amelia said. She began thinking of her days with him, his quirks and kindnesses, and the sense of loss when she got the telegram from her parents that he had died in the night.

"Was that sudden, out of the blue, like this?" Avery asked her.

"No, not really. He was old, and I watched him get weaker—but I never thought he would die. You just don't think about that."

Amelia could see that this situation was not like the death of her grandfather. She had happy memories of her days with him, felt his loss, but he died of old age when she was a college student. She had accepted it as a matter of course as she moved forward.

"This is shock, that's what it is," Amelia said. "And that awful man. I should have been able to stop him."

The picture of Curry Cumbie came to her in full focus—the first time she saw his face with its other-worldly fixed smile, her revulsion at just seeing him in this little town, his sinister appearance, out of place. Now she pictured him lying on a slab in the morgue.

"Think of it, Amelia—how could you have known?"

"I always knew."

"No you didn't," Avery said. "You didn't like him, but there was no way you could have anticipated—"

"I have seen evil."

"I can't argue with that, but that doesn't mean you had a hand in it. You were more perceptive than I ever was about that man, and that's surely a good thing—but you don't have magical powers."

"I am just one person," Amelia said, really to herself, trying to piece together in her mind the unfathomable events of the past few months. "And I wasn't charged with the responsibility of—"

"Saving the world." Avery completed her sentence for her.

Avery was right, of course. This incident did not stem from anything Amelia had done, and it was not up to her to make it right. Yet she was haunted by the thought that she might have warned Mrs. Johnson of her suspicion that the paradise of Fairhope might harbor at least one serpent. Now she tried to sort Fairhope and its images in her mind. Memories and images crowded each other out as she thought of them--the friendly faces of the old people who welcomed her when she first came to town, the new friends her age who taught at the school, the children of Fairhope climbing trees and playing marbles in the street. Even with the mosaic of smiles and kindly faces in her thoughts she could not erase the frozen expression Marietta Johnson wore in the hospital room.

She was thinking differently now—was this dream of utopia all that fragile? And the school—Mrs. Johnson and her extraordinary vision of changing the world through a new kind of education. Was it possible all this was an illusion?

Amelia let out a deep breath as she felt the moist breeze from the bay on her cheek for the first time on the trip. It was like the fresh wind of childhood, reminding her of the mission that had brought her to Fairhope. She was confronted with her own conflicts now, gradually becoming aware how fragile a dream can be.

🙦

Marietta Johnson knew, in the blur of her memories, that two of her young teachers, Miss Buchanan and Miss King, had been in the room trying to talk with her, and the very nice Dr. Blake had spoken with them. It was like a dream, but far worse than any dream she had ever had. She tried to talk but couldn't make anyone understand. She remembered who she was, at least, and made that clear to the doctors, nurses and police. They told her they would bring her friends from Fairhope on the next boat to take her home in the morning.

She would have little memory of that day or the next. The loss of George Ray, the hideous scene of his murder, the death of the deranged man—events faded in her mind and returned in flashes as gradually she began to experience grief, remorse and even self-doubt. It was simply unthinkable that she could have been in the middle of such a nightmare. She was given a sedative, and she rested somewhat during the night, but she had no thoughts of the brief visit of the two young teachers from her school. Her great, active mind was hobbled as she sought her way through the webs of mystery surrounding the horrific event. She seemed a different woman, subdued and uncommunicative, when Dr. Beatty and Lydia Comings came to take her back to Fairhope.

Weeks went by before she could sleep without some medication from Dr. Beatty.

Lydia spent hours with her every day, just as she had years ago when the two women suffered the great loss of loved ones in their lives within the same month. Mettie drew solace from Lydia, her own rock when times were difficult. They had been, Lydia said, through deep waters together before.

One by one, Mrs. Johnson's friends visited her at the School Home, bringing food and comfort as they could— yet the emotional pain was almost unbearable.

Lydia was able to remind her that she had survived terrible events before, but Marietta seemed to have only a dim awareness of the life surrounding her. The only thing that cheered her even slightly was the news that the school was running well.

"I know you would like to have been able to go to Greenwich," Lydia said to her. "We've heard from them, and they say things are going well. They look forward to your return early in the summer."

"I wanted to show it to George Ray," Marietta said.

"Yes, and that isn't going to happen now. I know how sad you feel," Lydia tried to reassure her. "The school is prospering, and your ideas are taking hold. Give yourself some time to sort all this out in your heart."

Marietta nodded. She knew that time was the answer. In time the school would give her hope and a reason to live. Only time could alleviate her grief and sense of guilt.

Twenty-Six

ONE MORNING EARLY in the week, Charles Rabold came to visit her.

"I've brought us some doughnuts from the Tea Tile," he said. The Tea Tile was the new café in town, and its doughnuts were quite the rage. She didn't eat things like that, he knew, but he gave her a smile and a wink.

"I checked with Dr. Beatty," he said. "And he says these would be good for you just this once. I've asked Auntie Co to brew us some tea."

Marietta tried to fathom how he could be making a friendly call at this time.

"I want to tell you of a project of mine," he said.

She was looking at him through her gleaming eyes, trying to smile or give him some encouragement but because she was dubious of his mission she could not tell if she was successful. She hoped the attempt to give him her attention would be taken as a measure of interest in what he had to say.

Just then Cora Myhers knocked lightly at the door and Charles went to it to get the tray of tea. He greeted her and thanked Cora, and took two doughnuts out of the paper bag he had brought them in, which now showed grease all the way through.

"I hope I'm not leading you astray," he said as he poured tea for both of them.

"Of course not, Charles," she said. "You are a ray of sunshine, as always."

This made him smile, which in an oblique way indicated he was concerned for her and trying not to show how much. They both sipped their tea and he took a big bite out of the doughnut. Mrs. Johnson felt it would be rude not to take a nibble, so she did.

"Delicious," she said.

"Glad you like it—now you must eat more of it than that," he said.

"I wanted to tell you of a plan," he said after he swallowed his second bite of doughnut and washed it down with a gulp of tea.

He then stared right into her eyes.

"The town, and the school as well, have been thunderstruck by the events of last weekend. I have no doubt that the adults will cope well, but to the boys in the school this is an almost unbearable situation."

She nodded and stared dully at her cup of tea.

"I have an idea of a way to help them, and I want to know what you think of it," he continued.

She looked up at him, at last engaged. Perhaps, even in her weakened state, she could be of some assistance in what he was asking. If only she could concentrate.

"You always say that boys are like puppy dogs," he said. "They need to run off their energy, to jump and frolic until they collapse in a heap."

She smiled slightly at the image. Yes, she did believe that, but it hardly applied to the current tragedy. She took another bite of the doughnut and a big sip of tea, which was soothing balm at last.

"George Ray's friends are at a loss. They are not in touch with their own grief and they are simply miserable."

"I'm sure they are," she said, trying to grasp his point.

"I want permission to take a truck load of them to the beach at the Gulf," he said. The Gulf of Mexico was a good long drive, but it offered a beautiful white sand beach and surf.

"And what will happen there?"

"We shall folk dance!" said Charles Rabold happily.

For the first time in weeks, Marietta Johnson laughed out loud. She was not laughing at her colleague's idea, but with joy at the rightness of it.

"Until they drop in a heap on the dunes!" she said.

"Exactly. Do you agree it's a good idea?"

"Yes, Charles," she said. "I think it's a very *organic* idea indeed!"

"I'll proceed with the arrangements, then," he said. "I'll get the kitchen to prepare us a lunch basket, and I'll pack all the swords we need for the sword dance, the sticks for the stick dance—and you'll see. I think it will shake them from their torpor and move them through their mourning right to the day of the memorial Saturday, when they will be able to weep outright if they need to and move on through their lives."

His eyes were shining at the thought of this. Marietta hardly noticed that she had finished her tea and eaten a whole doughnut.

"Puppy dogs on the beach," she said gently, a little sadly.

"Dancing puppy dogs," Rabold, thrilled to have made dancers out of ordinary boys, also enjoyed a feeling of being help to Marietta.

❦

The next day Charles helped Joe Cyrus, Wallace Hodges, Chauncey Wilson, Ronson Marshall, Zeke and Pat Arnold into the truck. He put young Chauncey next to himself in the cab. All the boys' faces were solemn and apprehensive.

"Relax, men," Mr. Rabold said to them. Then, after a moment, seriously: "This is what George Ray would want us to do."

They were not convinced as they sat in the back of the truck, the wind blowing their hair wildly. They could hardly look at each other. They would do anything Mr. Rabold suggested, but a picnic at the Gulf was not what they would have contemplated with such heavy hearts. They saw he had brought the folk dance swords and sticks, but they could not discern any purpose for them.

The Gulf beach was bare and bright, a huge sandbar that had been deposited, almost like a gift, by the big hurricane ten years before. A lone wooden hotel stood at the western end of the sandy dirt road they drove down, but Mr. Rabold was taking them in the other direction. As soon as they pulled up to a spot in the dunes where he could park, about a mile from the main highway, he stopped the truck in the middle of the road. No point in risking getting stuck in the sand. No other vehicles would come this way.

"You all know I want us to folk dance," Mr. Rabold said, piling the sticks out. "Let's start with 'Lads A Bunchum.'"

The boys formed a set of six. Mr. Rabold took a place at the head of the set and, as if to demonstrate the dance, he danced with them, exerting himself as much as possible. He urged them to jump higher, to sing the music with him, to dance harder, as they did dance after dance for an hour in the sun on the beach, sweating and tearing up inadvertantly as thoughts of their fallen friend came to their minds.

It was time for lunch and he could tell the plan was working. They had thrown themselves into the dancing and the masks of desperation and sorrow were giving way to a looks of the living—the look of normal boys on a day at the beach.

Auntie Co and the School Home staff had packed egg salad and tunafish sandwiches on white bread, and a few chicken sandwiches on whole wheat bread, a pitcher of fruit punch which was not cold but felt wonderful going down. They knew a lunch for six hungry boys would require plenty of sandwiches; they had allowed three for each, plus two pies—apple, and a mulberry from the trees by the driveway at the School Home. They filled the rest of the basket with fruits, including loquats and satsumas from the local trees.

Then they all sat on the dunes for a few minutes, and Ronson Marshall, the boarding student from Connecticut, suddenly blurted, "I wish George Ray could be here." They all began to cry overtly. Charles allowed them to do so for a few minutes and then he said, as simply and in as straightforward a manner as he could muster (as he himself was not far from tears) "He is here, you know. Every one of us will have him at our sides the rest of our lives. Now, let us do some of the Morris dances."

He demonstrated "Jockey To the Fair," a difficult challenge-dance they were learning for Spring Festival, and soon they all were trying it. They did a few more Morris dances, very strenuous, and then Charles announced it was time for the sword dance. They knew that this would be the last dance at the Festival and probably the last dance of the day. They each took swords, Charles sang the tune for them, and they clapped the wooden swords together as they went through the complicated manouevres of the dance, ending by weaving the swords into a star. As they brought the circle to the end Zeke, who held the star in the air, presented it to their teacher. He took it and smiled. There were tears in some of their eyes and two of the boys sank to the sand and lay flat on their backs. They were not in a heap like puppies, but they were spent, emotionally and physically.

"Very good work," he said. "I'm proud of you all."

At that, they all sat down on the sand to rest, and one by one they began to weep, even Mr. Rabold. Thinking of these boys and what would become of them, how each would go on to productive lives, and again of missing boy and the life that would not be his. He lay on the sand for a moment until he felt a tear run down his cheek and drop to the sand. He let out an audible sigh and began to realize they had all reached a point of awareness and grace.

Rabold got up, brushed sand off his clothes, and told them it was time to go home. The boys piled into the truck talking softly to each other. They thanked him and told him they felt better.

"I'm not worried about Spring Festival now," Zeke Arnold said, and all the boys nodded in assent and allowed as how they had all improved their folk dancing skill that day. Their spirits were lifted, too, although they didn't quite realize this at first. As they sat in the back of the bus they began to sing some of the old English songs they had learned at school, and all at once the Arnold boys burst into "Amazing Grace," which the whole group sang at top volume, so loud that Chauncey and Mr. Rabold heard it in the cab and joined in. Charles Rabold came to see he was not much more than a puppy dog himself.

⚜

Marietta and Lydia went for a walk on the beach and talked about the incredible recent events.

"I hate to think that that troubled man had hidden his feelings all this time, even from Ernestine," Marietta said.

"Do you know that?"

"She is quite beside herself with guilt," Marietta told her friend. "I could only say to her that she was not to blame in any way. I do not know if that helped her."

They walked in silence. Marietta picked up a limb of driftwood and used it to mark in the sand.

"This is the most tragic event of all, friend," Lydia said. "And I can but think, 'What if that man had achieved his goal?'"

"Life is full of what-ifs," Marietta said. "It was not to be. I shall always think, 'What if George Ray had survived?'"

Lydia reached for her friend's free hand, and they walked along the bayfront in silence.

Twenty-Seven

THE MEMORIAL FOR George Ray Collins was held the day before Easter at the Fairhope Christian Church. It was packed to the rafters. Marietta Johnson sat ramrod-straight in the group with the faculty of the school and the staff of the School Home. The colored help, solemn and silent, took their place at the rear of the sanctuary. They all had loved George Ray and knew his noble act had saved Mrs. Johnson from a madman's bullet.

Marietta Johnson wanted the simplest ceremony with a few hymns and she suggested Rev. Dickerson ask Mme. Morehead to sing.

When the program started, Mme. Morehead sang the poignant hymn she had chosen, "Let the Little One Sleep," which described the death of a child as sleep, a needed slumber from which he should not be roused. The song was sentimental and sad. This was the occasion for such emotions. In Fairhope nobody objected to overt sentimentality; the gentle, old-fashioned song moved the congregation to tears. Mercedes looked handsome in a long black skirt and waist, with a simple cameo at the neck. She ended the music for the program with "How Great Thou Art," always a hymn that elevated the spirits of a grieving congregation—and her trained soprano elevated the music to spiritual heights. The congregation sang a hymn Mrs. Johnson had requested

"This Is My Father's World," which she chose because she knew it was a hymn that George Ray had loved. His appreciation of this ode to nature and God's world was as innocent and pure as the boy himself had been.

As he and Mrs. Johnson had discussed, Rev. Dickerson spoke of the infinite wisdom of God and the difficulty of man in comprehending events such as those the people had endured the past week. He continued his sermon saying that in time the people of Fairhope would heal and they always would be grateful to the Almighty had spared the intended victim so that she might go on with the work she had begun. He admonished the gathering to pray for understanding, forgiveness and to thank God for Marietta Johnson.

Mrs. Johnson had not wanted him to overpraise her in this way but he was intent on including this section. To his mind affirmation of the person who exemplified the spirit of Fairhope was the only good that might come of the calamity. He insisted the people must be reminded that she survived, and her strength was the strength of the town itself, and that the town might go forward with greatness only with her leadership.

Ernestine did not go to the service, but she was with Curtis and Lou Ellen at the gravesite. Distraught and uncomprehending, she had nonetheless insisted on attending. It was the only way she knew to begin to make amends for the senseless killing. She did not admit to anyone that she could only feel relief that Curry was gone from the earth. If only she had known what he planned to do, maybe, she thought, she could have stopped him if it meant putting the bullet in him herself. In the last few weeks she hardly saw him, but she had known full well that he was up to something. She never could have imagined this.

The teachers stood together on one side of the grave as the coffin was lowered into the ground. They thought of the loss of this fine boy, but more than that they realized how close Marietta Johnson herself had come to being a victim of this unspeakable crime. Many wept outright, and those, like Maxwell and Jim, who did not, were visibly holding back tears.

Amelia and Avery talked of their visit with Marietta Johnson in the hospital, how shocking it was to see her in such a condition. Amelia's fear was that even though not hit by the madman's bullet, Mrs. Johnson might be indirectly taken by this incident after all. It was possible her heart would not hold. Seeing her without her usually aura of good spirits and total control of matters started Amelia questioning her own resolve.

Thoughts of the meaning of the utopia worried her. Nothing was as perfect as it had seemed at first.

Amelia thought of the shivers she always got when she saw the killer, Curry Cumbie. She had felt all along he was truly dangerous; she even had a premonition that he was going to go off the deep end and do something dreadful. All that she would have imagined was an act of domestic violence, perhaps, or a drunken fight, but his appearance betrayed a soul suffused with evil. Avery had always downplayed this, thinking he really couldn't help his appearance, but what Amelia saw was the reality of the man, and she knew it. It was just a matter of time before a full mental breakdown would cause him to act.

The four of them walked together from the cemetery to the cottage, the couples holding hands, all tearful. The atmosphere in Fairhope was more than sorrowful; it was permeated with a feeling that it was unsafe. Everybody shared a shaky vigilance, as if there were now dark forces in the shadows, lurking in the trees and bushes. It was comforting for Amelia to be between Avery and Max, with her shoulder brushing that of always calm Avery and her hand firmly gripped by Max's. The four of them alternated sighs as they put one foot in front of the other to reach the cottage that had meant so much to them all.

"I think there's a bottle of something in the kitchen somewhere." Avery crossed directly to the pantry area as soon as she entered the house.

"We need it," said Max. "The whole town needs it."

Amelia needed a chair, and she plopped into the shaggy carpet rocker.

"I'll help," said Jim, going right into the kitchen to uncork the bottle of the red liquid and bring a glass to Amelia while taking one for himself.

"This was so unexpected," Amelia said, closing her eyes. "Things were going so well."

"And they will again," said Avery, coming from the kitchen with glasses of wine for herself and Max.

"How?"

"We have to follow Mrs. Johnson's lead. Just see what she does and do the same."

Jim said, "I wonder where her strength comes from."

"She has a mission," said Max.

"Yes. Her life is her school." Amelia was well aware of that.

"She's been tested before," said Avery.

"Maybe," said Amelia. "But nothing like this."

"She lost her own baby 15 years ago—"

"I thought he was off at college?"

"There was another baby. Killed in a freak accident—a head injury, I heard."

"My God!" said Max.

Avery related what she knew of the story. It was during the early days of the school, Avery said, her youngest son, little more than a baby, had fallen from a table and hit his head. The fall was fatal.

"Probably the school and its mission were Mrs. Johnson's motivation to carry on even then," Avery said.

"And she had her husband," said Jim.

"Yes. Then she had to endure the loss of him."

"But that's not like a child," said Avery. "Mr. Johnson was ill for some time, I understand."

"It's interesting that she never speaks of the death of the baby. I wonder if she will speak of George Ray," Amelia said.

They were quiet while they all stared ahead and drank their wine. Amelia thought of Fairhope itself and all the cracks in its veneer of perfection.

It was not possible to achieve heaven on this earth after all.

"Did you hear about Mr. Rabold taking the boys to the beach?" Avery asked after a moment.

"Why was that, do you suppose?" Jim said.

"I think to help 'em let off steam," said Max. "And it worked too. They all were calmer—more at ease—today."

They all pictured the boys, how they'd gone from being miserable a few days ago, at a loss, to the straight-backed young men at the memorial, focused and solemn, suddenly almost grown up.

"They are readying themselves for Spring Festival," Max said.

"That's right," Amelia said, now realizing the visible change in the mood around school. "I even heard Zeke Arnold say it was what George Ray would have wanted."

"I had to replace him in *The School for Scandal*," Max said. "Small part, but we'll always think of him in it."

"Funny to think of the boys saying what George Ray would have wanted," said Jim. "George Ray was a tag-along—he always was on the edge of the crowd. Now they're deferring to him, doing what they think he would have wanted."

"And it was Ma Johnnie he tagged along behind the most," Avery said.

"He would want everything to go as usual," Max said. "So he could tag along."

Everybody laughed softly.

"I liked what the preacher said," Jim said, pouring another glass of wine.

"What else could he say?" Avery was staring at the floor.

"It was kind of upbeat, at least," Jim said. "We must carry on—that sort of thing."

"And we must thank God that Mrs. Johnson was spared," said Amelia.

Everybody nodded assent, still staring straight ahead, thinking. There was a knock at the door.

Avery got up and the group heard Sam Bradley, the man from next door.

"I don't want to disturb y'all," Bradley said. He had a bottle of home brew in his hand.

"No, you're not, not at all, Sam," Avery said.

"Thought you might appreciate a little drink about now," he said.

"We had the same idea," Avery told him, "But every little bit helps. Please join us."

"I wanted to say a few things to you," Sam said.

"Come on in," Avery said, walking him into the living room where the others were sitting. She picked up a glass for him in the kitchen and carried it with her.

"Thanks a lot, Mr. Bradley," Amelia said.

By now they all had some liquor in their glasses and Amelia took a swallow. It was stronger stuff than she was used to. The group laughed when they saw her face at her first sip.

"This is not what I'm accustomed to!" she said. Her throat burned but she was determined to be a good sport.

"I thought of that," Sam Bradley said. "But on a day like today, you have to have high octane."

The group laughed again.

"I know you're all grievin'," he said. "I am too. I feel—I guess I feel responsible."

"Oh, no," said Avery, and everybody chimed in, reinforcing her.

"I gave work to Curry Cumbie, even though I could see he was in a bad way. I guess that was why I gave him work. I just didn't know…"

"You did a good thing, Mr. Bradley," Avery said. "That is, you did what you did for a good reason."

He turned to her with a most mournful look on his face.

"I didn't have no idea."

"How could you have—of course you didn't—you were doing the man a favor!" were the comments the group made, all at once, so that it was indistinguishable who was doing the talking.

"I knowed Curry and Ernestine for years, back when their daughter was in that accident," he said. As he looked around the room he realized that none of these young people had known about Alice Ann or the landslide. That was back in '15, and the school kept the story quiet since then.

"What accident?" Jim said, so Sam Bradley laid it all out for them, how the child had gone up into a cave on a field trip to the gully, was smothered in a landslide, how Mrs. Johnson was nowhere in sight, not even in town, but when she got back she stopped all school trips to the gullies. The teacher in charge, he said, felt so bad she left the school for good. And, he said, Curry and Ernestine had moved away for years. Nobody thought they would ever come back, but when they did, Sam and everybody else thought their minds had healed.

"As I saw Curry git more and more unhinged, I just didn't make the connection. I allus thought it was just because he couldn't git a break, really, and maybe it 'us the drink. He got to drinkin' real bad.

"I hadn't seen him around for a coupla weeks. I didn't know he was in such a bad way." Bradley took a healthy swig of his drink. "I shoulda done something."

Everybody jumped on him for that. Of course there was nothing he could have done, they all agreed.

"I had the same feeling, and I couldn't even stand to look at the man," Amelia said.

"Everybody always thinks they could have done something to stop it when something like this happens," Max said. "But they never can. And they never could."

"I did know one thing about him that nobody else knew," Sam confided, and everybody turned to him.

"He was the only man in the world to hate Marietta Johnson," Sam said. "I think that hate just took his mind."

They all tried to think about it. Sam poured another round from his bottle, but Amelia wasn't up to it. The drink was making her dizzy to the point of nausea. Nobody had had any food since lunch.

Amelia was thinking about the utopian promise of the school and of Fairhope. To make it heaven, everybody had to be on board one hundred per cent. One slip and the whole concept would cave in, just like that wall of the gully with the Cumbie's child. There seemed to be something false about the experiment, something fragile at the very base of the structure.

Sam said again that he was sorry for all concerned. Most of all, he said, he was sorry for the school and Mrs. Johnson, but he knew they would do all right in time.

"Yeah," said Jim. "Hard to imagine now, but it's gonna get better."

At that point Bradley rose and picked up his bottle, which still had some of the home brewed whiskey in it. He took his leave of the group, saying he appreciated them letting him talk, and that he hoped and prayed everybody would feel better in the morning. Everybody noticed that he took his bottle with him when he left.

"Bring your bottle and leave with it—I don't know if that's an Alabama custom," Jim said. "But he left me wanting more liquor."

"Anybody who wants more is welcome to mine," Amelia said. "I don't know what's in this stuff, but if I have another swallow I'm pretty sure I'll be sick."

"That's alcohol," Max said. "Hard stuff. You have to have the stomach for it."

"And I don't."

"Think some fresh air might help?"

Some nights Amelia went home with Max and left the cottage to Avery and Jim. This was definitely a night she didn't want to spend alone, and the two couples had learned early on that both couples spending the night in that cottage didn't work. The walls upstairs were too thin.

Amelia thought for a moment through the haze in her mind.

"I think so, yes," she said. "I think I'll walk you home tonight." This was their code for spending the night together at his place, and Avery and Jim knew it well.

"I doubt if anyone in Fairhope will be sleeping much tonight," Avery said.

The walk through the town in the dark was different this night. Lights were on in most of the houses they passed, for one thing. People all over town were doing as Sam Bradley had done, visiting their neighbors, talking things over, trying to sort out between them the events of the day and the preceding week. Everybody needed understanding. House by house, they sought each other to help assuage their grief and disbelief.

Maxwell sensed her grief as he walked Amelia up Oak Street and on to Bancroft to his room. He could tell she was melancholy and she could not think of words to say to him. The bloom had faded since their first awakenings of passion, and she knew very well she did not want to make love to him this night.

MARY LOIS TIMBES

"I have to tell you, there was something in Mr. Bradley's home brew that apparently has rendered me impotent," Max said.

"It has rendered me decidedly woozy," Amelia said. She was glad the air was thus cleared. She wanted someone to lie down with, someone to embrace her, and she loved that it was Max, but she knew there were too many distractions in her mind this night for lovemaking.

As they walked through town they could only notice how many houses sat with their lights on, and wonder how many neighbors were comparing their stories of Curry Cumbie, Marietta Johnson, and George Ray Collins, the courageous young victim of the irrational act.

They slept in the bed, both of them fitfully, and in the night Amelia said, "Do you think we shall get over this?

"We have no choice," Max said. "But it won't be easy, and it won't be soon."

Marietta Johnson sat in the big room at the School Home, playing Patience with a fierce intensity. She felt she must restore serenity and positive action in the school by going through the motions of everyday life.

Boarding students milled about, and Auntie Co and Esther always saw to it that the curious children kept their distance when Mrs. Johnson played Patience. They understood her attitude and her need to be alone with her thoughts this night. They sat talking quietly in a corner of the room Paul holding Esther's hand as her baby, Paul Frederick III, slept soundly nearby in a cradle his father had made for him.

She turned the deck to find a red nine for her black ten, which gave her the opportunity to move a black seven with its row of alternating colors off its nest of face-down cards and on to the red jack the moved red nine revealed. Then she spotted the Queen of Hearts, which had been facing her on the board all along.

One thought came into her mind as she moved the Queen of Hearts onto the King of Spades and sighed with a deep breath that reverberated around the room: She was going to win this game.

And tomorrow would be Easter.

Twenty-Eight

THAT EASTER SUNDAY was a turning point for the citizens of Fairhope, with the memorial for George Ray just one day behind them. Ministers at the Methodist and Baptist congregations joined Rev. Dickerson of the Disciples of Christ in the topic of their Sunday messages, incorporating the hometown story with the resurrection of Christ. They all did what they could to impart an atmosphere of hope in the desolated town.

In Maxwell Taylor's room, the couple sat on the edge of the bed sipping coffee. Amelia told him that she felt a need to commune with the Quakers on this day. He nodded, understanding that she, like everybody else in Fairhope, needed some help in coping with recent events.

"I'm beginning to worry about myself," Amelia said.

"Why is that?"

"I actually think I'm beginning to like this coffee."

"That's a sign of something," he answered, but they agreed that they didn't know what. "I think we're all in a state of transition," she said.

"Flux."

"Yes, she continued, thinking abou it. When you're in that state you have no way of knowing what's coming next. It's a dangerous feeling."

"I do know what's coming next," Max said.

"What?

"*The School for Scandal.*"

Amelia walked from Max's place to Dr. Beatty's office to get a ride with him to the Friends' Meeting House. Sunday mornings always were quieter in Fairhope than in most places, and this Sunday was even quieter than usual but for the song of a few birds. The air was heavy with a fragrance Amelia did not recognize, being from a part of the country that was not overrun with gardenias in the springtime. Fairhope's gardenia bushes, dark green shrubs with the creamy white blossoms the size of a cat's face, gave off a distinctive, sweet smell. The cemetery was so full of them that some called the bushes "cemetery flowers." She had noted the smell that morning at the service.

Today the sun was bright, the sky was blue with white clouds around the horizon, and the combination of satsuma blossoms and gardenias filled the air with freshness and promise.

The doctor made it known that he drove his new motorcar to the meeting every Sunday and would carry everybody he could fit in. The car was full this morning, Amelia just one of the crowd who yearned to spend this particular Easter in silence and meditation. Quaker philosophy did not hold Easter as a separate holiday, but regarded its spirit of redemption and resurrection as the essence of everyday life for a true Christian. Hal and Martha Etheridge, not regular churchgoers, chose to attend this morning with Ally in tow. Passengers in the car on the way and on the return ride to Fairhope kept silent, but at the meeting a few chose to speak.

"Days like this make me more grateful than ever for life," Hal Etheridge said. "I thank God that I am alive, and on this morning I thank Him particularly that Marietta Johnson is alive."

✻

Mrs. Johnson had declared Monday a day off school, but she called a meeting of the faculty at 2 P.M. They all came, eager to hear anything she might have to say. She needed to talk to them, to clear the air, and to bolster them as best she could for the last six weeks of school.

They met in the library, as they had that first day of orientation in September. Amelia was struck with the difference of mood between the two meetings. There were obvious reasons for this. They all knew each other well now; they had just endured a crucible together. Yet here was the indomitable Mrs. Johnson, still at the helm, taking charge once more. There was not the expectant exuberance of the fall this morning, but a palpable mood of concern, tempered with some regret and a great deal of sorrow. The faculty shared some shards of optimism which they could not fully understand. Mrs. Johnson sat in the room, with chairs arranged in concentric semicircles around her, talking in a subdued manner to a few of her colleagues.

Amelia had felt detached when she entered the room, that somehow she was not a part of this, that she was watching from a distant vantage point. She was still dealing with the impact of her hospital visit. She was hesitant in approaching Mrs. Johnson, but she did. She walked up to her and said "Good morning," a little weakly, recalling their encounter in the hospital.

"So glad to see you, my dear," Mrs. Johnson said. Her gentle voice at once grounded Amelia and gave her confidence that maybe, after all, things would soon be back to normal.

The room was quiet as it filled up. In her mind Amelia contrasted the atmosphere today to the chattering, chaotic din at the welcoming meeting in the fall.

Mrs. Johnson walked to the front of the room, to the center of the first row of semcircles, to speak and they all seemed to hold their breath at once.

"Thank you all for your patience and your devotion," Mrs. Johnson said. "In this life, there is a great deal to be said for both." The teachers began to applaud spontaneously, unable to stop for at least a minute's time, which seemed like half an hour. It was exactly one minute, according to Max later, who, with his theatre expertise, was extremely precise about things like the timing of applause.

Mrs. Johnson held out her hands, palms down, to quiet them.

"You all may have noticed I have a few old saws at my fingertips at all times. I use them with students, teachers, and friends alike. Some are original—I don't know where I picked up others. I only know that when I say such things—when I repeat them—it is because I have found them to be true and useful in my own life.

"The one that I think applies now is—'It doesn't matter what may happen to you in life, what matters is how you meet the situation!'

"The recent tragedy happened to all of us in this room. We are all tested by it to different degrees. We must assess its effect upon our own lives. That is for you to do individually, and with each other. I myself am still struggling with it, through faith and contemplation. I cannot tell you its full meaning today. I have not arrived at it myself. If I did, perhaps I might express a message from it for all of us.

"Yet I stand before you today somewhat changed, very much chastened, enduring yet another terrible life transition, a dreadful and uninvited challenge.

Our students now have been thrust into the frightening reality of a random event that they should have been spared. We cannot choose the catastrophes that plague our lives or theirs. It is up to us to set examples, and we can only do that by being honest and having the courage to gain self-awareness through the most difficult trials.

"An example of that is Mr. Rabold," she said. "I think you all know what he did, taking the boys to the Gulf last week, and letting them dance their hearts out. This worked out as well as anything in helping them face the loss of their friend—"There was a catch in her voice for a moment. She cleared her throat and paused. "To get them in motion, to change the focus of their grief and confusion to something positive, something active in their lives.

"We don't have a lot of time left in this school year. But all of us have exciting projects in the works. I for one cannot wait to see Mr. Taylor's production of *The School for Scandal*. I look forward to our first Spring Festival under the direction of Mr. Rabold the first week of May. Soon after that we shall have a graduation ceremony and I hope many parties surrounding that event.

"Tomorrow will be an ordinary school day. The bell will toll from the Bell Building tower to start the day. First Lifers in Miss King's class will climb trees, and older ones will throw the ball over the science building calling, 'Annie Annie Over!' in a game made up by their older brothers and sisters. There will be arts and crafts, folk dancing, wood shop, recess, tales of the Greek myths, history, science and math.

"Through it all, for as long as I live and I hope for as long as any of us shall live, you teachers will find the strength and wisdom to do your best work. Your commitment to this place, this idea, this point of view toward education, will not only take root here, but will thrive in the world and bring mankind of a greater knowledge of the needs of childhood.

"It will start with little things. Do what you can here, today and tomorrow, and let us continue to build a better future for the world."

It was clear to the assembly that Mrs. Johnson's course would not falter. Not a soul who was in that room would dare to do less than his best to continue with the work he had planned for the rest of the school year.

※

Max was excited about the rehearsals for *The School for Scandal*. Sarah Willard Heistand had helped with the costumes and continued getting the students to stand and admonish the ocean to "Roll On!" along with her other vocal exercises while Max put the finishing touches on the comic moments of the play and guided the cast with learning lines, cueing each other, and walking properly in their 18th century costumes. Jim and his woodworking boys and girls constructed and painted sets for the production, and the day the play was to open, classes for the high school were all but curtailed as the final rehearsals took place.

Mr. Crane held forth on history, but excitement about the production kept most of his students from paying him much attention. It was all that those who were in the play could do to sit still for his class. But he was determined to follow Mrs. Johnson's dictum to keep them on track, business as usual.

The School for Scandal was to be presented on Friday night, April 28, and, in light of what the school had learned from its Christmas pageant, a second performance was scheduled the following evening to accommodate the overflow crowds.

Amelia was impressed with the enormity of the student body's commitment to events such a play production. Maxwell had the whole high school organized and participating at some level, although almost all his actors were from the junior and senior classes. He had bent his own rule by giving George Ray the role of Trip the servant who appears in a scene in Act III, and since the tragedy he had been working Chauncey into the part. Chauncey certainly had taken to heart the notion that George Ray would want him to do it; he had learned the lines right off and followed Max's directions and blocking to the letter.

Bessie was carrying the show, really, with her ability to absorb and portray the unsympathetic, superficial Lady Teazle.

"I think maybe she hasn't noticed that this character is unsympathetic," Max told Amelia. "Lady Teazle has taken her over her completely!"

That focus influenced the rest of the cast, making Ronson, as her husband, bedazzled at the same time he was exasperated. Ronson had been gradually shedding the fat he brought with him from Connecticut, whether from the better diet at the School Home, the added exercise of folk dancing every day, or simply the fact that he had grown about two inches in height since September. Max noted he was becoming less of a character actor than a leading man; he could use that in plays in the coming years.

Excitement enveloped the campus again on opening night of *The School for Scandal.* The students had run off programs on the school mimeograph machine and included a line "Dedicated to the memory of George Ray Collins" right after the title. They had asked Max about it and he agreed that it was a good thing to do.

Comings Hall filled up with Fairhope's citizens, whether they had anything to do with the school or not. The Crosses were there, and the Pilchers; also Dr. Beatty, Rev. Dickerson and his wife. Of course Lydia Comings was there, as were Mr. and Mrs. Gaston, Piney and Jim, along with all the parents of school-age children; and the students themselves who were not involved in backstage tasks or onstage.

From the rustle of skirts at the first entrance, the cast showed that they were ready for this play. Ronson dropped a line in an early scene and Bessie picked it up. She simply said it herself. The audience laughed and followed the mistaken-identity plot, full of young people in fancy dress bounding in and out of doors, clearly enjoying themselves.

"Great verve," E.B. Gaston said to Maxwell after the curtain calls. "You have given us a play with great verve."

"Thank you, Sir," Max said. "We could all use more of that."

"Indeed!" Mr. Gaston said. He sprinted to Marietta Johnson, saying "Great verve!" to her as well.

Max was exhilarated and stayed so for the next 24 hours, until the end of the second production. He had called for a strike party at the end of the evening, both to tear down and save what bits of the set they could use in future productions and to help the cast unwind, throwing lines of the play at each other, and laughing. He told Amelia that strike parties were an old theatre tradition. She, Avery, and Jim joined him and the kids as they spent several hours taking apart the set.

"Time to go home, everybody," Max said at an arbitrary point. "We can finish this tomorrow. I know tomorrow is Sunday. Those of you who are not going to go to church meet me here at 10—and others, come when you can during the day. A very important part of the theatre is the clean-up afterwards!

"Oh, and great show, everybody! This is one you'll re-member for the rest of your lives—I hope!" Then, almost under his breath he said, "I know I will."

They reluctantly put down their hammers and tools and filed out of Comings Hall. Joy permeated their talk, their movements—the joy of a job well done and, in spite or perhaps even because of their adapting to the loss of their beloved young comrade they experienced a feeling of close-ness even greater than before.

❧

Mr. Rabold went forward with plans for Spring Fes-tival. The Fairhope seamstresses, under the guidance of Mrs. Heistand and her costume builders, had come up with a dress design for the girls, that was different from the high-waisted traditional English gowns he had insisted upon for the Greenwich summer school. The Greenwich costumes were Wedgwood blue, had an Empire waist with three rosettes on the bodice, and trailing ribbons, modeled on the traditional English design. Mr. Rabold found them quite beautiful, but he was more than willing to allow a new tradition to spring up in Fairhope, one which would be more attuned to a Southern U.S. fashion. The Fairhope costume for folk dance was floral printed jumpers, gathered at the waist, with a white blouse beneath. Their mothers made the costumes, advised to look for drapery fabric with a light background and large flowers, all of which would read well from the dance floor. They were given specific instructions about the amount of fabric to use, how to gather the skirt, and the length of the skirts. The boys were to wear white from head to toe, decorated for different dances with baldrics and lanyards and sometimes bands of jingle bells. Mr. Rabold did not change the Organic School tradition of white tennis shoes and socks for both boys and girls.

Festival started at 2 P.M. on May 8, on the green between Comings Hall and the library. It was the perfect space, and the milling boys in their whites and girls in their flowered dresses added an almost unreal dimension of the beauty of youth. The large magnolia trees, with their dark green leaves, were now in blossom with the large, sensuous off-white flowers that gave off a slightly lemony scent. Here and there a few roses were blooming, and here and there a girl had one or two of them in her hair.

Such festivals begin, Mr. Rabold taught, with a "processional," a dance that involves all the participants of the festival, and Charles had concocted such a running dance for the whole school to the tune of "Helston Furry," an old English folk dance air. Dancers filed onto the grounds in couples, formed a simple pinwheel, and then danced forward four more steps until the field was full of whirling young people. By then the leading couples were dancing off, and once the whole school had been seen the Processional was over. Then began the simpler dances by the younger groups. Even kindergarteners—unable yet to learn the dance figures—charmed the viewers by coming on dressed as butterflies and flowers and skipping to music. Amelia's class did two dances, which she and her assistant Helen had taught them. One was the singing game "If All the World Were Paper," which she had learned at that first folk dance party at the beginning of school, and the second was called "Captain Jinks" which was also a circle dance and had a song to it. Her class was earnest as they reminded each other of the steps. She could not help but empathize with them. She stood on tiptoe until they finished and filed off the green space.

The meat of the program was, of course, the advanced dances done by older dancers, who demonstrated their skill with precision and even flair. Folk dancing was the perfect activity for Mrs. Johnson's school, as the dancers worked together as teams, forming figures in a flowing, ever-changing patterns. Notable dancers stood out but the dances did not emphasize particular stars. Mr. Rabold's boys who had been to the beach were the most outstanding, so seriously attempting the challenge dances, but Amelia was partial to the country dances in which partners, boys and girls, took hands and moved with grace. They danced "Christchurch Bells" and "Country Gardens." The Morris Dancers with their handkerchiefs essayed capers and hops to the flowing piano music of "Blue-Eyed Stranger" and "Lumps of Plum Pudding."

The program reached its high point when six of the high school boys grabbed their flat sticks of balsa wood for a rendition of the "sword dance," a rousing, hopping dance, jumping over the swords, twirling under the swords, and climaxing with the dancers in a circle weaving the swords into a star. Zeke Arnold held this star over his head in triumph as the boys danced off the green.

The Recessional marked the end of the daytime dance program. Dancers joined a serpentine single file line beginning with the high school and including every child in the school, ending with the kindergarteners, who, without comprehending the one-two-three-hop of the dance, simply skipped by, all waving handkerchiefs. The youngest ones were most touching, trailing the end of the line, visibly trying so hard to dance.

After this, the crowds filled the Arts and Crafts building to see some of the items the students had made, and a dinner, prepared by the Mothers' Round Table, was sold on the grounds where the folk dancing had been. It was a social time, truly a festival celebrating the advent of spring.

"Charles, you are a magician," Amelia said to Mr. Rabold as the two of them loaded their plates with fruit salad.

He smiled and responded, "Not a magician. I'm just everybody's friend."

"That's a fine thing to be, at this school," she said.

"Is there anybody here who is not everybody's friend?" he asked with a smile.

᭡

Amelia watched the festival thinking of home. The Alabama heat was already strong. As the boys and girls sweated performing folk dances from the hills of England and the folk music of other lands wafted across the campus, everything seemed as unreal and incongruous as it was beautiful. On one level she was euphoric about the way the festival was so elegant and right, while at the same time it caused something in her to yearn for the gritty train terminal in Hoboken, the immigrant children playing games on the sidewalks, the sight shoeshine boys and street vendors. She missed the atmosphere of Philadelphia, with its historic buildings, the stimulation of traffic and intellectual exchanges at the University.

She missed the sharp crispness of the Pennsylvania woods and the shock of the changing seasons. It would be cool in Pennsylvania today—here it was over 80 degrees. Standing in the hot, humid, floral-scented air of the deep South, she felt more and more out of place, like a visitor to a dreamlike Peaceable Kingdom that never really existed. She remembered her arguments throughout the year with those who believed that Fairhope itself was a place where people deceived themselves, believing they were special.

For a moment she too thought Fairhope might be, as Max once said, a mirage, a fragile bubble that could burst with a single gunshot. After the tragedy of Currie Cumbie and George Ray Collins she saw Fairhope's dark side in full focus. Unlike Hoboken with its demarcated dangerous side, here they had removed the boundaries and allowed the direct flow from evil to good. She recalled the arguments over politics by the elders, the level of strife as they railed about their devotion to a cause which was inconsequential in the rest of the world. She thought of the segregation of the races here, the downcast eyes of the blacks, the essential unfairness of mankind, even here. When she saw the dancing boys in their clean white dancing costumes, she remembered the yearly ritual of teen-aged boys throwing a pitiful old drunk into the bay. Boys will be boys. Indeed.

She caught herself in a moment of disorientation between her thoughts of Pennsylvania and Hoboken and the reality of her Fairhope life. On one hand, she asked herself, what nicer home could there be than this remote enclave where everybody cared about everybody and nobody judged what anybody else did? What finer people were there in the world than the leaders of this town, the thinkers and doers so intent on making the world a better place by reforming its basic institutions? What more beautiful home than this little town, so removed from the modern world yet so advanced in its thinking? Most important of all, it was the site of this particular, peculiar school, dreamed into existence as the source of education for all time to come.

How long would she stay, she wondered. She had seen Marietta Johnson endure the most traumatic experience one could have, and she had seen her and the school prevail beyond that terrible moment. Mrs. Johnson took a lesson from the tragedy, moving her forward. Was it truly forward, or simply deeper into the dream?

Amelia loved it here, there was no doubt, but now she realized it would not be home to her. More and more it seemed unreal. Thinking of Philadelphia and its surrounding countryside; perhaps it would be her destiny to return in order to achieve a reputation on her own.

Amelia barely thought of Max during this. She was more and more aware he was not to be in her future. She did not know if she would ever want to lose herself in love.

Maxwell Taylor saw Amelia across the crowd, standing alone and staring at the scene before her. He could see she was deep in thought, perhaps troubled, in conflict. He came up behind her, standing as close as he dared, yearning to put his arm around her shoulders. It was school time, broad daylight, and a big crowd surrounded them, so he restrained himself from reaching for her. There would be time for talk later.

Twenty-Nine

IN THE SUMMER Amelia visited the Chapmans in Philadelphia and her parents in Hoboken before embarking for the school in Greenwich, Connecticut, to take part in Mrs. Johnson's summer program. She loved transporting the "Fairhope idea in education," as Mrs. Johnson called it, to the Northeast, where so many New Yorkers and academics from major institutions observed Organic Education in the summer school. The same enthusiasm for the idea prevailed here as existed in Fairhope, but the pace of the Northeast and the caliber of the participants were at a different level. Rather than a casual, easygoing, remote place, Greenwich inhabited instead the vital center of a very advanced intellectual universe.

Well-known authors and artists enrolled their children in the Greenwich program, and many of them joined the hands-on summer projects. It was nothing to see the artist Rockwell Kent herding a group of youngsters in a outdoor Robin Hood extravaganza, or to hear music conducted by Walter Damrosch, followed by his folksy talks bringing music theory to a level everyone could understand. Language was taught by practical application—Mrs. Johnson joined the educators who believed children to be receptive to learning foreign languages at the same time they naturally acquired ease in their mother tongue. At Greenwich,

Mme. Fousier spoke only French to her preschoolers, and Sra. Colon spoke only in Spanish. The children picked up both languages quite naturally. The halls at Edgewood rang with activity, and the surrounding woodlands teemed with happy children.

Charles Rabold and Paul Frederick came up from Fairhope, bringing a few of the boys with them to help teach folk dancing. Zeke Arnold and Joe Cyrus were among them. It was right, Amelia thought, to connect Mrs. Johnson's two institutions, and to use her Fairhope group to demonstrate in this different location how well her system worked there. It was impossible not to think of what this exposure might have offered George Ray Collins, but Amelia resolved not to dwell on the tragedy and to follow Mrs Johnson's example.

Avery and Jim were along as well, taking a cottage together and announcing they were engaged to be married in the next school year. They would not have a big formal wedding, but Avery told Amelia they did plan to have the event in Boston with her family in attendance.

"And you must come, friend! I won't have attendants, but you and I know that you will be the secret maid of honor. We just won't tell my sisters!"

This appealed to Amelia, who suggested they set the date for some time during the Christmas break from school so she could arrange to visit all her relatives, in Philadelphia and Hoboken.

Maxwell Taylor had joined a theater company on Cape Cod for the summer, and all his time was taken. But as the summer drew to a close, he made a point of visiting Greenwich in order to spend time with Amelia. He was excited about the possibility but she faced it with a great deal of apprehension.

In their time apart she was more and more aware that she could not really reciprocate his feelings. With him, she had succumbed to the need to explore the world of passion and romance about which she had only heard. Max was committed to her, and she trusted him enough that she gave in both to her own curiosity and his desire. Yet she had come to feel that she was using his love in an unfair way. She knew she would have to tell him so. When he wrote her that he would be coming to Greenwich in August she was determined it was time to tell him how she felt.

꽃

She met him at the train station, and he was so full of talk of his theater experience that she was delighted. She began to reconsider her decision.

"We just produced a new work by one of our young playwrights by the name of Gene O'Neill," Max said. "He's a moody sort, but very talented as a writer. Hard to get to know. He's very exacting about how what he puts on the page gets played.

"Provincetown is essentially a summer workshop," Max went on. "The troupe has a performance space in Greenwich Village in New York. Some of the actors and the plays are clearly headed for Broadway, and there are other of us who are just there to learn—like good Organic students!"

"You think your friend Gene—?"

"Definitely New York. His father was an actor; he has connections. To say nothing of a huge talent."

"Not that good with people, though?"

"He's good with some people and not with others. I don't know whether that's a good thing. Time will tell."

Max looked more distracted than usual as he looked around the Greenwich campus.

"This is lovely, isn't it? Do you like this place?"

"I think it's wonderful in its way. But it's not quite the Fairhope way."

"What's the difference?"

"Probably that we're in Connecticut!"

Max smiled at that.

"Feels different, doesn't it?" he said.

It felt different seeing him in different circumstances too. Not the all-powerful teacher-director now, but a cog in a bigger wheel of theatre. Max had the ability to be creative and bossy at the same time.

"I want to talk with Mrs. Johnson if she has time," he said. "I have an idea about an all-school project including a pageant next year. Not at Christmas, but later on in the year when we have time for it. A study of ancient Rome. We can use costumes, theatre—in fact we can tie it in with history, geography, math—"

"It sounds right down her alley!"

"I thought so too. Must visit with her."

"They're doing Robin Hood here, with Rockwell Kent directing," Amelia told him.

"Rockwell Kent?"

"His children are in the program."

"Wish we could get them down to Fairhope…"

In his summer stock adventure he had made many friends with people he felt sure were going to shape a new American theatre. This group he was involved in was determined to produce new American plays, to eliminate the star system, and to function as a company. He said he was beginning to feel like Marietta Johnson himself.

He kept Amelia laughing and off her guard. It was good seeing him again, but she checked her emotional reactions and couldn't imagine going to bed with him again. Broaching that with him was going to be a difficult conversation.

Later that evening, after a light supper at the big table, she had her chance. They sat on a bench outside the dormitory and talked.

"We haven't discussed where I'll be staying tonight," Max said to her, perhaps sensing that there was some reason she had avoided the topic. "I've only got one night here, you know."

"I know."

The silence spoke volumes.

"I'm beginning to feel a little less than welcome," Max said.

"Oh, Max, it's not that."

"What is it then?"

"I need to talk to you."

He looked stricken, but shifted his shoulders in a way that suggested subconsciously he was expecting to receive a blow.

"Max, I don't think I've been being fair with you." This caused a startled look. "I mean, maybe I haven't been honest." She paused to organize her thoughts.

"It was so wonderful at first, that beautiful night when I dropped my books. I didn't know what to do or what not to do, so I acted."

"Yes you certainly did that," he said, clearly remembering their first morning together in his rented room.

"Are you saying you've changed your mind?" Maxwell asked.

Amelia had to think, remembering the whole constellation of events that had occurred in Fairhope over the past year—the Halloween party, the parties that flowed to the beach, the sunsets on the pier, the warm Christmas, and then the terrible moments learning of Mrs. Johnson's tragic event, trying to communicate with her in a state of shock in the hospital, and Spring Festival, where all the experiences had crystallized in her mind. Talking with Maxwell this night, however, what stood out in her memory was the evening in the park on the night he first kissed her and the morning when she went to his room and became a New Woman.

"Maybe," she said.

She wasn't sure what to say next. "I acted on my feelings of the moment."

"And you don't have those feelings now?"

"I have learned to care for you deeply."

"Why does that sound sort of ominous to me?"

"Well, what I'm trying to say is—"

"That you're not in love with me."

"Yes." She paused and he tried to read her face. "I'm not."

Perhaps he had sensed what she was going to say from the moment she met him at the train. For her part, she couldn't imagine what he would say now. There was another pause filled with the sounds of night. Not so loud as tree frogs. Probably crickets.

"I guess there's not much anybody can do about that," he said.

"Max, please don't get me wrong—"

"Wrong? You're being perfectly clear."

"I don't want to hurt your feelings."

"I guess it would be more hurtful if you kept going the way you were, feeling the way you feel—or don't feel."

"I'm so sorry."

"Yeah, well. These things happen."

He stood up and said, "I'm sure there's a place where I can find lodgings for the night."

"Oh, there's a big dormitory," Amelia said.

"I'll see if I can find the person in charge before it gets too late," he said, starting off. Amelia walked beside him and took his hand until they got to the front door of the dormitory building. Max turned to her.

"Look," he said. "I'm not going to say I'm not hurt. But it was worth it."

That was that. He had come up with just what Amelia needed to hear. She understood that she had done the right thing. She had almost expected a cataclysm, a breakdown. He looked stunned, but he turned away from her quickly and walked into the big building.

She had made a grown-up move. She must take care of herself by herself now. Max was walking steadily away, the end of an episode. They would be traveling separately, but they would both be moving forward.

❧

The next fall all was busy at the school as it had been the year before, a gathering of the new teachers with the old—which now included Amelia. A folk dance party engaged the whole town, followed by a pot luck supper, and soon there was the all-school Halloween Party.

Max was at work planning his big event, Roman Day, to take place early in the second semester, but he had to organize the Christmas pageant first. He and Mrs. Johnson had planned the Roman Day and had meetings with all the teachers to work on Italian and ancient Rome projects for months in advance of the day. The high school students already studied Latin, and this year the whole school would add many more Italy-related subjects and studies of ancient Rome, and display what they'd learned on Roman Day. The senior class would perform an excerpt from the Roman playwright Terence's *The Girl from Andros*.

Amelia, Avery and Jim thought of little besides the up-coming wedding scheduled for December 27th in Boston. Max would attend. The ceremony was to be modest, held in the Congregational chapel Avery's family had attended for generations. The bride chose a formal-looking suit and wore her hair curled and bobbed especially for the occasion.

Avery was more girlish than usual, and Jim all but fell apart—but these transformations of behavior felt perfectly natural to Amelia. A wedding was going to change every-thing. Avery did not carry a bouquet, which Amelia was grateful for. She did not want to have to pretend to want to catch it.

After the ceremony there was a reception at the home of the Buchanans. This was a fine old Boston house—not on Beacon Hill, but in a very respectable neighborhood. Jim Holloway dressed for the occasion, somehow managing not to look out of place, and Amelia was pleased that Max was composed, formal, and more serious than usual at the event.

Avery and Jim's wedding signaled a sea change in the lives of the young teachers in Fairhope, particularly Ame-lia. Avery Buchanan was now Mrs. Holloway. They were a couple, committed to each other and to a future. It hadn't gone that way for Amelia and Max. She was still sorting that out, but felt she was doing the right thing for herself facing her future alone. She had lived through so much in Fairhope, and yet there was so much to come.

Avery and Jim planned to leave Fairhope after the current school year and move to Kentucky where they would start a genuine folk school, emphasizing woodworking, pottery and local handcrafts such as weaving and needlework. Avery would be in charge of the academic studies. She had been spending more and more time with Mrs. Johnson, getting advice.

Maxwell knew he would go into the theatre full-time soon. He had made friends with an idealistic young man named Jasper Deeter who wanted to establish a theatre of his own outside the commercial mainstream—in the wilds of Pennsylvania. One of his actresses said, "We shall perform in the hedgerows if we find it necessary," and they decided to call the group the Hedgerow Theatre Company. The company was able to secure a deserted community hall that had been converted from a gristmill and took it a step further to become an artistic center and theater space.

Amelia talked with the citizens of Moylan in Pennsylvania, coincidentally very near to Hedgerow, about a school similar to the Organic School. She stayed in Fairhope, working with Mrs. Johnson for five more years, and by then the Moylan group had connected with some important funding sources and offered the job of director to Amelia, who had apprenticed with the best.

From time to time she would have a visit from Maxwell, as he carved out a successful life in the theatre, both offstage and on. He loved Deeter's commitment to a theatre as a company of actors rather than a training ground for stars. Max almost always had one actress or another with him when Amelia saw him. He put women on a pedestal in his mind, as he had done with Amelia. This did not work well for him, particularly with actresses, who felt entitled to it yet not inclined to be wives. He would wed two actresses and finally settle down with a gentle woman named Ann Bennett Scott, a playwright who all but gave up writing and bore him a son and a daughter. It occurred to him to name the girl Amelia, but he thought better of it.

Marietta Johnson remained available for counsel to the young teachers who left the fold and founded schools of their own. She felt, as they did, that they were all in on the ground floor of a movement that would change the world through its children. The children of the future were to be educated in a radically different way from any generation before—they were all convinced of that. They in turn would start schools that reflected Mrs Johnson's philosophy, and future generations of children would grow up with a broader understanding of what education was. They would insist on such education for their own children, and then the battle for minds and hearts of the education community would be won.

When Mrs Johnson was in the Philadelphia area, she occasionally visited Amelia and listened with great interest to the stories of how her school was doing. Avery and Jim still worked at Greenwich in the summers and often visited Fairhope during Christmas vacation. Running a school was challenging to them both, and they were determined to make both their school and their marriage work.

Marietta Johnson was on a trip to Greenwich when she stopped in at Amelia's school at the beginning of the term in the late 1920s. A contingent of parents in Bridgeport had invited her to explain her theory and to help them start a similar school and she wanted to see how her protégée was doing.

"I like what I see here, Amelia," she said after a day observing Amelia's school children at work and play. "You understand how to apply what you learned at Fairhope."

"It's very 'organic,' isn't it, Aunt Mettie?" Amelia found herself using the term of affection for her mentor for the first time.

Mrs. Johnson took the remark in stride, but there was a glint of pride in her eyes.

Amelia felt it had been an honor to have worked in her formative years as a teacher at the side of Marietta Johnson. She spoke of her days in Fairhope often, whenever she was invited to describe the new approach to education. As she became a school administrator and fundraiser as well as a teacher, Amelia had to develop skill in public speaking. She yearned for the facility with words that Mrs. Johnson had. She would use that talent in so many ways—including finding a way to describe Marietta Johnson herself.

Amelia's school thrived among the intelligensia of the Philadelphia area. Among them she met a number of young men who, like Max Taylor, had wanted to pin her down, define her, capture her in the way she most resisted. Her commitment was to children and to young teachers, and to starting a school like Marietta Johnson's. She always saw herself as a New Woman, constantly growing, changing as she faced the good and the difficult situations that life offered. She thought it very modern that she didn't have any interest in marriage.

She forged contacts among those she had met through Mrs. Johnson, and built her school and her reputation as an educational innovator on the radical ideas of the early reformers of Fairhope. She always felt the same joy from watching the eyes of children and young people light up as ideas hatched in their minds.

Sometimes she was taken with memories of a place where ideas proliferated like mushrooms, a place where the elderly perceived themselves as young and the young thought they held the wisdom of the ages. The world of tomorrow had seemed to be at their fingertips in those days. The future was the one thing they had all been certain of, with that conviction of the young and the idealistic, that they were in front of the parade.

After Word

THAT WAS TOMORROW is fiction. Most of the characters never lived except in the author's imagination. But there is such a town—Fairhope—an isolated single tax utopia on the eastern shore of Mobile Bay. I have attempted to recapture the atmosphere it once might have had when it was in what some consider its heyday.

Some of the people depicted here did live in Fairhope at that time. They moved to the settlement with the express purpose of changing the world by creating a demonstration of Henry George's theory of the single tax, which with some personal tweaking by their leader E.B. Gaston, they considered to be one of the best ideas for reforming world governments. Fairhope was at that time a locale for the growth and cross-fertilization of ideas, and, as something of a byproduct of this, it became a retreat for dreamers and those on the fringe of the mainstream. More than one hermit found his way to Fairhope at different points in time, and lived on the outskirts of the settlement. It was a haven for outsiders, nonconformists, and reformers, most of whom really believed they had the one idea that might save mankind.

The song, "Fairhope," by J.M. and A.W. Pilcher, was always sung to herald the end of public gatherings in town. It has five verses and a rousing chorus that brought tears to many of the citizens of Fairhope in its early days. Marietta Johnson loved the song and requested that it be sung at her memorial service, which it certainly was.

E.B. Gaston was the founder of the town and the leading exponent of the theory of Cooperative Individualism, which was his adaptation of Henry George's theory as outlined in *Progress and Poverty*. Gaston was a newspaperman, as I have written here, and used his *Fairhope Courier* as a direct-mail piece to convert others the world over to his ideas—and as promotion for his utopian colony of Fairhope.

Capt. Jack Cross and his wife did run The Gables, a big, rambling hotel occupying the lot at the corner of Fairhope Avenue and Church Street. There was wooded land around the building; however, no picture of The Gables itself still exists that I know of, although it can be seen on the edges of some of the old photos of the town. It looked to be a spacious and inviting hostelry. I created the character of Idella Cross in my own imagination. I did not know Capt. Cross' wife's name—only that she was known as one of the best cooks in town.

Lydia Comings and Marie Howland were very real, very unconventional women for their day and both were close friends of Marietta Johnson. Paul Gaston has written the histories of both Mrs. Howland and Mrs. Johnson in *Women of Fair Hope*, a book which gives an idea what both women were like.

The biggest fiction in the book is the attempted assassination of Marietta Johnson. This was entirely a device to pull my stories together with dramatic tension, and to reveal yet another affirmation of the character of Marietta Johnson. Almost all of the anecdotes about her and descriptions of her are based on those I heard from her contemporaries.

For example, "Do you love all children?" was said to be a question she asked all prospective teachers in her interviews. From a woman who had attended the school in the 1930s I got the anecdote about Mrs. Johnson asking, "Where'd you get that outfit?" that I attributed to Avery.

There was a landslide in one of the gullies near the school when there was a class exploring there, in the mid 1910s, and a child was accidentally killed. The Cumbies, however, are fictional.

The character of Amelia King was loosely based on a young teacher named Grace Rotzel, who lived in Fairhope in the 1920s, leaving it to start her own similar school in Rose Valley, PA. Miss Rotzel wrote a short essay about the cottage in which she lived in Fairhope with a roommate named Avery, and besides the name of her roommate I co-opted some of her descriptions, including the battles with cockroaches, and the name "The Sieve" from her article. I do not know much about the real Miss Rotzel except that her school still survives, and that she always credited Marietta Johnson with her theory of Progressive Education. When Mrs. Johnson died in 1938, the board of the school offered her job to Miss Rotzel, who had to refuse because she was so engaged in the management of her own school, The School in Rose Valley, that she would not leave it.

Max Taylor is fictional, but in creating him I used some information from a teacher who had taught at the Organic School in the 1930s and returned to live out his days in Fairhope when I was in the school in the late 1950s, dying in the 1960s. This teacher of drama, English, psychology and other courses had worked with Jasper Deeter at the Hedgerow Theater in the 1930s. He directed a production of *The School for Scandal* at the Organic School in 1938, and I transplanted that production to the year 1922. This teacher remembered Marietta Johnson, and he was the one who told me of her habit of charging through town to Knoll Park when she had an idea for a speech, stopping in the shops on the way to round up a crowd.

Wharton Esherick and Sherwood Anderson were indeed good buddies who met in Fairhope in 1919. Esherick, who later became known as the dean of American craftsmen, taught art at the school, and he told friends in the Philadelphia area the stories here about his wanting to teach the local Fairhope blacks and being advised to do it after hours. A painter when he came to Fairhope, Esherick became a carpenter and designer of furniture after he left. He was given his first set of carving tools in Fairhope, probably by Marietta Johnson. Sherwood Anderson, author of *Winesburg, Ohio*, and other books, lived in Fairhope for a year and palled around with some of his friends from the Dil Pickle Club of Chicago who wintered in Fairhope. This was a wild, bohemian bunch. There is much evidence of the fact that they spent a lot of time splashing about in the bay in the nude. I touch on that without making it central to the story. I think in those days, although the population was small, everybody was welcome and there was very much an attitude of live-and-let-live. Anderson wrote that he never did figure out what the single tax theory was all about.

I trust the Arnold family will forgive my transporting them from the era in which they did live in Fairhope (the 1930s to the present) to the time frame of my book. The real Arnold family and their offspring were central to the student body of the School of Organic Education from then through the present day, so much so that my mind's eye could not picture activities at the school without some students named Arnold participating. They were all good at folk dancing, and they were (and are) a loving, wholesome family of the kind Mrs. Johnson sought for her school. I added a brother Zeke and did not mention all the names of the children, but could not resist including a Mordecai, who is a special hero of mine, and Pat, the beloved brother killed in World War II that the women in the family told me was their favorite. Both these men came along a great deal later than I have placed them in the book. I did not name all the family, mostly for the sake of space. Although they were not in Fairhope in the time frame of this work, the Arnolds are so integral to my own emotional attachment to the school that I felt compelled to write them in.

You'll be happy to learn that the model for George Ray Collins lived a long and full life, had a happy marriage and raised two fine sons. He was devoted to Marietta Johnson and I have no doubt he would have taken a bullet for her.

Minor characters in the book, like Esther and Paul Frederick, Piney and Jim Gaston (and their babies) were real and would have been involved in school affairs in the time of the book. Madame—Mercedes Morehead—was a citizen of Fairhope in the 1920s and 30s, and she was a trained opera singer and veterinarian who rode about town on a white horse. "Auntie Co" Myhers and Charles Rabold were very real. Mr. Rabold did take a group of boys to the Gulf beach one day many years ago when a friend of theirs was killed in a gun accident. Mr. Rabold folk danced with them on that beach—I don't believe I could have dreamed that up—and they held that memory for their whole lives.

Sarah Willard Hiestand was a Shakespearean scholar who directed what she called The Alabama Shakespeare Festival in Fairhope through the decade of the 1920s. Walter Damrosch did teach music appreciation at the School of Organic Education on a temporary basis during this period. There were other well known names who were in Fairhope in its early days, but did not make it to these pages because they were there a few years away from my story one way or the other—for instance, the Socialist writer Upton Sinclair, who came in 1909 for over a year and Clarence Darrow who spent a few weeks in Fairhope in 1927.

Mr. Rabold and his accompaniest Hannah Bottstein were killed in a plane crash in 1930. It was another of the close scrapes of Mrs. Johnson's life; she had been in California with them and decided at the last minute not to take that plane. The loss of Rabold dealt a blow to the school that can never be measured. Marietta Johnson was grooming him to take over the school as director when she retired.

The words I have attributed to Mrs. Johnson were almost all based on those she was known to have uttered. The speeches were lifted almost verbatim from her own, and the offhand comments were remembered by people who knew her. The last speech, however, honoring George Ray, was not hers but based upon her writings about the children in her school. It is also a fact that she did play a lot of Solitaire, and when she was doing so, it was *verboten* to interrupt her. She also enjoyed participating in folk dance parties and felt strongly that this was the most wholesome kind of dancing for young people. She was a raw foodist as were many in Fairhope in the early days.

Marietta Johnson was a spellbinding speaker, most compellingly when she spoke extemporaneously. After making a speech many times, she wrote it down, so there are a number of copies on record at the Marietta Johnson Museum in Fairhope and in the digital Marietta Johnson collection at the Fairhope Public Library. People who remember her have said over and over that her speeches do not read as well on the page as they sounded when she delivered them. She was persuasive and charismatic, and apparently the full force of her personality and mind came into play when she was before a crowd. She wrote two books, which are out of print but have been reprinted as one paperback volume, available through the museum in Fairhope.

In these pages I wanted to capture her elusive personality, and not have her come over as pompous no matter how formal her words were. It remains to the reader to decide whether or not I succeeded.

Acknowledgments

THE WRITING OF this book was a result of years in Fairhope and was influenced by so many of the elders in Fairhope who related stories of how it once was. After I came up with the first draft there were specific people who participated in its creation.

Mary Gardner and Bonnie Walker took on the daunting job of editing, steering me away from my emphasis on historical backstory and toward a more dynamic piece of fiction. Bonnie spent hours poring over my text and editing out details more appropriate to a history text than to a coming of age story of a young teacher in 1920's America. After its first presentation in electronic format, Rex Howard Anderson was a tremendous help with reworking the prose and helping with proofreading.

For my knowledge of Marietta Johnson and her work, I thank the Marietta Johnson Museum of Fairhope, Alabama, where I worked for several years as director. This background was a tremendous help in my research for *Meet Me at The Butterfly Tree* and *The Fair Hope of Heaven*, two non-fiction books which inform the stories in *That Was Tomorrow*. I was inspired by a number of people over the years who remember Mrs. Johnson, including the late Dorothy Beiser Cain, Helen Porter Dyson, Claude Arnold, and others who attended the school in the 1920s and 30s.

Their remarks and anecdotes about past eras in Fairhope and at the school grounded me in myths and reality about old Fairhope. Graduating from the school in 1958 gave me a lifelong interest in its unique history and approach to education. Donnie Barrett, director of the Fairhope Museum of History, is a good friend with whom many conversations about Fairhope in the days represented here helped provide me with a story.

I thank Paul Gaston, Michelle Feltman Strider, and Jonathan Odell for their patience in wading through the original draft of *That Was Tomorrow*, at the point where it was wearing a different shape and a different title. Their suggestions put me on the road to editing and rewriting the book. I attended a workshop Jonathan taught at the Loft Literary Center in Minneapolis, which was a spur to keep going in the writing of this book.

I attended a symposium in Philadelphia about Wharton Esherick, the woodcarver who lived in Fairhope briefly. The visit to the Esherick museum in Paoli, PA, and the many lectures and exhibits of his work inspired me to include him and his friend Sherwood Anderson in my story. Esherick's experience of working with blacks was related by the many scholars and sculptors I met at that symposium. Alan Samry at the Fairhope Library was a great source of information about Lydia Comings.

Sources

T HE MARIETTA JOHNSON Museum in Fairhope, Alabama was a source of much of the information in this book. Among the treasures I found there was a brochure about Organic education with an essay by Grace Rotzel about her time in Fairhope. I wrapped the novel around these anecdotes, including the battles she and her roommate Avery had with cockroaches and a leaky roof. Some of the words appear verbatim from Miss Rotzel, but much was rewritten and edited to fit the story of my fictional heroine. By the time the book was finished very little of the real Grace Rotzel remained.

Information about the bay boats came from Sam Dyson's book *Fairhope, A Universal Community,* and from *Montrose,* published in 1959 by Florence Scott. Mr. Dyson's book included a lot of useful descriptions of characters and the atmosphere of Fairhope during this time period.

The Internet confirmed a lot of my research about Wharton Esherick and some of Fairhope's other visitors during the time period of this book. I attended a symposium on Esherick at the University of Pennsylvania in 2010, where members of his family and many students and teachers of his work and history revealed what they knew about his time in Fairhope.

The Fairhope Public Library's collection of *Fairhope Couriers* provided information of the news of Fairhope in 1921-22.

A number of books about Fairhope history, including the following, have been invaluable in my lifelong research about Fairhope and had a great deal to do with the writing of this work. My thanks to the many people over the years who have shared their memories of what the town was like in the early 20th century.

Allums, Larry, *Fairhope 1894-1994*, The Donning Company, 1994.

Alyea, Paul E. and Blanche R., *Fairhope, 1894-1954, The Story of a Single Tax Colony*, University of Alabama Press, 1956.

Bell, Robert E., *The Butterfly Tree*, J.P. Lippincott Co., New York and Philadelphia, 1959.

Buchan, Perdita, *Utopia, New Jersey, Travels in the Nearest Eden*, Rutgers University Press, 2007.

Dyson, Sam, *Fairhope, A Universal Community*, Sam Dyson, 1990.

Ewing, Marjorie Edwards, *Out of Russia*, unpublished manuscript, Marietta Johnson Museum, 1992.

Gaston, Paul., *Man and Mission, E.B. Gaston and the Origins of the Fairhope Single Tax Colony*, The Black Belt Press, Montgomery, Ala., 1993.

Gaston, Paul, *Women of Fair Hope*, University of Georgia Press, 1984.

George, Henry, *Progress and Poverty*, Roberty Schalkenberg Foundation, New York, 1960, 1879.

Johnson, Marietta, *Organic Education, Teaching Without Failure*. Published by The Marietta Johnson Museum, Fairhope, Ala., 1990. Originally published as *Youth in a World of Men* and *Thirty Years with an Idea*.

McGrath, Janet, *A School for Utopia*, unpublished thesis, Marietta Johnson Museum, 1991.

Rosemont, Franklin, *The Rise and Fall of the Dil Pickle*. Charles H. Kerr Publishing Co., Chicago, 2004.

Scott, Florence, *Montrose*. Published by the Montrose Garden Club, Paragon Press, Montgomery, Al, 1959, 1960, 1976.

Mary Lois Timbes Adshead
New Paltz, New York
April 2013